Kate O'Riordan

was brought up in the West of Ireland, but now lives in London. She is an award-winning novelist, playwright and television screenwriter, and has been a recipient of the Sunday Tribune/Hennessy Prize for 'Best Emerging Writer'. *Involved* was shortlisted for the Dillons First Fiction Prize.

From the reviews:

'A striking debut by an origin~~al~~ ~~writer.~~'

~~DER~~MOT BOLGER

'A truthfully ~~...~~ novel from a terrific storyte~~...~~ ~~...~~ O'CONNOR

'A writer with t~~...~~ ~~...~~ it how it is, not how we think it ought to be, a~~nd to~~ tell it passionately, yet with humour and a sense of the power of language to move and change us.'

FAY WELDON

'Kate O'Riordan has the gift of creating complex characters whose emotions are both real and moving. She is not afraid to shock; her description of violence and sex leaves little room for glamour or sentimentality. A writer of originality and huge promise.' JONATHAN MOORE, *Irish Post*

'A witty and moving dissection of young love across internal political borders in Ireland, *Involved* is packed with subtly inflected violence. A passionate portrait of familial strife, with no sentimental short cuts or half measures.' *Vogue*

'A contemporary Irish love story and a very compelling first novel, one that tells an old story in a fresh new way. An auspicious debut for a fine artist.' RONAN SHEEHAN, *Irish Press*

Further reviews overleaf

'From the brutal description of a puppy dog's entrails being sliced out, to the erotic depiction of lips playing on the petals of a rose, Kate O'Riordan's writing has a power and authenticity which makes this an unusually assured debut.'

MAXINE JONES, *The Tribune*

'The action moves between Dublin, Belfast, London and rural Cork, all four places lovingly described and convincingly evoked. This is an eminently readable, warmly written novel which should leave you wanting to hear more from this writer.'

TINA OGLE, *Time Out*

'For her first novel, Kate O'Riordan ignores the well-trodden areas of tribes and sovereignty. Instead, she explores a very different characteristic; that ancient mentality gap which separates Ulster from the rest of the island and keeps Ireland like a bear with a sore head. In a new version of Troubles thriller mixed with a love story, O'Riordan pours out her exasperation at Northern Irish insularity and poses some interesting questions about just how united Ireland or its inhabitants can be.'

AISLING FOSTER, *TLS*

'A strong first novel, with some scenes that are bound to churn weak stomachs. But also one that shows insight and displays a deep compassion for those caught up in affairs not of their own choosing. And there is a coda in the tail that is truly chilling.'

VINCENT BANVILLE

'Kate O'Riordan's courage in confronting the uncomfortable is stunning and not for a moment sensational. She is merciless in her perception.'

Cork Examiner

'Boiling with energy and invention.'

Image Magazine

'O'Riordan is a find, one of those very talented writers that turn up maybe once in ten or twenty years in Ireland.'

Irish World

KATE O'RIORDAN

Involved

Flamingo
An Imprint of HarperCollinsPublishers

Flamingo
An Imprint of HarperCollins*Publishers*
77–85 Fulham Palace Road,
Hammersmith, London W6 8JB

First published in Great Britain by
Flamingo 1995

9 8 7 6 5 4 3 2

ISBN 0 00 654761 3

Set in Galliard

Printed and bound in Great Britain by
Caledonian International Book Manufacturing Ltd, Glasgow

For Donal

December

A sharp high wind rattled the roofs and clattered against window-panes along the narrow street as he closed the front door to the small terraced house behind him. It was bitterly cold; tiny ice crystals formed around his nostrils. He pulled on his nose and blew a warming breath on his exposed hand.

For a moment, Eamon O'Neill contemplated using his car. He eyed the white Sierra parked across the road, hesitating with his back to the wind. He jangled the keys within his coat pocket then allowed them to drop. He decided to walk and drop by the church on his way. Martin Fogarty's house was less than fifteen minutes' fast stride away, and besides it was probably a wiser decision to leave his car where it was.

With his head down and hands plunged deep within his coat pockets, Eamon faced the wind and walked briskly past the dark rows of almost identical houses; street after street, anonymous in their red brickness or greyness and air of tired dilapidation, until he reached the modern grotesque church of bald brick and long narrow windows. It sat on the confluence of similar streets, glowing brazenly in the only operative streetlight.

He was just on time. Inside, Fr. Bennett was dimming the lights and checking the candles. The priest genuflected each time he passed the central tabernacle on the altar above him. Eamon watched him open the confessional cubicles to check that no one remained inside; a wino perhaps, hoping to escape one cold night or a youngster reluctant to return home after a fight with his father.

The priest peered through the gloom and nodded toward the solitary genuflecting figure at the back of the church. He was a familiar sight at about this time every evening. Eamon signalled that he would only be a few minutes, and Fr. Bennett raised his hand in a habitual waving motion as if to say: 'Take your time. Take your time.' Then he grinned broadly. Behind Eamon, who was kneeling in the third to last pew, two women had entered, muttering and nudging one another. The mother and daughter waited most nights until Eamon entered, and followed him inside.

The transparency of their motive was at times hideous to Eamon; subtlety being a luxury that desperate elderly women with unwed thirty-seven-year-old daughters, and single, plain thirty-seven-year-old daughters, could ill afford. They invested in candour at no expense.

Eamon could hear their whispers and his name being mentioned. No doubt they were discussing his new grey overcoat. There was little about him that they had not discussed at one time or another. He did not have to turn around to know that the widow wore a scarf around her head which made a triangle of her face not dissimilar, he always thought, to those little triangles of children's processed cheese his mother sometimes bought – milky-white and putty-like. He had wondered if a finger prod would dint her face like the cheese. The daughter with her gapped smile and pleated brow would be wearing a black or navy blue beret. He took a surreptitious glance over his shoulder on the pretext of brushing dandruff away. Navy blue. He smiled and peered ahead again toward the statue of the Virgin Mary which stood with widespread arms to the left of the altar; in the gloomy light she appeared luminous. He closed his eyes and tried to concentrate but the women were twittering. Sighing heavily, he made the sign of the cross and rose. He genuflected in the aisle and inclined his head sideways toward the women who peered up at him out of the corners of their eyes, with what he considered that wretched flirtatious look of truly ugly women.

At the door, Fr. Bennett was indicating with a backward motion of his head that he wished to speak with Eamon. The priest looked furtively over Eamon's shoulder to check that the women could not hear him.

'The young lad I was telling you about . . . ?' Fr. Bennett spoke directly into Eamon's ear.

'McCaffrey – aye . . . ?'

'Well, he's holed up in some sort of squat off Dugan Place – He's done the whole area in the last couple of weeks, so they tell me.'

'What age?'

'Fourteen. Or nearly fourteen leastways.'

'Old enough.'

'I'm only passing the information on mind . . . like I promised. He's a danger to himself that boy. Ye'll go easy . . .'

But Eamon was waving a hand, he had no time for the man's conscience salving.

'Enough said,' he muttered, walking away as the priest opened and closed his mouth repeatedly, cut off as he was in mid-flow.

Outside, a freezing rain spitted against the pavement. Within moments Eamon's hands felt like two raw lumps of meat. He quickly buried them in his pockets once more, felt for his keys and that other icy metal object within. Turning it over with his stiffened fingers, he grunted with satisfaction.

Further along the street he turned up to the left casting an indifferent eye inside the yellow squares of window on both sides of the street. Some windows, though uncurtained, were decorated along the inside frames by layers of entwined crepe paper or green white and gold tinsel, meshed with care and some artistry. He peered past the thin films of soiled, dingy nets at the bodies inside, huddled around their fires and blue television screens. The front rooms were uniformly small. Enough room for a sofa, two arm-chairs, a television and an occasional cabinet in teak veneer, stuck against a wall. Some rooms offered a fake Christmas tree in a corner or by the window, and little wooden figurines and St Brigid crosses on window ledges, signifying that this was the home of a craftsman spending Christmas in the Maze.

Many of these houses were home to his pupils. He recognized a young lad's gaunt figure and shaven head coming out through one of the doors; he had pulled up the collar of his flimsy denim jacket against the wind. The boy almost collided with Eamon before he recognized his teacher.

'How's it going, Sir?' he said. 'Bloody freezin' in't it?'

'It is that all right.' Eamon smiled and saluted the boy's father who reeled out after his son. He instantly recalled that this was

3

a house where an older brother had recently acquired a bullet in the base of his spine for joy riding. He had been on his second warning.

'Don't forget my fucking cigarettes mind.' The father's voice was thick with liquor. 'Mr O'Neill – is that you? Hoi, is it you I said?'

'Aye. It is.' Eamon's voice carried back to the doorway.

'God blast it – passing the door without a word – come back, come back I say – for a cup of tea or something. Sure it's Christmas.' He bawled up the street after Eamon's receding figure.

Eamon raised a hand in a casual manner without turning around.

'No time tonight Michael. Another time. For sure.'

As he rounded the corner and passed into another identical street, row upon row of two- or three-ups, two-downs, the bricked line broken here and there by grey pebble dash, the last house with its windowless flank daubed in slogans, all political, none pornographic, he began to hum to himself:

'Drink, drink, drink to eyes that shine ever brightly . . .'

In two weeks he would be singing his role in *The Student Prince*, a production by the Choral Society, of which he was a leading founder member. This year, Eamon was himself the producer as well. He was pleased with their progress and anticipated a successful show. The costumes could be better he conceded, being old and rehashed each year, but in general he felt that he had done a good job.

He was coming into a newer part of town. The streets widened slightly, some offered an erratic line of plane trees outside houses which were semi-detached, many with garages, many with a layer of bright paint covering their breeze block anatomy. The houses had wide windows, aluminium-framed with green fascia boards between the ground and first storeys. To him, they seemed impermanent compared to the solid brick of his district. There were front gardens neatly manicured with herbaceous borders. All the windows were curtained fully, some had Austrian blinds as well, pulled down to undulate between lined dralon drapes.

A man passed him walking his dog and nodded. Eamon grunted. His face was by now quite frozen. He licked a few drops of icy sleet from his lips. Something was nagging. A thought, like a fly, waiting to land. Then, he realized the source of the pleasurable nagging. He was almost erect. He sighed and tried to concentrate on the cold.

He stopped to stare up the street into which he had just entered. Streetlights trailed yellow broken dashes of light along the wet footpaths and dipped into black sockets on the lumpy road surface. The night was silent except for the barking of a dog nearby. A car passed and sluiced his feet in a wet icy puddle. With disdain, his mouth turned down in a grimace, Eamon shook his shoes and glared after the car.

He was there. He knew the house, fourth from the end on the right of the street. He knew it well.

It was always like this. A certain reluctance borne of familiarity, distaste, a degree of lassitude and most recently, boredom. It was cold. His feet were wet. And the erections. They had begun to bother him. They smacked of perversity. But he was clean. He was ready and willing and clean he told himself. He believed that a man should believe in something. For that reason, he was often misjudged he considered. But then, believers were often misjudged. If anything, he was a Missionary. Smiling at that thought he approached the house slowly. The erection swelled between his legs.

He shook his head in a physical effort to remove his thoughts, a knack he had acquired and honed to perfection, so that, at times, other times, as now, he could approach anyone or anything with a mind without clutter and therefore without shadows.

He pushed open the wrought iron gate. A dark-haired boy, about eleven, ran out of the garage door followed by a golden cocker spaniel pup. Eamon liked dogs and children. He smiled. The boy stopped and eyed him warily. The pup ran forward and sniffed at Eamon's feet, wagging its tail in a frenzy of excitement. Someone new to enchant. Eamon knelt immediately and cupped the dog's head.

'Hello little fella. Hello small thing. Friendly little bugger, aren't you?' he crooned.

The pup licked his face. He was good with dogs. He looked up and smiled again at the young boy, who relaxed visibly but still studied the stranger with caution. He was sure he had seen this man before. Late one night from his bedroom window coming into the house with other men to speak with his father. The man was his father's age – thirty-eight or -nine. He remembered the brushed back full head of pewter hair, the eyes he saw now were brown and set wide apart in the squarish face, the lips were well defined and fleshy, like a woman's. Handsome, the boy supposed, for an old man.

'What's his name?' Eamon asked. Deep laughter lines creased under his eyes.

'Rusty,' the boy replied, careful not to appear to be melting too quickly. He had the worldly-wise air of most eleven-year-old boys in Belfast. He did not trust easily.

'Good name. Nice little animal.' Eamon stroked the pup's long silky ears, shifting his weight to his haunches in an unhurried fashion. At least he did not appear to be in a hurry as he stroked idly and mused on the pup's antics. Rising slowly, creaking himself up, he grinned at the boy, engaging his eyes, he said:

'Your da in?'

'Dunno.' The boy shrugged.

Eamon smiled to himself. He was pleased with the lad. Suddenly, he had passed the boy with no apparent haste so that the boy was still turning his head as Eamon's hand turned the key. The pup scampered through in a flurry of tailbeats and elated whimpers.

'Sure we'll have to have a look so,' Eamon tossed over his shoulder in a friendly voice to the boy who, transfixed for a moment, now bolted ahead of Eamon.

Eamon made his way to the living room. It was not far. The boy shouted up the stairs, his eyes fixed on the visitor who reclined with insolent familiarity upon his father's easy chair.

'Dad . . . Da-a-a – Some man here to see you,' the boy's reedy voice called up the stairs. 'Are you there?' He remembered and blushed. Eamon smiled good-naturedly. The pup was on his lap covering his face with wet salty licks. He chuckled.

'What a nice wee thing you are. You are indeed.' The pup rolled onto its back and offered its belly for tickles. Eamon complied with a grunt of delight. 'You are indeed.'

Martin Fogarty descended the stairs and stared past his son toward the visitor. Eamon did not look up immediately, preferring to imagine the expression on the other man's face.

When he did look up, he found what he had expected. Fogarty was terrified. His soft brown eyes shimmered under straight black eyebrows which met in the middle. A pink tongue like a newborn hairless mouse, darted from side to side across the small open gash of mouth. The tremulous smile he attempted from the bottom stair made Eamon look away again in disgust. Now, at least, he could be certain . . . Sometimes there was reasonable cause for doubt. He leaned further back into his host's chair, content in his rectitude. He liked to be sure, to be absolutely sure. He believed himself to be a fair man. Until this moment, he had allowed a tiny thread of doubt to lace his certainty. But he always knew in the end. It was in a man's gaze, in his stance, in the sweat that glistened on his brow at the moment of confrontation and that almost imperceptible spark of relief at the back of the petrified glazed eyes. The traitor's percipience as he tumbled toward inevitable exposure. What Eamon liked to think of as salvation. The inverse bravery of cowards who put themselves in greater danger through their cowardice than they would ever have deemed conceivable through bravery. It was all there in Martin Fogarty's cornered stare.

Eamon pursed his lips up tightly then flexed them wide again, he plucked at specks of fluff on his trouser legs. When he glanced up his gaze appeared unfocused, cloudy at first, then his eyes fixed keenly onto Fogarty and remained there. A tight little smile sketched his lips, he raised a finger to his eye and rubbed the eyelid wearily.

'Martin.' He inclined his head. The man he addressed wrestled with his face and body in the hall. Eamon continued to rub one eye while the other watched the ungainly body, the twitchings and comical, unconscious handwringing of the other man. Fogarty approached with dragging footsteps. Eamon had to suppress a snort. He took the trembling, outstretched hand and lightly grazed it with his own palm.

'Eamon,' a pause to swallow, 'what brings you to this neck of the woods? – you should have called – I might have missed you

7

. . . Ahh, you've met our wee pup then. Nice little thing, isn't he?' Fogarty having found his voice, could not be parted from it. He was doing well, Eamon conceded, as he studied him from under his long lashes.

'Aye. That it is.'

Heartened, Martin Fogarty rubbed his hands together, pulled his nose and replaced the mouselike tongue within his cheek. It still darted about inside. He threw himself into the armchair usually occupied by his wife, leaning across to examine the spaniel as if for the first time.

'Good animal that.' He leapt to his feet again. He could not bring himself to ask outright the reason for the unexpected visit. Though he should. If unexpected, he was surely expected to ask. But he could not bring himself to tempt fate. His eyes darted between the pup and Eamon, a rivulet of sweat streamed down the side of his cheek. He brushed the arm of his sweater along his brow and opened his mouth to speak, but a solitary, harsh, cracked sound was all that he could emit. He swallowed the rock in his throat and tried again:

'Well what'll it be? A hot whiskey – that's it. Need it on a night like this. Freeze the balls off a brass monkey . . . a night like this . . . Liam, flick on the kettle, there's a good lad,' he commanded the boy, who had remained at the bottom of the stairs, staring silent questions toward his father. He had done the wrong thing, letting this man into the house. But he had not let the man into the house, the man had simply walked right in. It was not his fault, but he looked as if he wanted to cry.

'Not for me.' Eamon raised a hand and lifted his gaze to meet Fogarty's eyes. The latter slumped back into his chair again.

'A cup of tea then . . . ?'

'Nothing.'

The boy poised on one foot, unsure where to place himself. His father's tongue was out again. Eamon wondered if the boy could smell the fear as he could. A rancid cold-sweat smell. Unmistakable to one who knows. He wanted to blow his nose to rid it of the sickening odour.

In the ensuing silence, Eamon idly stroked the pup while his eyes raked Fogarty's face. The pup looked around with curiosity at the unmoving, unspeaking men. He hopped from Eamon's lap and circled Fogarty's ankles. The latter hung his head in a gesture of submission; as he stroked the spaniel's head a wry defeated smile played on his thin lips. His bony shoulders heaved up and down as if the effort of breathing was painful.

Eamon leaned forward. He clasped his hands. He wore the deeply serious concerned expression of one encumbered with bad news.

'You know why I'm here.'

For a moment, Fogarty's black curly head poised in hesitation. Then he nodded.

'Good.' Eamon settled back into his chair again. 'Now, where's Sinead?'

'Sinead?'

'Yes. Sinead. Your wife.'

'She's . . . ahh . . . she's upstairs. Putting the babby down for the night.'

'Get her.'

'What for? Can't she . . . can't she just . . . ? Oh Jesus Holy Christ. And Liam . . . ?' Tears streamed down his cheeks.

'Liam can stay here for a while and keep me company.' Eamon offered a clenched smile. His voice had remained soft and low and conspiratorial. He pulled words from his mouth on a length of velvet-covered elastic. While he watched everyone and everything, he appeared to keep one eye trained on himself. He deliberated on movement, a casual throw of his arm, an insistent drumming of fingers on the chair arm, an uncrossing of the legs now, then a crossing again.

Martin Fogarty stumbled to his feet. The pup whined impatiently for more attention, then ran to the boy.

'Liam . . .' The father gestured to his son to take his chair. His nose dripped onto the carpet as he staggered toward the stairs. Halfway up he leaned on the bannister and wept aloud, his shoulders heaving like an exhausted child.

Eamon stared at the boy who stared at his father, an expression of horror tinged with shame, Eamon noted, spreading over the freckled features. From upstairs the sound of a hushed, terse exchange drifted down to them. The boy slowly rolled his wide brown eyes toward Eamon, his mouth had opened into a little 'O'. Eamon smiled, which made the boy flinch, and gazed upstairs again. The little mouth closed and set into a rigid line. He approached Eamon with his head down. He came closer until the top of his trainers touched the toes of Eamon's black lace-ups. The boy twisted his mouth from side to side then he looked up to meet Eamon's eyes. His head jerked several times before he could get the words out:

'If you hurt my Da – I'll get you.' The boy hissed.

Eamon pursed his mouth and nodded. Then he smiled, a broad easy grin which encompassed the boy in his benign approbation. He liked to charm people even when they hated him. He stretched.

'And so you should, Liam. So you should.'

Martin Fogarty descended, followed by his wife, her small sharp eyes blinking rapidly. She carried an infant in her arms, the child was asleep.

'Have a seat, Sinead.' Eamon gestured toward the sofa to his right. She was pitiable in her agitation, scurrying past him to sit as directed. Eamon wondered if she knew about her husband. Perhaps. Perhaps not. He decided it did not matter. Sometimes it was important to know or learn these things, but she was weak. It showed in her small pursed mouth and little nodule of chin. Her face puckered – she was about to cry. A reaction to her husband's obvious terror. She knew nothing much, Eamon decided. She might be dismissed.

He dismissed her and returned his gaze to the hapless figure of Martin Fogarty who stood in the doorway, still weeping, still trailing snot from his nostrils. The sight was repugnant to Eamon. He elected to watch the boy instead. To his surprise, he found the boy was staring at him instead of his father. He was strong. Only eleven and already twice the man his father would ever be. Eamon grunted and shifted in his chair.

'Are you a good boy, Liam?' he asked. 'Do you love your Da?'

The boy started, taken unawares. But he recovered quickly, he took a little step backwards.

'Fuck – off – you,' he snarled.

'Liam!' his mother remonstrated.

'No. No, Sinead.' Eamon raised his hand, he returned the boy's stare. 'Let him be. Let him be. He's a fine lad.' His own glare had taken on a rapt fixated glint.

'Eamon – please . . .' Martin Fogarty snorted through the fog of his misery.

'Shut up,' Eamon barked, his voice harsh, raised for the first time. Fogarty pawed his wet cheeks like a chastened child told to stop crying but unable to control the hiccoughs.

Eamon leaned forward toward the boy.

'Do you know what your Da is, Liam?' he whispered.

The question met measured silence and the narrow, slitted gaze of a suspicious schoolboy.

'He's an informer, Liam. That's what he is. Touting for two years now the bastard. Do you know what an informer is, Liam? No? I'm sure you do - a bright, intelligent lad like yourself, and may I say brave too, but I'll tell you anyway. An informer, Liam, is a traitor, a coward, pretty much the most contemptible, despicable species known to man – or woman for that matter. A breed all to themselves, Liam. Informers screw their grandmothers, Liam, oh yes, and they eat little boys like you for breakfast. And bigger boys than you too. They believe in nothing. They are worth – nothing. Look, look at me – See this . . .' Eamon motioned, picking something out of his nose. He flicked the imaginary speck toward the boy's father. His eyes glowed but the voice was low, steady, persuasive. 'They're not even worth that – what I get up my nose.' He leaned back to study his new pupil. 'Now, Liam. Now d'you see?'

The boy remained mute but Eamon observed the flicker of uncertainty waver behind the rigid stare. The boy knew about informers, Eamon felt sure. Not many eleven-year-olds of his background did not.

Sinead Fogarty began to cry. Now she understood.

Her husband slumped against the doorframe. A thousand denials ebbed and flowed but he could not gather his mouth around the lies he should be offering. He was on the point of collapse. He stared at Eamon with swooning eyes, his breath came in short, wet gurgles. They had set a trap for him. He had even suspected it at the time. But the money had been tempting. To anyone it would have seemed as if his garage business was simply doing well and he had paid his dividends from that too with monies gained from touting, but there was nothing too crazy, too absurd, these days.

He had wanted a new life. Away from the grime, the fanaticism, the never being able to say no. He could never believe the way Eamon O'Neill and others did. Like religious zealots they clung to their fundamentalist doctrines, unable to sway for a solitary moment, unable to falter or question or doubt because that would render their lives meaningless and all the deaths, meaningless, and they would become, yes, ordinary.

He knew that Eamon had been suspicious for well over a year now, but he had covered his tracks well. They were always suspicious in any case. He had wanted to stop, but found he could not. Someone always owned him. He had jumped from the tight embrace of the fundamentalists into the even tighter embrace of the risibly-raincoated Special Branch men who met him in the early hours of the morning at the city dump, walking even then at an angle to each other as they approached him, from years of practice at avoiding the sniper's gun. One down, they had explained, as if he didn't already know, the other had a chance if they were not picked off in a straight line. They were friendly enough to him but Fogarty trusted them as little as he trusted his own kind. The money had increased as the stakes had increased, and now Eamon O'Neill was here.

Fogarty passed a hand over his face and hung his head in defeat. Then he heard his son's voice piercing the cloud around him.

'My father's no informer. He's not. He never was. You've got it all wrong, Mister.' Liam's eyes blazed with belief.

Eamon laughed with pleasure. He clapped his hands.

'You're right about one thing there lad – he isn't . . . any more.' He turned from the boy, who in the process of backing away, had met a chair and collapsed into it. He gripped the chair arms fiercely.

'You should be proud of your boy, Martin,' Eamon sighed. 'And grateful too. You should be shot for what you've done. You should die like a whimpering dog in the street. I should take you outside and whip you like the cur you are. Show you the top of my shoe. Spit on your face and roll you over in the gutter. Something for Liam to remember, eh? What a fine sight you'd make, you snivelling cur. Aye, that's what I ought to do. There are others who would do worse. A lot worse. But not tonight. Not tonight . . . but maybe. You know that. I know that. Now Liam here knows that too. Just one more word – word, mind – and I'll come for you. They couldn't hide you from me. The world's a small place. Remember Gerry Hennessy? Yes? We found him didn't we? He had to be identified by his teeth. Yes, the world is a small enough place to find a whimpering dog if you have to – d'you understand? D'you get my meaning, Martin?'

Eamon was on his feet. His face strained toward Fogarty, veins bulging on his temples. He shuddered in silence for a moment as his fists clenched and unclenched by his side.

Martin Fogarty cowered in abject relief. He was saved. His son had saved him. He could not meet their eyes. His wife retching with terror on the sofa, his son, now poker-faced, rigid in his chair like a small Buddha, doubt permeating his stony expression even as his father peered from under his lashes. He groaned with relief and shame. The boy's eyes burned through him. Questioning, questioning, questioning.

Eamon thrust his hands into his pockets. Searched, found what he was looking for. He encircled it with his fingers. It had all been so much easier than he had expected. Thanks to the boy. He smiled reassuringly at him.

'Well that's that. You'll keep an eye on your Da for me won't you, Liam?'

The boy blinked. The pup returned from a foray to the kitchen, and wagged itself around Eamon's ankles again.

'Nice animal,' he intoned and bent to pick up the excited spaniel. He held it up by the scruff of its neck and playfully brought the dog toward his face. He nuzzled the shiny wet black nose with his own. The pup flailed short legs in the air and whined with pleasure. Its forehead was wrinkled with the loose skin pushed up from the neck so that the eyes, half concealed in layers of puppy fat, gleamed irresistibly. Eamon smiled and conceded to the seemingly endless capacity of dogs and small children to charm at will. He allowed the pup to lick his nose.

Then he pulled something slender and glinting from his pocket. He held the blade to the dog's throat which provoked yips of delight. The yip turned into a high-pitched scream, almost human in its unearthly tone as the blade sliced through soft folds of neck down its full fat belly, through small furry testicles to come out dripping at the other side. The pup shuddered. For a moment, the flailing legs pawed the space between them as the wail pierced through its opened frothing mouth: high, shocked and confused, then the resonance of agony. The scream subsided. A moment passed as the liquid eyes clouded and glazed. A quiver and the hot bloody entrails poured out of the cleft. The animal was still wriggling, slightly, though silent in its death throes as its long gut followed by various dark red, bluish and bright orange viscera slapped onto the carpet in a steaming, spreading puddle.

Eamon shook the dog's neck. Another glossy pile of brown sacs fell to the floor, followed by a spray of blood. He was careful to stand well back to avoid the surge but a few splatters caught his coat and shoes. The eyes stared at him, glassy and shadowed.

Eamon looked around the room. Sinead Fogarty was choking, about to vomit. Trickles of blood veined the beige carpet and lapped at her shoes. She hugged the sleeping child to her and moaned into the folds of her shawl.

Martin Fogarty had fallen to his knees. He babbled, dispossessed of his senses. The blade might as well have sliced him through. A wet stain spread around the front of his trousers.

Silently, Eamon turned to face the boy. He nodded at the carcass still raised in his hand and inclined his head toward the boy's father. The boy, though speechless with shock, understood the message. His lower lip trembled. He wanted to cry out, to scream, yet managed to contain himself. His pup. His beautiful pup, Rusty. He could not hate this man any more if he had done that to his father.

The blood flowed relentlessly in every direction. It mingled with the wet urine stains between Martin Fogarty's spread thighs. Eamon eyed the man with dispassion as Fogarty's hands groped along the ground as if in search of something. It was strange that no one had screamed, but Eamon had often found that to be the case.

Now the son, too, eyed his father. That kneeling, moaning mass of flesh, wallowing in piss and dog's blood. Martin Fogarty's snorts of anguish graduated into a cacophony of mewled whimpers. Eamon peered closely at the boy's face. The expression of shock, horror and scalding shame might have mirrored his own face, the night his father died. He hissed an intake of breath as the image of his father on his knees, begging, returned to his mind. But his face only registered a bland curiosity as he cocked his head to one side while he studied the boy. He spoke gently:

'You see how it is, Liam, eh?' he whispered. 'This is how it is – tell your father, won't you? There's a good lad.'

He carried the wretched evisceration to Martin Fogarty, and with a grimace threw the pulpy mess on top of him.

Blood poured from the long gash still. Fogarty moaned in disbelief. The body was still warm against his thighs. Small white teeth pressed against his hand through the opened mouth.

The boy looked, then dropped his eyes. Two livid spots spread hot and scarlet across his cheeks, the lower lip trembled still but he controlled his mouth by biting down hard on the bottom lip. His eyes flickered up toward a corner in the ceiling, and he stopped himself blinking by biting ever harder on the lower lip. To blink would be to cry and the man appeared to be waiting for that.

Eamon observed the telltale flickers in the otherwise impassive stare. He glowered down at the quaking heap at his feet, then with deliberate care, almost fussily, he extended a foot and stubbed the dog's slit belly into Martin Fogarty's crotch.

'Poor beast should be eating your liver,' he hissed.

He looked around for the last time to view the boy, but his stare was unreturned. He noticed that the lower lip was bitten so hard by now that it seeped blood. A few drops spilled onto the boy's chin.

It would have to be for others to comfort him. Eamon's work was done. His duty executed. He felt, as he walked toward the front door trailing a path of bloody footprints behind him, that, if in a sense, Missionary was what he was, then he had converted them well.

*   *   *

Outside, the cold northeasterly wind sliced into his face. It had dropped another couple of degrees since he had entered the warm cocoon of Fogarty's house. Icy rain washed the blood from his shoes but only succeeded in darkening the patches on his coat. He inspected his new overcoat ruefully, but at least the rain was cold so the stains might be removed quite easily once soaked. A small price to pay for a job well done. He sighed with contentment and ran his forefinger down the sharp wet blade inside his pocket.

He spat at the thought of Fogarty's miserable face. It was one thing to be a coward and a traitor, but to be a fool as well . . . What did the wretched creature think that Eamon would do to him in a house with witnesses whose reactions would be at best unknowable, at worst, unpredictable? If the party had wanted him dead, he would be dead. Instead they had fed him on a diet of useless information, and he had eaten and regurgitated to their satisfaction. Now, he might be used – for a while longer anyway. There was justice in feeding pigs with pigs. Alone, he might have threatened Fogarty with the knife. Just a little, if required. But that was unnecessary once he had seen that awful fear-filled face. Still. The boy was handy. The dog was useful. Later, doubtless, Fogarty would realize his own foolishness, but still he would not run. Wherever he went, he would have to take himself with him – and the boy. He would vacillate, waver, between the talked-about and the talked-to's, mouth quivering, eyes watering, belly churning, until one side or the other terminated the porcine jig.

Despite the cold, Eamon knew that his cheeks were burning. He felt his face. A hot flush had crept up his thick short neck to suffuse his cheeks. He walked, head down, feet crunching the pavement. The echo of his footfalls followed him.

He stopped to spit again. It was still there. Throbbing, insistent in its nagging. He tried to concentrate on the song – 'Drink, drink, drink . . .' but a few streets along, it still swelled between his legs.

Betrayed by his own body, it was unseemly. He recognized the burning cheeks not as the flush of success, though that too, but rather as the blush of desire and shame. He had to stop for a moment to breathe in deep gusts of stinging air. He shook his head, but still the recollection persisted – it always did at times like this. He was approaching his thirteenth year at the time, not long after his first confusing wet dream. A lad from out of town, a great big shaven-headed country boy, brought a jar of chopped pigs' livers to school with him. In the outside toilet in the schoolyard, he lined the boys up and told them to stick their dicks into the jar. He told them that 'it' felt just like that. The same consistency. The same feeling. Or words to that effect. A few boys demurred but others eagerly pulled themselves erect and plunged inside. Eamon had watched in silent horror as boy after boy shuddered and spilled themselves into the jar. The contents did not look quite so red or liverish by the time it was passed to him. He managed an erection but kept his hands tightly cupped around himself to avoid the curious slitted eyes – each boy was comparing – but at the last moment he wilted and turned from the jar with his hand clamped over his mouth. For months afterwards he vomited at the thought.

Months had passed now since he had resorted to self-abuse. Those covert moments between the sheets when he felt that he was entirely alone in the world, lying there with a handful of white, viscous, sticky loneliness, desperate to wipe his sin onto a crumpled tissue. A man should be strong. Strong enough to resist. He would read St Paul before sleep tonight.

But Maureen crept into his mind. Slinking like a moulting cat around a corner in his brain. She was only a few streets away, a short walk.

He could feel his nerve ends quivering. The sordid tumescence poked through his flies. He would have to go.

With cool familiarity, Eamon reached inside the letter box on the door to Maureen's small redbricked end of terrace house. He pulled through the key on a string and opened the door. He could hear voices coming from the kitchen at the back.

The door was open. Maureen was standing by the kitchen table, slicing a sandwich in two for her son, a blonde cherub-faced boy

17

of nine, who stood beside her. The pair looked up, unstartled, as Eamon entered.

Maureen's hands continued cutting, placing the sandwich quarters carefully upright on the plate as she eyed her visitor surreptitiously, took in the blood-splattered coat, wet hair, the flared nostrils steaming still with cold fog and the dark brown eyes fixed upon her, ignoring the boy. She had seen that gaze before, dark and needy and ruthless as a newborn baby's.

Maureen smiled, a tentative questioning smile that merely traced her thin top lip, turning it up at the corners. She was a heavy woman in her mid-thirties. Weight disguised the full ravages of the years, until close up, the tight etched lines under grey pallid eyes might be seen. Eyes that were slightly bulbous, cheeks soft and loose, a protrusion of the upper teeth which overlapped in front, short brown hair frizzed at the edges from too many bad home perms, all merging to give the appearance of a benign chipmunk.

Eamon could tell that she was dressed to go out: she wore a short red skirt, at least one size too tight under which her fat knees and calves wobbled like jellies stuck into her black patent stilettoes. In stockinged feet, she would be just under five feet tall. The white blouse unbuttoned sufficiently to reveal the huge swell of her breasts. Her nipples protruded through the white brassiere and polyester blouse. Eamon caught his breath.

A knowing, cunning look flickered briefly over Maureen's features before she applied her concentration again to the sandwich, absorbed, or so it appeared, in her endeavour to make each triangle fall in identical sequence one upon the other.

With her head down, she said, in her breathless voice that rose at the end of every sentence, as though in permanent query:

'Well, well, Mr O'Neill. Long time no see-ee.'

The boy stared sullenly at Eamon. He wanted his sandwich whenever his mother would stop playing with it.

'About six months, I'd say, Maureen,' Eamon grunted from the doorway.

'Oh at least, I'd sa-ay.'

'You're going out?'

18

'I was aye.'

'Was?'

'Well. I am. I will be that is. In a whi-ile. You know?' She giggled like a young girl. Eamon flushed with embarrassment. If she winked he would turn on his heel immediately. She did not.

Instead she modified her lascivious expression to one of practised innocuousness. She slid the plate toward her son, and indicated the television in the next room with a nod of her head. The boy took the plate and slowly added salt to the sandwich. He liked to make it clear by such small gestures, to visitors, that it was in the end, his house. Maureen nudged him with her elbow and he left.

When he was gone, Maureen leaned forward, smiling broadly. The nipples thrust out as she had intended.

'And what can I do for you-ooo?'

Eamon shuffled toward her. He opened his coat and dropped his eyes to the obvious bulge in the front of his trousers. Maureen's eyes followed his glance and she grinned with feigned surprise.

'Oh dear,' she said. She might have been talking to a child who had cut his knee and had come for a bandage. She knew how Eamon liked her to talk. And how to act. Sometimes she was confused in the preamble, so many preferences to keep on file, but in general, through memory and intuition, she employed reasonably effective tactics. The competition, like the clientele, was stiff; any edge was worth exploiting.

'Need some help,' Eamon grunted. He stared shamefaced at the swollen gland and pulled the corners of his mouth down. 'What about . . . ?' He gestured toward the boy in the other room.

'He's grand. His programme'll be on in a minute.'

Maureen took him by the hand and led him upstairs into her small pink room. She was pleased Eamon had returned, fearing him lost to a competitor. There was a certain cachet to be had from having Eamon O'Neill frequent her house, and he was quick, direct, and paid in full and on time.

Her room was filled with white cane furniture, bedstead, chair, chest of drawers all in white rattan, covered for the most part in satin or lace cushions in the shape of hearts or squares with inscriptions on them.

'Love is never having to say you're sorry', and 'I love you this much', this latter on a heart held by a small fluffy bear.

Maureen lit a dim lamp on the dressing table and swept all the cushions off the bed with her arm. She pulled down the pink floral bedspread and turned to Eamon.

'C'mon then,' she giggled, unbuttoning her blouse.

He hesitated for a moment, watching her undress with the hooded eyes of a hungry, nervous cat. His cheeks burned. He shrugged his coat off and threw it on top of the cushions on the cane chair.

'Not there,' Maureen remonstrated. She was a confident mistress in her own territory. 'You'll get blood on my cushions – just leave everything in a pile on the ground.'

'Sorry.'

Her blouse lay at her feet, wet with sweat under the armpits. She kicked it away. Eamon pulled his sweater over his head and stood in his vest and trousers. He pulled his stomach in and watched her wrestle with the zip of the tight red skirt. She wriggled it down along her meaty thighs and kicked it to join the blouse. She was wearing white suspenders and panties above black stockings over which white soft flesh spilled generously. Layers of belly, wrinkled in the middle and scarred below the navel, quivered beneath the white brassiere. With a coy smile, the crossed front teeth peeping beaver-like over the lower lip, she removed the brassiere and unleashed the oscillating breasts traced with blue veins around the purple, goosepimpled nipples. She kept her stilettoes on, which added to the grotesque proportions of her frame, the short fat legs peeled apart only at the ankles. With a groan, as if the effort might be all too much, she pared herself from the rind of white panties, thrusting it downwards with her thumbs. Halfway down, she looked up and added another toothy smile to the performance.

Eamon was entranced. It seemed to him at that moment, at all such moments with Maureen, that she was the most beautiful and the most intrinsically evil thing he had ever seen. He groaned and removed his shoes and socks, then unbuckled his belt and

20

slid his trousers down. He approached her in his shorts, the stub poking out through the blue material. He never removed his shorts until underneath the bedcovers.

Maureen's bulging eyes widened. Her mouth made a salacious *moue*. In the half-light, her skin shone with a sickly mustard pallor. He stopped to look at her for a moment, then buried his head in the enormous bosom. He placed his hands over each nipple, barely touching, feeling the warmth of her. The palms of his hands whispered against the dark tips.

'Oh,' he said. 'Oh. Oh.' He nuzzled slack flesh, interring his nose in the sweaty cleft. 'Oh God.' She exuded a musky, high, perspiratory odour, redolent of greasy mutton.

'There's a good lad,' she coaxed, rubbing the back of his head. Still cradling the head against her breast, she lowered herself onto the bed, shunting her shoes off with her toes.

'There's a good boy,' as he lay on top of her moaning. Her left hand slipped him out of the slit of his shorts.

'Oh,' he cried. 'Good God.'

'Oh now. Who's a big boy,' she crooned. Her right arm extended and deftly pulled open a drawer on the cane bedside cabinet.

'Here. Put this on.' She slipped a small foil package in under his spread palm.

'What is it?'

'You know what it is, for God's sake.'

Head entombed in cleavage, shook.

'We don't need that,' it muttered. 'You know I'm clean.'

'Aye darling. But what about me-ee?' She laughed. 'Anyways, look it, they're all using them these days. AIDS and stuff. Pigs in Hawaii and the like . . .'

'. . . Haiti.'

'Wha-aa?'

'Nothing.'

'Well?'

Eamon groaned. She was tanklike in her resolve. Maybe she was right though, he knew it to be unclean up there. With a sigh, he swung himself around on the bed, and with his back to her, began to fumble with the offensive package. He did not like her

21

to see him naked but she crept around his shoulder and peered down, smiling. He shut his eyes and braced himself. The urge to reach up his hand behind him and snap her stupid neck was almost overwhelming. Instead, he sat rigidly still and willed his mind into a cool blank canvas, the one without the clutter and shadows. When he could trust himself, he opened his eyes and spoke quietly:

'Get – off – my – shoulders. Now.'

She pulled back in haste, aware that she had forgotten the contents of the file.

'Sorr-eee.'

He flinched.

'I think I'll go home now,' he said. She watched the wounded shoulders, stiff as chairbacks, and wondered what way to play him.

'Ah love. I'm sorry. I am really. I just forgot you don't like me lookin'. Sure you're a grand man. You are truly. C'mon now. C'mon.'

She ran a tentative hand up his back and patted the bed beside her. The shoulders relaxed after a few seconds. He swung around again, pulling the covers with him to hide his nakedness.

As he pushed into her he was aware that it would all be over in a matter of minutes – if that – and he would regain his freedom for another while. In a short time now, after the sucking in, the plunging in, the nightmare that was loving or all he knew of loving, would be over and he would cry. He always cried.

She was used to that. He was not alone there. Weeping like babies in her arms, recoiling their flaccid worms to creep home, frightened as rabbits. A few wanted another go or even to stay the night, the latter usually true of the younger, less experienced lads. But she charged for seconds. It didn't matter to her the amount of helpings. Her pudding paid the rent and thus could never be free. Even at Christmas.

Eamon grunted. He sweated. His eyes remained tightly shut.

'Oh,' he moaned. 'Oh, oh . . .' But it just slipped out. Seeped out in a skulking trickle when he had prepared himself for a geyser-like eruption. Still, it was over now, until the next time –

22

if there was a next time. He always hoped that there might not be, he could manage for several months at a time now.

Maureen's hand patted his back in a mechanical motion as he lay on top of her, crushing his post-coital sobs into the space on the pillow beside her head. She regulated her breathing to accommodate the dead weight. Short, fast pants, two in, two out. He was heavy.

While she waited for him to finish, moans gradually dying away, a subsidence into ragged tired breath, she wondered, not for the first time, about this man who cried like a baby after sex, an act which he performed with the startled thrusts of a bullish teenager on the sofa of his girlfriend's home.

Her fingers feigned a drumming upon the heaving shoulders. Not long now. It looked like he wasn't going to talk – sometimes he rambled on, muttering like a schoolboy while she waited, but he did not appear to be in a garrulous mood tonight. She would hardly be late – only ten minutes or so after all – at the Working Men's Club, where nobody worked.

Maureen considered condoms the best thing ever. Now she wouldn't even have to bother with douching or showering; a quick pat with the powder puff in the bathroom and she would be right as rain for the night, and what's more she smiled to herself, she would have a decent sum of money in her pocket.

It was an effort not to drum her fingers in impatient allegro. He was so damn heavy. Slabbering and grunting like a pig. So strange, a man like him to be such a wain. Maureen recalled the only time she had ever seen Eamon outside her own house – it was at some Easter service or other, the Stations of the Cross on Good Friday maybe, at the Redemptorist's. He was at the Monastery with his mother. Both stiff-backed, heads bowed, up and down they went, on two knees, genuflecting. Yes, it was the Stations all right. Maureen went to keep her sister happy who lived nearby. Afterwards, in the cold, pallid afternoon, he passed right by her. It was almost dark. She nodded or blinked an acknowledgement, perceptible only to one who might expect to perceive it, but he blinked at the driving rain and showed her only the corner of his eye. She expected neither more nor less. And yet, occasionally the softer ones cast her a surreptitious eye to show that if all things were equal, they might have tried a smile.

Maureen had observed under heavy eyelids to hide the direction of her glance, how easily Eamon O'Neill seemed to glide from this person to that, he had a handshake for many, a smile for a few, just like a politician. That full slow smile, cracking his face on the cheeks, sketching friendly grooves around eyes that crinkled in soft amusement. Those shining liquid brown eyes taking you in, giving you time and face and sometimes respect and the benefit of his good humour which was, after all, a thing to be desired, a thing to see – that smile – as his head cocked to the side to listen to his mother as she whispered in his ear. The dark eyebrows raised in polite, slightly ironical attention. The mother did not smile, Maureen recalled. But she watched her son smiling and seemed content.

The slobbering desisted and Eamon rolled off. He snorted.

'Ah God.'

'Are you all right now, Eamon?'

'I'm fine. Grand,' the voice quavered. 'It's just – it's just that . . .' He squeezed his voice out but broke off as a voluptuous sob overcame him.

Maureen sighed heavily. Perhaps he was going to talk after all. Her teeth bit into her lower lip, the entire bottom half of her face crumpled and folded into layers, chin dissolving into bands of neck. She lay rigid, droll-eyed, like weeks old unkneaded dough.

Eamon shifted onto his elbow and stared down at her. He could barely disguise his disgust. He wanted to say something but she took his voice away.

He emitted a long groan and turned away. She so resembled a hapless sheep when she rolled her eyes and offered that vacuous smile. As ever, he was wondering how he could possibly have entered her. Right now, a jar of pig's liver seemed an eminently more attractive proposition. He could not help himself:

'Tch, tch,' he said.

Maureen remained in bed as he quickly dressed and threw two crisp ten pound notes on the cane dressing table. She sighed.

'I suppose it'll be another few months before you call on us again?'

'Maybe.'

'I see yeah.'

'What?'

'I said – yeah.'

He cinched his belt tight in anger, cast her a last look –'God' – and ran down the stairs.

The boy was still watching television. He did not look up but his back was straight. He was always prepared for trouble. The half-eaten sandwich lay upon his lap.

In freezing night, Eamon stalked homeward. Several times, he hawked and spat. His body still shook in huge rolling paroxysmic shudders which seemed to emanate from his bowels. Within his pockets, his hands trembled. The smells of the night lingered on his clothing and on his body. He could have split his skull against a lamppost. But then, in no time at all, or so it seemed, he was standing outside the door to his own house. He waited a moment, leaning forward to rest his hands on his knees. He lifted his head and watched the sleet slanting across the darkness. A cat called up an alleyway nearby.

Bloated with deep breaths, Eamon entered the house. He passed the small living room on his left and went on to the kitchen behind. They were still waiting for him, pretending not to be. Their eyes full of questions.

'I'm tired,' he announced, banging the kettle on the gas ring.

Agnes O'Neill – Ma – filled her kitchen with herself. She stood there, head down, ironing, her hand moving back and forth in fast, aggressive strokes. When she folded a pillowslip to iron in quarters, the motion of her palm creasing the fabric was like a punishment. Her lips pursed in concentration.

The others sat around the square table nursing mugs of cold tea. A priest, and a middle-aged man with a lined and crusty face.

The priest eyed Eamon's stiffened back, took in the specks of blood, added and subtracted and reckoned in his head. He had the well scrubbed appearance of clerics and small children, with full purple lips that constantly threshed together as he performed his mental arithmetic. He had salty clipped hair, a pink bald pate high on his long peanut-shaped head and eyes of palest blue that could, at times, appear to dissolve into a startling white. He had the appearance of a man who had been pasteurised, and relished the experience. He was Eamon's uncle, Agnes's older brother, Fr. Joseph MacGinn.

'We're here for a while Eamon,' the priest broke into the silence. 'What kept you?' His voice was low and insinuating.

The iron clattered over the ironing board.

Eamon's back ramrodded further in irritation. He wanted a mug of hot tea, he wanted to bathe, maybe say his prayers for a while, maybe not. More than anything, he wanted to be alone. He did not want their bleatings or their prurient curiosity. Fr. Joe was the worst, but he had to be tolerated. The little things they told him just to keep him happy. So that he could pretend. Ma said they should keep him happy. And quiet.

'Never mind what kept me,' Eamon barked, after a long sigh to show that he was prepared to tolerate only so much.

'Well, then. How did you get on?' Fr. Joe would not be put off the scent that easily.

'I got on grand.'

'Is he sorted out then?'

'Yeah.'

'What?'

'I said yeah.' Eamon grimaced to himself at the absurd repetition of almost the same conversation he had had with Maureen earlier. He was leaning against the Formica dresser, cradling his mug of steaming tea. His face was closed against them, but softened slightly as his mother cast him an encouraging look while she straightened her spine to fold a shirt against her chest, pinning it with her chin.

'Not too much trouble, I hope?' Fr. Joe was saying, for the benefit of his crony, Eamon surmised. Eamon rolled his eyes toward his mother. It was nearly time for her to intervene to end this charade.

'No trouble at all,' he replied.

'Well, you might tell us – he was touting then? No doubt about it, eh? How d'you handle him?'

Eamon winced. Enough was enough. Ma's iron struck the board forcefully.

'Don't you mind about that now.' Thump went her iron-filled

fist, up and down, her voice like her brother's was low and sibilant. She issued words from the side of her mouth, staccato-like, threw them toward the ground, divested them of any inflection as they reached her lips, so that it seemed that everything she said, quickly, hurriedly, was in effect a sort of secret.

'Eamon said it was handled. He said so. Thank God for that much. Yous can be going home now, let yous. We should all be in our beds long ago.'

Fr. Joe might have protested, but he noted the firm line of his sister's thin lips, the reciprocal gleam in eyes blue-white as his own. The man beside him mumbled in agreement about the lateness of the hour, adding thanks for the tea. He was sorry to give them all so much bother but the times that were in it and so on.

Eamon nodded the man from the room, placing a hand sympathetically against the small of his back to hasten him toward the door.

The feel of the man's jacket against Eamon's insistent fingers was enough to make him squirm. He could not abide the weak, unctuous features, drooping mouth and shifting eyes of this drunk. But he had a good son, a man, not yet twenty-four, put away as a consequence of Fogarty's touting. The man had a right to be interested in the night's outcome. Besides Fr. Joe had been the one to raise the initial suspicions about Fogarty. Confessional secrets passed on from one priest to another, neither above a little touting themselves.

When they had left – Fr. Joe with a show of reluctance – Eamon slurped back his tea. He stayed a good distance away from his mother. The salt smell of sex was so strong in his nostrils he felt sure that she must smell it too. The thought made him shake again.

She continued with her ironing. Th-ump up, thu-ump down the board, a quick flick of the garment with her left hand, sometimes a press so hard on a section that steam hissed and spitted in fury from the iron, encircling her wrist.

'You know Joe,' she said, 'he was always a bit of an old woman. A bit of a busybody really. No harm done.'

Eamon could sense her anger but that was as much as she could show for now, and as far as she could go toward an apology for having the priest and his crony there in the first place.

'Busybodies talk,' Eamon muttered, draining the mug for a last sip.

'Ach, he's all right. You know that yourself. He just wants to be involved is all. I'll talk to him tomorrow.'

'I don't mind him but the other . . . that's asking for trouble. That's just plain bloody stupid if I may say so.' He slammed the mug down.

'You're right. Of course you're right.' She ironed with renewed vigour. 'I'll speak to him tomorrow. Now go to bed, let you. Look it, I'll hang the white shirt with the navy stripe on the back of the chair there for the morning. That grease stain came out with a boil. I told you it would.'

The intricacies of their relationship dictated that he hang around for a little while longer to savour her kindnesses. She was not often gentle with him. Her soft, low voice droned sideways about this and that and nothing while he sipped a second mug of tea. She had a capacity for endless idle talk when it suited her and now it took the sting out of the evening for her son. He was momentarily soothed, massaged by chatter. She did not ask questions, just like Maureen, but for different reasons. Ma O'Neill found it impossible as a rule to talk about important matters. She had learned to look to the side of things, above or just below; money problems or deaths, it was all the same, she did not look straight ahead at the thing itself, not because she could not face it – she could – but to face it, look at it head on, so to speak, meant facing whatever lay or lurked behind. She believed the problem of today staved off the problem of tomorrow, which to her mind was always worse.

It was warm in the small yellow kitchen. Condensation trickled down the back window, lapping into little pools on the rotted lintel. Steam rose from Eamon's coat. He could still smell himself but an ease had crept into his limbs, and he was reluctant now to climb the stairs.

'Any hot water there, Ma?' he asked.

'For what?'

'For a bath.'

'At this hour?'

'What of it?'

'Nothing. Nothing. I'd have said it's a bit late for baths. Still . . . it's up to yourself.'

His spine stiffened again. He shuffled his coat off before she could tell him to do so.

She had not once looked up from her ironing; the blue eyes darted from side to side as she spoke, but never fixed on his face.

'There's plenty water,' she said, and, 'your brother's coming up next weekend.'

'Who told you?'

'He telephoned Mrs Neeson tonight. She came round herself and gave me the message. He's bringing someone with him.'

'Is he indeed.'

'A girl.'

'A girl?'

'For the weekend. Some doctor's daughter from County Cork, by all accounts.'

'What else did Mrs Neeson have to say?'

'A Kitty, she said. Short for Kathleen, I suppose. No fuss needed, she said. The girl's not a bit like that.' Eamon could only stand and admire his mother's implacability, not for the first time. His younger brother might have brought girls home every weekend for all she showed. Still, there was that telltale, breathless quality to her voice.

'Kept her a secret didn't he?'

'Aye.' A frown transferred itself to the ironing board; she crunched a shirt collar flat with one solid deft movement. Eamon waited. He knew from the pursing of her lips that she had more to relate. 'Her mother kicks with the other foot by all accounts,' she said lightly.

'What? A Prod?'

'Aye. According to Girlie Neeson anyways.'

'And how does she know?'

'Dan must have told her, I suppose. You know what he's like. He'd enjoy shocking the likes of Girlie.'

'And what about the father – this Doctor?'

'A Taig.'

'Well she'll be brought up a Taig, so I suppose.'

'I suppose.' Ma's mouth unpursed. 'You'll have to give her your room and bunk in with Dan. We'd never manage to tidy his room up enough in time. Your room is grand. You don't mind – do you?' Two sleeves were flattened in the blink of an eye.

'S'pose not.'

'Good. That's settled then.' She clicked the iron's control off. He might go.

Eamon went. First, he ran the water for his bath downstairs in the small bathroom addition that was once a back kitchen. Then he trudged upstairs, realizing with each step the extent of his exhaustion. He would have stepped out of his skin if he could. A vision of Sinead Fogarty's tearstained face entered his head. Just once, he had seen his mother cry. One time. The same night his hands had dripped with his father's blood. In daylight, you could still quite clearly see the faded stains on the stair carpet. Someone, a neighbour probably, had used water from the boiled kettle to try and dissolve the stains. Months later, Ma on her knees, no longer crying, wrestling with the stains, scrubbing, as aggressively as she ironed. Everyone knew, or should know, she said, that you treated blood with cold water, not hot. It's a protein stain, she said, like egg – it sets in hot water, we'll never get the blood off now, she said to her young son, the eldest, watching.

Years later, his eyes sought without thinking, the dark spot shaped like Italy on the third stair, the dots like small islands on the fifth stair, the just perceptible boy's handprint at the top. Stains he knew well. Since he had made them. They had become in some ways comforting in their immutability.

He had caught the inflection through the dry plains of her voice when she spoke of Danny. Eamon rubbed his open palms down his face and moaned. He was too weary for prayer. Best to start afresh tomorrow. From force of habit he dipped his forefinger in the holy water font hanging on the wall that separated his bedroom from his mother's. The sign of the cross was made on his forehead before he remembered, and once more was consumed by guilt. He would scrub the sign off in the bath. It was the least he could do. He slumped against the doorframe and buried his face in his hands.

From the kitchen his mother's voice called up to him.

'Eamon. It's run already. Your bath is run. You haven't gone asleep have you? Eamon – answer me.'

'I'll be down in a sec,' he shouted. She would not go to bed, he knew, while he was still up. She had yet to intone her night prayers by the kitchen table, then set the table for the morning though there was just the two of them. She had the television to unplug, the fire to check and recheck for sparking embers and the lights to switch off. It did not matter that these things might be done by someone else, namely himself, she would run through the checklist again anyway.

He had passed her on the way to the bathroom when she stopped him. She indicated his coat on the chair with her head.

'There's blood on your coat.'

'Aye.' A sigh.

'I'll dab it with cold water while you're having your bath. Cold water for blood, you know.'

'I know.'

He slammed the door behind him and locked it. He was frantic to be cleansed. Impatient to have done with the night. She wore him out, from time to time.

September

Kitty stretched and shunted up on the bed. She lit a cigarette and followed the blue stream of smoke upwards with her eyes. It was raining again. Lightly at first, just a drizzle barely clinging to the windowpanes, then as a strong wind blew up out of nowhere rattling the windowframes, the rain pelted down. She listened to it beat against the glass and to the sound of car tyres sloshing through the wet streets outside, yellow beams circling and illuminating the bedroom for an instant, then darkness again. A distant siren sounded nearby, raucous and intrusive for a few teeth-gritting moments, then dissolved into the city's swell somewhere to the north. She was remembering nights like this from her childhood when she would lie awake for hours just listening to the rain, safe and warm in her single bed; now, the feeling was similar except the bed was larger and Danny lay beside her. His breathing was regular, he was finally asleep, but she knew that if she touched him, he would awaken instantly. She stubbed out the cigarette and leaned sideways to kiss his cheek.

He pulled her closer and she laid her head on his chest.

'Shh,' she said, 'I didn't mean to wake you.'

'Yes you did,' he said, drowsily.

'Well, are you awake now or what?' she asked.

'If I say "or what", does that mean I can go back to sleep?'

'No.'

'I'm awake then.'

'I've been thinking,' she said, smiling already at the expected response.

'Did it hurt?' he complied.

'Just a bit but I'll get over it – now if you're finished smartassing you can ask me what I was thinking about.'

'I don't need to ask, you were thinking about me I know,' he said, chuckling as she raised a hand to lightly cuff his cheek.

Kitty sighed with contentment. She loved these moments entwined together under the bedcovers when they could indulge in a silly idle banter that would have made them cringe by day, when the need to maintain a certain distance, a certain degree of coolness, still prevailed. She often woke Danny several times a night, sometimes just to check that she had the power to do so but also for the pleasure of listening to his sleep-filled voice tease her or answer her questions without the wary self-consciousness that accompanied his daytime responses.

'Well,' he said, raising his head slightly, 'what were you thinking about then?'

'I was remembering our first night together – it was raining like this, do you remember?'

'No. I can't say that I do. All I remember is thinking – I hope she's not like her snotty friends . . . Can I go back to sleep now please?'

'One more thing.' Kitty raised her head.

He bent his head down to kiss her forehead.

'Yes. I love you,' he said. 'Now, go to sleep.'

They drifted down again beneath the bedcovers. Kitty sighed aloud and waited until his draped arm felt limp and lifeless around her midriff. When she heard the constant rhythmic inhalation and exhalation of his deep sleep, she moved up on the bed with folded arms and stared down at his supine form. She could not sleep. Not yet at any rate. She rubbed her cheek along the bristles of his chin. He moaned softly in his sleep, but she hushed him with a finger to his lips. His mouth opened and his tongue snaked along her finger.

'Sleep,' she commanded.

'Come here,' he said, burrowing against her.

'Sleep,' she said sternly, smiling when a little snore escaped his lips. She brushed her lips gently along his, drawing her hair over his face in long sweeps.

A cat-like squeal sounded from the flat next door. Kitty lay back and stretched. The couple, she reckoned they had to be in their sixties if they were a day, were at it again. She pulled her mouth down at the corners and moved her head in time to the elderly woman's moans. Usually Danny listened with her, snorting into the pillow and timing himself with the man's thrusts, but he was finally unconscious. She traced the outline of his face with her finger and decided to let him sleep on. She chuckled to herself remembering again that first night together over two years ago.

Now twenty-four, Danny was a year older than her. They met at some house party or other, not long after leaving college. It had been one of those all-night affairs of the type Kitty usually avoided like the plague. Roaring music, ersatz disco lighting, the sweet acridity of reefer smoke drifting in swathes around the room, wilting queues for the bathroom; fag-ashed, limp sandwiches and little surreptitious pools of vomit in every corner. She found herself standing by one such pool, nursing yet another bottle of tasteless beer, watching her flatmates and ex-college friends; like her, they were new to their jobs, unlike her they wore square-shouldered late-eighties' power suits which she still eschewed for her college uniform of slashed jeans and oversized sweaters. Then she spotted Danny standing in another corner across the room. It was really his similar uniform which caught her eye at first.

She watched him for a while through the strata of grey-blue smoke. He appeared to be alone. He was unshaven, shabbily dressed even by student standards and his hair stood on end where he had rested the side of his head against the wall. It was this observation, that he did not automatically raise a hand to smooth his hair, which held her attention. She approached cautiously, prepared to veer off course in an instant should a proprietress suddenly loom into view by his side.

They slumped together by the wall for a while before Kitty ventured some small talk, the inanity of its content sticking in her throat even as she tried. She had realized too late that he was monstrously good-looking; the fog in the room and his scruffy appearance had managed to conceal this fact at a distance. Now that she could see the crisp blue eyes, sharply defined cheekbones and wide, flexible mouth, she felt intimidated and predatory. She closed her eyes and wished that she was dead or at the very least

34

suffering from some incurable, terminal disease so that she might tell him this immediately and thus alleviate her acute embarrassment. Instead, she found herself wittering on interminably about college and parties and collegeparties and partyparties until, flushed with scorched cheeks, she finally ground to a halt, took a deep breath, expelled the air, shrugged and gazed helplessly at him.

'Will we go so?' he asked casually, as if he had been waiting for her to pause for a second, and she realized he had a soft Northern Ireland accent. She further realized that he hadn't spoken a word up to this point and she placed the palms of her hands against her cheeks to cool them.

They walked for hours. Stepping in and out of doorways to dodge the light powdery rain that dusted the pavements. Kitty felt lightheaded, she knew that she was doing most of the talking, about her home in West Cork, her parents, life in college, her editorial duties at work, which were minor in comparison to the mundane clerical day-to-day drudgery she had to contend with, fending off calls from irate authors in pursuit of payment in the main, she did not tell him that the small publishing firm was owned by her father's cousin. She noticed that he seemed to deliberately avoid the subject of Belfast, telling her instead of life in the solicitor's office where he was doing his apprenticeship. His time was spent on conveyancing, punctuated by days of letter stamping; he was bored senseless, it wasn't at all as he had expected it to be. He was even unsure why he had chosen Law in the first place, he appeared even less sure now. He did not care for Dublin much. When he spoke, he studied the ground in front of him and rarely met her eye.

As they walked, Kitty began to wonder if she might invite him back to her flat in Ballsbridge, to sleep with him. The persistence of her virginity had begun to trouble her greatly once she had reached the age of twenty. It was not that she lacked offers, neither was it the sleeping or not sleeping with anyone that troubled her, it was the waking up with someone. The 'what kind of music do you like?' preamble bored her, and a second sense told her that it would only intensify next morning. Contrary to her expectations, so far, she had found the young men she dated almost ridiculously romantic in that they appeared to suffer from some sort of compulsion to declare love. They said 'I love you' after a few salty tongue probes, 'I really love you' after a breast grope, she could not bring herself to imagine what they might say after sex. This at any rate was the excuse she had given herself for her pristine state, when most of her friends could hardly walk straight since they had discovered the joys of sex in the big city, away from the upstairs inhibiting creak of Mammy's and Daddy's bed.

In the early hours of the morning, as a spear of orange light moved across the sky to the east, she did invite Danny back to her flat. She gave him a mug of coffee which he nursed between his cupped hands while he stared in bemused silence at her increasing agitation. She could not sit down. But when she stood, her legs shook so badly she had to press her toes painfully to the ground to stop the trembling. She plumped the beanbag and turned on and off the electric fire constantly so that they baked or froze alternately.

Finally she clicked her tongue, grabbed his hand and led him into her small bedroom. They did not speak, he still appeared bemused and hesitant; she stood in the dim light staring at him, wishing she could either die instantly or think of something to say. He looked at his watch again and she thought she heard a bored sigh escape his lips.

'You can sleep here if you like.' She pointed to her bed. 'It's very late. I mean, early. I'll sleep on – on the beanbag.'

'You can't do that,' he protested. 'I'll sleep on the beanbag.'

'Oh no, I'm used to it really,' she lied. 'It's very comfortable.'

'It can't be.'

'It is.'

'Then I'll sleep on it,' he insisted, 'or I'll go, if you'd rather that . . .'

'No, no, there's no need for that. Look – actually – it's quite a large bed, we can both sleep on it . . .' She flushed in misery. Now what was she supposed to do? Take off her clothes or sleep in them or what? She felt certain that he must be laughing at her. Tomorrow he would tell his friends about the tight little West Cork virgin, a species long thought extinct, that he had really slept with the night before. Hilarious. Standing there in a fugue of uncertainty, she felt a sharp spasm of hatred toward him for a moment. She watched from the corner of her eye to see what he would do next – he blithely undressed down to his boxer shorts so she quickly followed suit to her underwear. They scuttled under the bedcovers. And when he reached for her, gently and reassuringly, she almost fainted with relief.

It turned out that he was in and up so quickly, easily, and slickly that she felt constrained toward a measure of embarrassment afterwards. She said:

'I don't know if you know or not . . . I was a . . .' She could not bring herself to use that Barbara Cartland term, '. . . It was my first time . . .'

He rested himself on an elbow and stared hard at her. Her heart sank. Now he would feel obliged to profess his love. She waited wearily.

'You'll be glad that's over then,' he said, and she blinked. His shoulders were heaving. She stared incredulously for a moment at him then threw her head back to roar with laughter. The tone was set. She could relax.

In the morning she watched him sleeping. His eyes opened slowly, fixed on her, he yawned and stretched, sleepily pulling her toward him. And still there was no stilted post-sex conversation. He seemed surprised to discover that she was not on the Pill, even if it was her first time.

'Shit,' she said, 'I never even thought of that.' She panicked for a moment, then calculated that she should be on the safe side of her cycle. He agreed to withdraw in time in any case. It all seemed so easy and natural that Kitty could hardly believe that this was her first morning waking up beside him.

'Kathleen or Katherine . . . ?' He murmured before drifting into a satisfied sleep again.

'Kitty,' she said. 'Just Kitty – My father called me after the Kitty in *Anna Karenina* – his favourite book.' Somehow the customary question did not irritate quite as much as it usually did.

'Oh aye,' he said. 'Kitty . . . I like it.' Within moments he was deeply asleep.

A week went by before he called her after that first night together. Her ego was dinted but not sufficiently so for her to tell him to piss off as she had intended. They met twice, or occasionally three times weekly from then on. Both anxious to appear as casual as possible at first, feigning a degree of detachment, until lying in bed at night they turned to one another with an honest, unequivocal hunger. And then by day again, the skirting, the nervous shuffles, the sideways glances to check, to always check, how much distance covered, how far left to go. Lying awake at night going over every conversation. Sleepless in anticipation of the next meeting. It took a while before Danny could admit that he felt like that too. When she was not with Danny, his over-sensitivity irritated her. Like many sensitive people he often displayed a gross insensitivity toward others. His shy diffidence concealed an arrogance. But when she was with him, alone in her room together (she rarely visited his flat, finding it offensively dirty), he was capable of a warmth that at first surprised her. He liked to touch, to be touched. Yet shied in public from the simplest of gestures such as holding hands, something which meant less than nothing to her. She discovered that he had not been well liked at Trinity, his shyness often being misconstrued as hubris, and she could sympathize with him there. Initially, she would invite him along with her friends, but grew too uncomfortable watching him watch every word he uttered, spending each syllable at such cost, it set her teeth on edge. In company, he would focus all his attention on her, to diminish his own awkwardness and she began to find the process draining.

He rarely discussed his family with her. She knew that he had an older brother, a teacher, and an older sister, a housewife, and that his father had died of an early heart attack while Danny's mother was carrying him. She knew that his mother called him every Sunday after Mass from a call box. Danny went to Mass every Sunday too, but never asked her to join him, safe in the knowledge that she would not. She knew that he came to Trinity on a grant, wore a threadbare coat and afforded a seedy flat across town. Last year, she bought him a pure new wool coat for Christmas. He said nothing when he opened the box but shrivelled her with a look of contempt. She never saw him wear the coat since; he continued to wear the other though the elbows were shiny and his sweater showed through a hole near the collar.

38

Often, she would think of him walking beside her in Phoenix Park. Shoulders hunched against the wind, head down, feet kicking leaves, that tattered coat handed down from his older brother, barely putting up a pretence at keeping the cold at bay. The cobalt blue eyes misting over, a sideways glance at her, and somewhere behind the confusion, a pain that lurked behind the pupils. Danny suffered. From what she did not know. Thoughts flitting through his head would cause him to frown, sometimes he would reach out and grasp, try to convey a thought to her but just as he would try, it seemed to evaporate, dissipate, land somewhere in the recess of his mind to lie in confusion. He appeared to her to exist on a periphery, the boundaries of an unknown landscape. At times, it was as if there was no living being behind the cerulean gaze. Then the vacant look would be replaced by eyes flashing in amusement as he teased her mercilessly about her posh flat in Ballsbridge paid for by 'Daddy', she had made the mistake of telling him that. In response, she teased him about the chips on his shoulders. Sometimes, the lighthearted taunting spilled over into a darker, more bitter region, and they would tacitly agree to withdraw to lick their respective wounds in silence.

Dublin was strange to both of them. A city full of paradoxes and contradictions. Perfectly square Georgian squares, gleaming doors to the end of the row and then a ruin, the skeleton of a house crumbled into a dilapidation that showed the uneasy tension behind the smoothness all around. Holes defaced every road, lay gaping like hideous mouths, for years it seemed. The north side of the city was tenemented to an almost ridiculous degree. Lines of washing strung up across bricked balconies, rubbish piled on narrow winding streets. Then, Southside, luxury villas overlooking the Bay. And in the centre, a young woman with a blanket-wrapped baby on every corner, begging. 'Ah go on love, just a couple of coins for the babby.' Kitty turned from them not because she did not wish to give them money, she did at Christmas and on her birthday, but because she could not look them in the eye and she could not bring herself to give them money without doing so. The look of the mendicant. Sleazy, disturbing and accusative. She saw herself judged in their eyes.

Danny on the other hand, who had so much less to give, could do so with a degree of savoir-faire that irritated her intensely. Poverty did not cause him any discomfort.

Now, as the couple next door blundered toward a noisy climax, she moved into the waiting cradle of his body. He moaned and stroked her breast. Kitty wrapped his arm around her body, she did not want to give in to sleep, she wanted the night to go on forever.

He smacked his lips.

'Remind me,' he said, in a voice drunk with sleep, 'I want to show you something tomorrow.'

'What?' she whispered.

'Nothing. Just remind me, okay?'

'Okay. Sleep now, sleep . . .' She was about to fall asleep herself when a thought struck her. She raised her head and looked down at him.

'Danny?'

'What?'

'You said a moment ago that you hoped I wouldn't be like my "snotty" friends – How did you know, or why did you presume they were snotty?'

'I knew they were snotty.'

'Why? Because you thought that I was?'

'No.'

'Why then?'

'Because I knew them – or knew of them.'

'But how?'

'Because I made it my business to know.'

'What are you saying?'

'Why do you think I was at that party in the first place, huh?'

'You mean . . .'

'Yeah. Sure. It took me two years from the first time I saw you on campus with your hair flying behind you and a deadly serious expression on your face – but I got there in the end . . .'

'. . . And you never told me,' she interrupted, sitting up again.

'I'm telling you now.'

'Jesus. You're full of surprises.' She was wide awake again. She poked him in the ribcage. He groaned and wearily shuffled his body up to sit beside her, his arms crossed over his chest.

'Well, that's that I suppose – no chance of a kip now,' he said.

'Bloody right,' she said. 'All this time and you never said a word . . . You let me think that I was the one to make the first move . . .' She laughed, delighted with his revelation.

'And now you want to know all about what I was thinking when I saw you first and what attracted me, right?'

'Something like that.'

'What'll I get?'

'What do you want?'

'What do you think . . . ?'

Kitty squealed when he grabbed her and he told her to hush, Maria or Joan, her flatmates, would be in on top of them if she didn't shut up and what did a fellow have to do to get an hour's sleep around here; this spoken in a feigned Texas drawl. Kitty gasped for air as he tickled her.

'Lawdy!' she cried, playing the game. 'I do declare the boy's embarrassed – secretly lusting after his belle indeed . . .'

'Shut up,' he groaned, moving on top of her.

'But I thought you wanted to sleep . . .' she teased, pinning his hips away from her with her hands. 'So what was it then – did you see me being nice to a puppy or something?'

'Worse than that.'

'Well? . . . You're not moving until you tell me.'

'I was at the cinema with a few mates and I recognized you a few seats ahead – you had a big box of popcorn and you were laughing your head off. People were telling you to shut up all round but you took no notice. I was the only other person laughing as well so I thought then that I'd like to – you know – get to know you better. That's it. No big deal.'

'What was the movie?'

'*The Exorcist.*'

Kitty laughed. That explained everything for some reason. Her hands fell away from his hips.

* * *

They watched a mother duck and her brood of five swim under the wooden bridge in St Stephen's Green. It was a fresh, crisp

Saturday afternoon. A rich yellow autumnal light spilled through the canopy of leaves just turning colour, to chequer the pathways ahead. Strollers passed by with coats draped over their arms. Kitty blinked rapidly in the sunlight, her eyes were stinging with tiredness. They barely slept the night before, as usual spending more time talking about going to sleep than actually asleep. It was just as well that Danny only overnighted two to three nights a week.

She stared at his profile as he clasped his hands over the bridge railing. Casually, he said:

'Did you read it then?'

'I did.' She had been hoping he wouldn't ask just yet.

'Well what do you think . . . ?'

Kitty hesitated. He understood her hesitation and muttered under his breath, cursing himself for showing it to her in the first place. It was a mistake. But he had wanted to share something with her.

'It's only a stupid speech, for Christ's sake. No big deal. You don't have to give me the big "look". I won't even be the one reading it tonight. You're always on at me to tell you about life "up there" as you put it. Well. There you have it. A stupid little speech to raise a stupid little amount of money and you give me that look. Who do you think you are?' His mouth twisted to the side bitterly.

Kitty winced, taken aback by his vehemence. How was she to know that when he presented her with the draft for his speech that he really meant to offer more than that?

It was a stupid speech. Badly written and overtly sentimental, which surprised her. She had known that he was involved in some sort of fundraising committee for the families of prisoners in the North, but she had assumed his membership to be couched in his usual vagueness and half-heartedness. It was somewhere to go to meet a few acquaintances from Belfast, she thought. It never occurred to her to question him further on the subject. She felt angry and dejected. Now, she said:

'If you want the truth – I didn't think much of it.'

'Thanks for being so honest.' He spat out the words. He was very upset she realized. The clasped hands trembled, he would not look at her. Kitty expelled a loud sigh.

'What do you want me to say? That it's a wonderful speech? Moved me to tears? Fine. If that's what you want . . . It's a great speech, Danny. Really inspiring. I understand everything now. Imagine the effect on a roomful of the converted anyway.' She was harder than she had meant to be, as usual. It was his turn to wince. He stared broodily down at the stream, daring her to continue so that he might stalk off. She compressed her lips. The loveliness of the afternoon faded.

'You just dismiss anything you don't like or believe in . . .'

'That's not . . .'

'Shut up,' he hissed across her. 'Let me finish. You don't know the first thing about where I come from, it might just as well be the other side of the moon for all you know with your pretty little pictures of grimy streets full of fanatics and madmen. I laugh when I hear you talking about Belfast. Laugh – d'you hear me? To the likes of you and bloody "Daddy" we're all not much better than some strain of fucking – I don't know what – mongrel, yes, that's it. Fucking mongrels. Not part of that lot and not part of your lot. With our funny accents and lust for killing.' He raised a hand to quell her outrage. 'No. Don't bother to deny it. I've seen the way you look at the lads in my flat. Like they were bacteria or something . . . I'm not a fool you know. I know what you think of them . . . of us,' he added, spitting into the swirling water.

Hot blood singed Kitty's cheeks.

'Oh it's "the things I've seen compared to you" horseshit now, is it?'

He spun around to face her. Blue eyes pierced, checked her when she would have gone on.

'Look Dan. Look Dan . . .' she said.

'Don't look Dan me. Not today. Please. Not now.' He turned away again.

Often she had found his silence stronger than her words. That was the thing about silence, it could insinuate anything. But today she found his words more disturbing.

'Let's just drop it,' he said. 'I want to go home.'

'Piss off then,' she barked and walked away from him.

Halfway across the park she stopped and turned back again.

43

He was still staring sullenly into the water. She raised a hand and stroked the space between them in a limp gesture, unable to touch him as she had intended.

'What now?' she whispered.

He worried a thumbnail. The ducks returned. A child threw lumps of bread through the wooden slats of the railing. The ducks swam past without a pause. She waited for the blue stare, the one that would tell her that it was really over. A look of regret, extinguishing love, perhaps a hint of contempt. Kitty waited, aware that she had given him the choice. Aware too that she had, without meaning to, renounced her right to choice. She peered up at the sun sifting through the high branches. She felt sick with self-disgust, but she had to know. Had she so entirely misunderstood him? Could he, after all, cast her off with a blue look? She wanted to cry. Seduced already by the image of the pain ahead.

'There would be too much crying. I couldn't bear it,' he responded after a while, and smiled. He did not say who would be doing the crying so Kitty gratefully assumed he meant himself. She hooded her eyes so that he would not see the extent of her relief.

'Buy you a pint?' she said softly.

'Where?'

'Why not just say yes, then ask where?'

'Yes. Where?'

'Across the road maybe?'

'The Shelbourne?'

'Why not? The Guinness is good there you always say.'

'All those West Brit types give me the creeps. I don't know what you see in the place. Let's go down the road to Mullins'.' He stared beyond her.

Kitty felt compelled toward further confrontation if only to punish herself for her earlier stab of terror. Now that she believed the point of danger past, she could gamble again. She began to walk away.

'C'mon. Hurry up, I'm gasping,' she called over her shoulder.

'Right. Right.' His voice throbbed with unspoken criticism. Kitty laughed to herself at the sound. She stretched as she walked, drawing the tension from her neck and shoulderblades with wide arcs of her arms. She stopped and turned to study his hunched and wounded back from the distance.

The ducks were heading downstream again, still busy, still going nowhere in particular.

'Stupid fucking ducks,' Danny muttered and kicked the railing.

'Hey.' The young child, a boy, protested, half-laughing.

Danny, startled at first, laughed aloud too. He looked up and caught Kitty's eye. She was smiling indulgently with her head to one side. She took a few steps backwards, clapping her hands against her thighs, then she turned and walked through the black wrought iron gates onto the street beyond. Inside the dimly lit womb of the Horseshoe Bar, she ordered half a Guinness from the curly haired barman from County Mayo. He beamed broadly at her. She sat and looked around. She liked the burnished gleam of the bar counter, the shiny brass rail and glinting optics behind. The Major-type in hounds-tooth jacket was perched on his habitual stool by the bar; two women overdressed for shopping sat amid their smart, shiny carrier bags, delicately sipping coffee, fingers straying up to pat new hair cuts from time to time. The darker, taller woman reminded Kitty of her own mother – she decided in the end that it was the over-application of make-up which did it.

She waited for a while then told Micheal of Mayo that he could start pulling Danny's pint. She lit a cigarette, exhaled and sat back, aware that she was under scrutiny by the women. No doubt they were discussing her jeans and the darns in the old ribbed sweater which had once been her father's. Her long darkbrown hair was wilder than usual; normally, she gathered it at the nape of her neck but she had forgotten the elastic that morning. Kitty smiled to herself at the contrast of her pale, make-up-free face and tousled hair with the dark beige foundation faces of the women and their symmetrical, shiny caps. She glanced up and peered directly toward them, through the curls of smoke. She raised her eyebrows questioningly, and they hastily sipped from their cups, clinking them onto their saucers in synchronization.

Danny slouched in with his hands buried deep within his pockets. Kitty handed him his pint and he took a deep slug, wiping the cream from the top of his lip with the back of his hand. He moved his stool so that his back was facing the bar and the women.

'God, it's warm in here,' he said.

'A bit stuffy all right,' she interpreted.

She gazed at him from the corner of her eye. He was swallowing, searching for words. He sipped again, shifted on the stool then leant forward confidentially.

'I'm a bastard,' he whispered, conscious of alien eyes upon them.

'Hmmm?'

'Ah Kit. Don't play with me. I'm sorry. I'm a bastard. Always having a go at you . . . forgive me?' He reached across and cradled her chin to turn her face toward him. She knew what such a simple gesture in public cost him, and smiled easily.

'Forget it,' she said, and stroked his hand which he withdrew gently, the gesture made, he had no wish to prolong it.

She grabbed the slinking hand and held it tight. She raised it to her lips, kissed it and smiled at his discomfort. The Major type humphed into his whiskey and soda. He often watched them. Too young, too modern to be in his local. Their youth and good looks were a mite unseemly, he considered.

Danny rose to order another drink as the bar began to fill up with the first shift of Saturday workers. A few well-suited, middle-aged executives overtiming. They spoke with good Dublin accents, lined up beside Danny, holding furled five or ten pound notes between their fore and middle fingers with a foot casually placed on the lower brass railing, a hand lightly touching their established stools behind them.

Kitty chewed her lower lip and watched Danny's slim, denim clad body, singular amidst the grey. She knew by the stiffness of his back that he was ill at ease. He would start talking next with a pronounced Belfast accent, much harsher than his usual soft tones. She observed the way he flicked his hair back several times self-consciously. His profile when he turned to glance at the man beside him showed his haughtily pursed mouth and raised eyebrows, as if he disagreed in principle with whatever the man might be saying. He dug a hand into his back pocket and pulled out a few scrunched-up notes; she caught his quick sideways flicker to check if the condition of his money had been noticed. He flattened the notes on the bar counter. Kitty observed with sadness his discomfort and self-alienation. Amongst countrymen to whom he purported to belong. Or did they too fall into sections and sub-sections and categories of brotherhood? Since she had met him, apart from his Belfast flatmates, Kitty had never really seen Danny at ease with anyone but her, and then primarily in the privacy of her room. At times, it felt as though the entire world was intent on offending Danny. She had often wondered how much of it he feigned, because taking offence was a way of being right all the time. She had wondered too, what he might be like in Belfast.

She listened to him thank Mayo in the brash accent she had anticipated. He was so vulnerable when unaware of her scrutiny, she had to look away. She wished she could somehow ease his pain. He approached her with rolling eyes and a jerk of the head backwards, indicating she understood, that bullshit was being expended by the bar again. She clicked her tongue in sympathetic agreement.

'I think.' He sipped and licked his lips of the creamy froth. 'I think. Maybe. Maybe you should come to Belfast with me next time.'

'You mean it?'

'Yes. Yes. I think I do.'

'And you? Will you come home with me? Look, I'm going next month – maybe you could come down for a weekend.'

'Aye.' He sighed. 'But do you think people might get the wrong idea?'

'What do you mean?' She asked though she knew perfectly well what he meant.

'You know . . .' He hesitated. 'About us. Will they think it's more serious than we want them to think?'

'Of course not.' Offhand. But her eyes registered hurt.

'You're right. It's no big deal really. Don't expect too much though, I'm telling you now. It's only a small house . . .'

'As long as there's a bidet in the bathroom, I don't mind,' she interjected harshly.

'You're mocking me now.'

'You deserve it.'

'Sorry.'

'Stop saying sorry. It doesn't suit you.'

He laughed. His knees had begun to jiggle up and down nervously. She could sense a myriad explanations, equivocations, anxiously tripping on the edge of his tongue, but thankfully he desisted. She did not want to hear his excuses for his home.

'Try not to be such a snob,' she offered gently. He scowled and chewed his words, turning them over in his mouth, enjoying the bitter taste.

'There are some things you just couldn't understand,' he said primly.

'Bollocks!' she said aloud, but smiling.

'Shhh.'

'Shhh yourself.'

'Ah damn it all, Kitty . . .' He floundered. His fingers entangled in a familiar motion, making and breaking steeples. She knew he would change the subject any minute now. Scalded yet again by simple words, simple observations. Once, when she had asked him to try and be more friendly toward her flatmates, his ensuing effort nearly made her cringe; it was as though his tongue thickened in his mouth and every sentence came out as if practised in his mind first.

'Listen Kit . . .' He was still struggling. 'Let's just do it. Don't say anything and I won't say anything. We'll just go. All right?'

'All right,' she replied. So there was to be no preamble. No animated conversations on trains about this person or that person they would or should meet. It was disappointing. But she realized that if she pushed it, he would simply abandon the whole idea. She was too much in love with the prospect to allow that to happen, her mind already enacting the first meeting scenario. She envisaged immediate enchantment of his family, Danny staring at her with a rosy glow of satisfaction and contentment. She would neither talk too much nor too little. She would bring only jeans and sweatshirts to wear. She would above all, be ordinary. Extraordinarily ordinary. So that a mother, his mother, might be inclined to say: 'A nice ordinary girl. The kind you'd be comfortable with. The kind that would suit me grand.' She checked her reverie. Why should she require the approval of his family anyway? Back to jeans and sweatshirts and measured talk. Kitty drained her glass and sighed with satisfaction.

'Danny?' she said.

'What?' He beamed expectantly.

'I love you.'

'I love you too.'

'How much?'

'More than I could say.'

'You never say,' she laughed happily. 'You never say anything.'

'You say enough for the both of us,' he responded, but the gleam of pleasure in his eyes belied his gruff tone. He was pleased with her. She was pleased that he was pleased but more especially that she was the cause. She liked to please him as much as she liked to taunt him.

Kitty's head remained on one side as she studied him through narrowed thoughtful eyes. She lit a cigarette, cupping her hands around the match, a habit acquired and remembered from furtive smoking at boarding school. She peered through the curls of smoke as she sucked vigorously. The first drag was always the deepest.

'Tell me about this speech.' She expelled the demand on a stream of smoke.

'Forget it,' he said, then was compelled to go on by her glance. 'I just did it to please the guys in the flat if you must know. They think I could do it better than them just because I have a degree is all.'

'Maybe they're right. But you wouldn't have done it unless you wanted to. Why can't you talk to me about this committee – Maybe I could help?'

'Kitty.' Eyebrows raised. Pint sipped. 'Forget it I said. Really. It's no . . .'

'. . . big deal.' She continued his habitual phrase.

'. . . Business of yours,' he said archly. She flushed. The hand holding her cigarette trembled slightly. He noticed and his face coloured too. He opened his mouth to speak but she cut across him:

49

'Just don't say sorry,' she said.

'All right. I won't . . . But I am sorry. Kitty? Kit . . .' He put his head to one side.

'Ah forget it.' She stubbed her cigarette into the ashtray, grinding the butt with repressed anger. 'Savage isn't it?' she said, shrugging in confusion. 'This – this whole – thing . . .'

Danny thought for a moment, then nodded soberly. 'Aye. It is that,' he sighed.

October

Since they left the train station Kitty had answered her mother's perfunctory questions with a series of monosyllabic grunts, and now they both sat poker-faced, enjoying the sour silence.

Short of speaking, which she was not about to do, Kitty was finding it difficult to convey by means of frowns and sighs, the intensity of her anger. Her mother hummed to herself, and kept both hands on the steering wheel while staring straight ahead with an air of resolute implacability.

As they passed the last village on the way home, Kitty studied her mother from the corner of her eye. The soft white skin (testament to a lifetime's avoidance of the sun) was still sufficiently unlined as to suggest a woman approaching her mid-forties rather than her mid-fifties. She was, as ever, immaculately made-up. Kitty could barely remember the occasions, if indeed they did exist, when she had seen her mother without her applied face. It was always peach-powdered and bow-lipped from early morning. Even on the rare occasions when her father did not drive her back to boarding school, Kitty could remember her mother showing at the very last moment, standing in the doorway, fully made-up, arm linked in the crook of her husband's in the bleak grey light of just past sunrise, waving to her daughter in the back of someone's car. Kitty found there was something comical and grotesque about the receding vision of her father's half-closed eyes, dishevelled hair and weary wave, beside whom the gargoyle stood, grinning from ear to ear, ruby lips peeled back in a fixed, calculated smile.

Kitty now observed that while the application was as flawless and meticulous as ever, the heavy powder was inclined to crust around the nose and chin. Blue eyeshadow over dull brown eyes

51

and matt red lipstick (visible on closer inspection above the lipline) appeared to be outdated. The effect was all too much; Eleanor Fitzgerald clearly did not aspire to a 'natural' look. Her thin, high-cheekboned face appeared gaunt beneath uncompromisingly dyed black hair worn short and severely permed. But despite the overall harsh effect, she was still an inherently attractive woman.

The perpetual half-smile on her painted lips incensed her daughter above everything else. The fixed, vacuous crescents of once pretty, ageing, embittered women with tinkling voices behind smiles which say: 'Here I am, safe. Here I am, untouched.'

Untouchable. Kitty had always found her mother to be so. She had searched the vapid brown gaze on countless occasions for something, any little thing, that might betray the woman's humanity, a hesitant blink, a look of pain, any attempt to convey a message through the eyes that her voice could not carry, but the glazed veneer was impenetrable. The voice tinkled, the smile smiled, and the eyes said nothing, ever.

Either Eleanor hid herself well or there was truly nothing to hide; she looked at her daughter candidly only in anger or recrimination, and those came regularly. For a long time Kitty had latched onto that. So much unspoken rage, vented by means of petty tantrums, or so Kitty had assumed. There had to be more, but if there was more, it remained locked tightly away behind the bland brown gaze.

She observed her mother in company, women who believed in the pursuit of good perms and lifelong happiness in that order, and Kitty would find herself surprised to see her mother laugh so frequently. She laughed a lot but found nothing funny. It was what one did in company.

As a young girl Kitty occasionally berated herself for the jaundiced eye with which she viewed her mother's every movement, but as years went by she gave up trying to humanize the inhuman and surrendered instead to her cartoon-like vision of the woman she called 'Mother', and even that with a degree of irony. It was no easy task belittling 'Mother' in order to confront her hardness, but Kitty worked at it sedulously, and with a measure of venom which sometimes made her feel ashamed.

The car wound around the narrow coastal road. To the left on the far shore, an ivy-clad stone facade, which was all that remained of the former grainstore, cast a long early evening shadow on the calm sea. The waters were rarely tumultuous here, being quite shallow and caught in a strait between two peninsulas. They passed a small stone chapel with a renovated clocktower. The Protestant church, a local Catholic would say in no pejorative manner; Church of Ireland, a Protestant would differ. Here, anyone who was not Catholic acquired the nebulous appellation of 'Protestant': Anglicans, Methodists, even Buddhists notwithstanding.

They pulled into a long narrow avenue. The car slowed to crawling pace to compensate for the holes in the gravelled track. Overhead, the oaks still wore their yellowed mantles, their branches tangling to form a canopy which coupled with the dense wild undergrowth to give a luminous greenness to the makeshift tunnel.

Kitty rolled down her window and stuck her head outside. She was immediately struck by the full, rich odour of the dying foliage. The rotting smell of autumn. So familiar it made her stomach churn. Autumn dragged itself along with little haste in West Cork. She looked up at the sallow, misty sky showing through the scalloped oak leaves. Her anger began to dissolve until she heard:

'Kitty. Put your head inside the car please, dear. Those brambles would pluck your eyes out in an instant. This avenue will have to be seen to. It's a disgrace. An utter disgrace.' The tone was light, but Kitty immediately detected that inevitable afternote of censure. She clenched her teeth and ignored the command.

'Kitty.' As the car rutted along.

'Kitty . . . please dear.'

'Why didn't you tell me?' It would have been all right if she hadn't been 'please deared', she might have made it until she had at least spoken with her father. As it was, she had just managed over sixty miles in virtual silence. But 'please dear' had done for her in the end.

'I explained to you on the phone how it was. Daddy asked me himself not to tell you. He . . . we, didn't want you to be overworried. You were coming home in a couple of weeks anyway, and he didn't . . . well, he didn't actually die dear, so when he began to recover so quickly – truly it was nothing short of miraculous, the way he just sort of stood up so fast again, he had fallen down of course – and well . . . that was it really. We just sort of said . . . you know . . .'

'No, I don't know. Tell me.'

'We just sort of said . . . what's the point of worrying her? She has her job to think of, doesn't she? Maybe it was the wrong thing to do. I'm always doing the wrong thing.'

'Christ.'

'Don't be vulgar.'

'Is Christ vulgar?'

'Don't be smart.'

'I *am* smart.'

'Here we are, thank goodness. I can see we're going to have a splendid time together.'

'We won't be together.'

'No? You're intending to stay elsewhere then?'

'I might . . . if I have to.'

'There's no have to about it, Kitty dear. No one makes you have to do anything. Least of all me, I should have said.'

'And they're off', hustled through Kitty's mind. 'They're off, they're off, they're off . . .'

'Just park the car please, Mother.'

'That is my intention. Now before you rush up to see him, I must ask you – don't kill me – I must ask you to exercise some little bit of restraint. He's still recovering. His heart . . . you know the way you . . . Kitty . . . Kitty . . .' She added 'please dear' to the open door swinging on its hinges.

Kitty took the stairs two at a time. She flung open the door to her father's room on the first floor – it adjoined his wife's room; like royalty, Kitty used to laugh and later wondered who crept into whose room by means of the connecting door. It was gloomy inside, light shut out by the almost closed shutters inside the sash windows. Without looking at the bed, Kitty ran and pulled the shutters back. Then she turned.

He was squinting like a sleepy rabbit in the onslaught of light. Kitty suppressed a gasp on seeing his atrophied features. The extreme slightness of him. The fluffy, downy hair white and awry like a baby's over such a flaccid face, wizened like an old sultana.

His mouth slackened slightly to one side above which the nose appeared like some strange excrescence, too large and bony for the sunken face. A thin line of spittle drooled like a snail's trail from the downturned corner of his mouth. His eyes, tobacco-coloured like hers, gleamed too brightly from underneath the still incongruously dark bushy eyebrows as if they pierced a dense haze. It was only a couple of months since she last saw him but he appeared to have aged ten years.

He was peering at her, measuring himself, what was left of his life, in her eyes. Her horrified gaze did not instill false hope. He smiled at his daughter, as if glad in a way for her honesty. Reassured too that he might now countervail the chintzy cheeriness of wives and medics.

Kitty shambled forward and heaved herself onto the high bed. She held his limp hands.

'Jesus Christ,' she exploded.

'Indeed.' His speech, though slurred, was comprehensible.

'So you're going to – to . . .' Kitty was kissing his hands, little mottled slabs of useless flesh, dormant in her grasp. 'You're really going to . . .'

'Die? . . . Appears so.' He tried a wry smile, conscious of the risible result as the operative side of his mouth pulled down to match the defective lee.

'I had it in my head – I don't know – I just thought that we'd all go together somehow. I presumed the end of the world would come or something. No. That's not true. I never gave it any thought at all. I just never thought you'd do anything so . . . so ordinary as just . . .'

'Die?'

'Yes.'

'I had similar thoughts myself until the stroke.' Stroke sounded like 'ssshtrook'.

Kitty had to look away. She tried hard not to cry but her face twisted, the lump in her throat could not be swallowed, she covered the lower half of her face with a hand and squeezed, expelling breaths in loud grunts. His hands flapped awkwardly like feeble blotched flippers and gestured her toward him.

'Come here,' he beckoned, and as she laid her head upon his

55

chest, a few loud unsuppressible sobs straggled their way through her vocal chords.

The sound shivered across the vast unaired room. Eleanor believed in darkness, closed windows, too many blankets, whatever the illness. He would have allowed her whatever claustrophobia-inducing measures she resorted to, Kitty surmised.

'It's good to see you,' he whispered.

'Why wouldn't you let her tell me?'

'I didn't not let her. She decided. She was probably right.'

'You might have died. I wouldn't see you again. Ever. How could you just agree with her like that?'

'It was easy.'

They laughed. Now was not the time for chastisement, Kitty conceded.

'Look,' he said, flapping his hands again. 'It's not so bad, speech is a bit tipsy but not so bad. Not so bad at all. How do I look?'

'Dreadful.'

'Thought so. Still, what can you expect? Just don't say "Physician heal thyself", I beg of you. I've promised myself the pleasure of emptying the contents of the pisspot over the next person to say it. So be warned.'

Kitty sat crosslegged and wiped her cheeks. His fingers fluttered her toward the box of tissues on the table beside him.

'I have to say you do look worse than I'd expected. To hear Mother tell it – you fell to the ground and just sort of hopped back up again.' She blew her nose.

'It wasn't quite like that. You know she always sees what she wants to see. Always has.'

'Except with me.'

'Yes. Well.'

'What if I told you that I'm not ready for you to die yet,' she said lightly.

'I'll bear it in mind of course.'

'Is that the best you can do?'

'For the moment.' He laughed. 'God you're a hard child. So de-manding . . .' He mimicked his wife's voice, but with his new slurred speech the effect was not as funny as Kitty usually found it. She had to look away and pinch the bridge of her nose.

56

'Don't . . .' he said gently, and stroked his overlapping hands as if they were her face. Then he was crying too. Tears rolled down his puckered face. He groaned with the effort of suppression, a ragged sigh making his bony chest shudder. He clamped his lips tightly, looked around the room, glad of space and light and objects to focus on. It had not seemed worth the bother of trying to explain to his wife that dim light in itself did not induce sleep. To be fair to her, she had heard him often enough – 'A healthy diet and plenty of rest.' Plenty of rest . . . All the dying men he had neither helped nor comforted with those words. But what to say to dying men? He still did not know.

'It's so absurd. Preposterous.' He suddenly choked. 'Utterly absurd. I should expect this – even be prepared for it. You'd think that being a doctor would mean something after all. I'm not so young they won't say "taken in his prime", or God forbid, the one that really gets me: "Only the good die young." How many times I've heard it all and seen that look on the faces of men my age and older, and I was surprised that they were surprised. That's the joke of it. And here I am – surprised for God's sake. Surprised. At my age.' He passed a hand across his forehead and up to pat a few wisps flat. 'I thought it would be dignified. Or hoped I suppose. Somehow I saw myself thinking up important things to say before I shuffled the old coil. Dignified things. I thought I'd spend the end days in contemplation, you know – the human condition, the meaning of life, art and maybe Beckett's plays, and instead I lie here wondering what will be on the tray she brings up and will I last till pudding and if I don't, I hope that it's mushy rhubarb and custard. They can even make a custard these days you know, without the carbohestorols that used to be the essence of a good custard. Custard without carbohestorols! I ask you . . . might as well be dead.'

'Tomorrow I'll make you real custard – thick enough for flies to walk on – and I'll read to you. Would you like that?'

'And a cigar?' His eyes lit up.

'After a heart attack?'

'Stroke.'

'Stroke – whatever.'

'Just one. One half-corona. Half a half-corona. Look, you smoke it, I'll just lie here and smell it.'

'What kind of doctor are you at all?'

'A bad one.' They laughed at the old joke. He was a bad doctor of sorts, a fact he readily admitted. 'What do you think yourself?', was a well known catchphrase of his; but that vague, slightly puzzled demeanour was in some ways reassuring to those who suspected but wished to sidestep the inevitable, and equally reassuring to those who believed that every visit to a physician meant certain death. He had come to expect self-diagnosis from his patients and was rarely disappointed. Nine times out of ten, they got it right. More than anything he detested broken limbs. The element of doubt was removed.

'Please Kitty.' He spoke now consciously employing an old man's wheedle.

'She'd kill me.'

'Well then, if you refuse, I must insist on dying. That's all there is to it. You leave me no alternative. Say your goodbyes now, darling, let's get this over with as painlessly as possible . . .'

Kitty laughed. From midway up the stairs a censorious voice could be heard:

'Kitty dear. Please. Not too much longer with your father now. He needs his rest. Please.'

They winced in unison.

'She would have made a good nurse,' he said dolefully.

'Efficient not kindly.'

'Now, now.' He tried to conceal the gleam of amusement in his eyes. 'She's been very good in fact. Credit where credit is due . . . It's never been entirely her fault you know . . .'

'What?'

'The whole damnable thing.' He waved an arm. 'We should never have married. She was too young, too pretty for me. But she wanted to marry a doctor and marry a doctor she did. She thought moving to Ireland was the equivalent of leaving London for the Cotsworlds.'

'Wolds.'

'I know.'

'Go on,' Kitty urged. He did not often allude to his wife with candour, usually tempering any vague opinions with the more familiar note of resigned irony.

'What's there to go on about?'

'Go on anyway – maybe it's cathartic.'

'Maybe so is a good shite.' He laughed. Then sucked in his cheeks. He looked away – ashamed. 'I've had a lot of time to think. Not an altogether pleasant experience,' he added.

'And . . . ?'

He stared at her for a moment. Unsure whether to go on or not. Then:

'Yes. Maybe we might have gone our separate ways if you hadn't come along. After so many years – you were the last thing we expected . . . Still. Here you are – thank God. And here I lie. Lying and dying . . .' He closed his eyes. 'But believe you me, if I could at this very moment set Rome on fire – I would. If only to singe my fingers. And a few other fingers as well . . . Listen to me now, so you'll remember. The main feeling is this feeling of absurdity, as I said. The voice that goes on saying "Was that it?" And every time you blink, every time you shut your eyes – "Is this it?" And I can't help but feel ashamed. All the people I might have helped if I had known – how afraid they were.' He pursed the crooked lips, and stared through bleary eyes. Then, a sigh, a smile and a wave of his hand through the air above his head as if to erase his own words. 'Ah would you listen to me . . .'

'You'll be fine. Just fine.'

'I'll be fine . . . Kitty?'

'Yes?'

'Don't just go along with things, there's a good girl. Don't fool yourself. Try to see things clearly. For what they are.'

Kitty shook her head in bemusement.

'I don't know what you mean.'

'I don't know exactly what I mean myself to tell the truth – Just don't be too proud – or too weak like me . . .'

'I don't have a clue what you're talking about.'

'Sure if I had a clue myself – I wouldn't be talking,' he smiled. Suddenly he gripped her hand as fiercely as he could. 'God, I've been a useless husband. A useless father. A pretty useless doctor too if it comes down to it . . .'

'Now you're just feeling sorry for yourself. Stop it.'

'I'll feel sorry for myself if I want to, young lady. I've a lot to feel sorry for.'

'What exactly?' But she knew to what he was referring. He raised his eyebrows and cast her a knowing glance. Kitty lowered her eyes. He did not have to apologize for his weakness. His wife was strong. But she had made Kitty strong, too – in resistance. None of that mattered now. It was past. There had been times when she could have shaken him, caught him by the shoulders and shaken him into facing the truth, confronted him with his wife's cruelty. But instinctively as children often do, she had taken the measure of the parent and protected him.

'I'm just going to close my eyes for a few minutes,' he was saying. 'Don't go.'

The thick black eyebrows, so comical now, drew together. His breathing was laboured. He was exhausted. Kitty stretched herself across him, supporting her body on her elbows. She gently kissed the pouched eyelids. The smell of him was unbearably familiar, sweaty with a faint tang of oranges, urine, and even now, cigar smoke. His face relaxed into sleep.

Kitty stood by the window. Outside, a couple of magpies rattled from their branch like old jeering women. She hugged herself, aware of a sort of abject, crushing love for the vestigial creature lying on the bed behind. Love of a father tainted everything, she thought.

She turned to gaze out the window once more. From the first floor she could see all the way down the mile or so they were set back from the main road, such as it was. From this elevation, the sea and far coastline were visible. Cattle grazed in the fields that lay ahead of the not very impeccable lawns. The grounds were ragged. There was too much land to landscape. For years the surrounding acres, about fifty in all, had been let out to farmers for grazing while the immediate environs of the house were supposed to be cultivated and manicured. But growth was too prolific – the result of prodigious rainfall and the proximity of the coast to the Gulf Stream.

Tropical and sub-tropical species grew here. An illusion of Mediterranean landscape, formed by the tall, gaunt Scots Pines in the distance and the squat Stone Pines – like grey opened umbrellas behind solitary pencil cypresses – was quickly dispelled once the eye carried on to the other shore. There the fields were small and rugged, surrounded by wild hedgerows of blackthorn, holly and sallow interspersed with stacks of naked grey stone.

It was darkening slowly outside. A sliver of moon, tremulous as a gold shaving, glinted through the horizontal slats of the Cedar of Lebanon to the left. Behind, she could just make out the silhouette of the castle ruin – just a wall with two slits – redundant once supplanted by the house, which was early Georgian. It was a wide house, not deep, flat-fronted with long, narrow sash windows set into the manila walls. Kitty's room was on the third floor, the attic floor. Despite the long climb she preferred it up there; the view was at its most expansive, cresting the peninsula to the purple hills beyond.

She surrendered to a bittersweet melancholia as she watched the small squares of butteryellow light come on in the houses on the opposite shore. Nothing much changed here. The same windows reflected the same light, night after night, and she could recall so many nights when she had wondered what lay beyond those comforting glows in the dark. In the city, there were so many lights, so many windows. But none to fix upon.

'Precious. Precious,' she whispered to herself, not in allusion to the scene outside but to the idle drift of her thoughts. Homes were like that, strange in their familiarity like the body smells of familiar people.

He moaned in his sleep. Kitty turned to watch the lengthening shadows glide across the room. With its red and gilt flock wallpaper and gleaming rosewood furniture it was as if someone had said, 'And make this one masculine'. Which to a degree, someone had. 'Parodic Homes & Gardens' her father had once described the interior decor.

Dr Con came from a long distinguished line of doctors. Or a long line of distinguished doctors. State your preference, as he put it. He had exhausted all the comic possibilities provided by his name with his predilection for punning, so that if he was not conning his patients, he was conjuring up a remedy. Bantering references to conjugal rights had been silenced quickly by his wife's gelid glance. He had accepted the house with the same

61

good grace as his father, who had in turn accepted it from his father, and all with the same resignation toward the nightly lucubrations required of those who follow unquestioningly a predestined profession. He was not a good doctor because he cared little for doctoring. He cared less for farming as the fallow acres testified.

Peering through the gloom, Kitty felt consumed by a tearing pity. He was right. He was weak. Weak and frightened. Consigned to the tender and most assiduous mercies of one who had been ignored for a lifetime. His wife would be ruthless in her mercy.

The lights of a car sliced into the violet haze below. A well-dressed woman greeted Eleanor who had evidently been expecting a visitor. From the hallway her voice sounded more English in accent than usual. Someone to impress, Kitty surmised.

'Who is it?' her father asked sleepily.

'No one. Just another of the living dead.'

'Bitch,' he chuckled. 'What does she look like? I take it it's a she?'

'Short, thin, dark hair, fat ankles . . .'

'That'll be Elsa O'Connor, the new rector's wife.'

'O'Connor?'

'He's Irish. She's English. She's your mother's new buddy.' He licked his caked lips. 'Pass me a glass of water would you?'

He sipped delicately as Kitty held the glass for him and cradled his neck. He lay back.

'Oh yes. Great pals the pair of them. Your mother has taken to attending "services" again if you don't mind.'

A peremptory knock on the door halted their giggles. The brightness of Eleanor's eyes was matched by her voice:

'Enjoying yourselves?' She had the look of a woman conscious of every word appearing inane. Kitty felt a sharp pang of pity for a second, but quickly suffocated it behind an equally bright smile.

'Will your friend be staying long?' Kitty asked.

'No. No. Not long. Half an hour at most.' She hesitated at the door. 'I thought you might like some mussels for your first night home . . . So – so I got some.' The clumsy attempt was wince-making for all of them. Eleanor's face clouded over. She hooded her brown eyes and stuck her tongue in the side of her cheek.

'Well.' She shrugged. Kitty giggled nervously. The thanks she meant to say stuck in her throat and lodged there, wriggling.

Eleanor suddenly covered the room in a few paces and without looking directly at him, she pulled her husband toward her, lifted and shook his pillows and replaced him as one would a budgie in a freshened cage.

'There,' she said. Her eyes glittered then hooded again. Her husband was wearing his bemused baby expression.

'Not *too* much longer,' Eleanor enunciated with precision from the doorway. She cast her daughter a meaningful look as if to say – 'if he has another attack tonight . . .' She swung the door after her but stemmed the slam just in time with her elbow.

They watched the closed door in silence.

'Don't be so hard on her, Kitty. You know she's trying.'

'Isn't she though.'

'You'll want to come home won't you?' He voiced what Kitty would rather have ignored for a while yet.

'Not to her. I'll never come home to her. She hates me. I hate her too,' she added, aware of the foolish note in her voice.

He was chuckling.

'I've never met such a pair. Dancing around each other like two boxers in a ring. But you'll come back for more, believe me, you will. When I'm gone you might think the last bell finally rung and before you know it, before you've even thought about it – you'll be back in the ring, ready for the off. And you know what? She'll be waiting. Sooner or later one of you will have to take the gloves off. Grow up, Kitty – let it be you, there's a girl . . . This is a messy business. Don't let it get bloody too.'

His serious tone again shocked Kitty. It was so rare for him to be entirely serious. Unsure if anything at all was worth saying or if anything was worth saying by him, he mocked his own words even as he uttered them. He had been playing the grand old man since boyhood.

Kitty opened her mouth to disagree, then abruptly closed it again. She was tired of the old whine. The old wrongs. What point? None. He knew. He knew it all. And he had played his part. He knew better than anyone how his weakness had played its part. He had seen the dull brown gaze rest on Kitty with almost childlike animosity. There were times when he felt certain that his wife could have killed her daughter. But something stopped her, so she killed her cat instead, poisoned it with strychnine, though no one ever accused her.

His wife hated mess more than she hated cats so she burned every book, every toy, once; in a glorious bonfire at the back of the house because her daughter had not tidied her room sufficiently. She had called them out to watch. They looked on in silence. And Kitty had cried out to her father as the last doll, her favourite, hit the flames. He would not look at her but spent the next week buying replacements which she accepted with tearful smiles. He knew too that Kitty had spent hours, once a whole day and night, locked in her room, ostensibly as punishment, in reality because her mother simply could not bear the sight of her. He knew it all. Now, his eyes met Kitty's and he nodded. He was grateful for her silence and she was pleased to offer it, this once.

'I think, if the truth be told, she's always been a bit – a small bit mad,' he whispered.

Kitty held his hands and raised them to her lips. His punctured face twisted. She lowered her eyes at the sight of him, crumpled and somehow distasteful, like a cheap forgotten suit left at the dry-cleaners.

'She's not mad,' she said with care. 'She's the wicked witch.'

'You'll kill me for saying this – but you're more like her than you know my dear,' he said, pulling a face at Kitty's horrified expression.

They giggled again. Happy to be back on giggling ground. His eyes were moist.

'How come you and I are always laughing or crying? There's no hope for me if you haven't grown up yet, you silly man. You silly, silly man. I love you so much.' She leaned across and gently wiped his eyelids with her thumbs. His breath upon her face reeked of creamy milk and decay.

His smile was grateful, complicitous. He tried to stroke her hair but his hand fell limply on the bedcover. He hissed with frustration, and she lifted the hand for him and glided it along her cheek. Then she slid off the bed again, smoothing the covers with trailing fingers.

64

'Mussels then,' she said.

'Mussels,' he repeated.

At the door she looked over her shoulder. 'Stop a second,' he slurred.

'What is it?'

'I don't know . . . it must be the light.' He appeared confused. 'For a moment there, I had the strangest feeling . . . You looked – I don't know – ghostly or something. As if you had died, not me. Am I losing my mind, do you think?'

Kitty smiled.

'Probably,' she said. He had not asked how long she would stay but, as if reading his thoughts, she said:

'I'll stay a week.'

'But work . . .' His voice trailed off. They both knew that it would not matter. Her employment with his cousin had become an extended stopgap prior to her Masters degree. Another forgotten hazy detail.

'What books for tomorrow?' she asked.

'Oh I don't know. Anything at all. Whatever you like.'

She waited.

'Lots of words, I think. Yes, that's it. A couple of chapters of the old *Brothers Karamazov* maybe. Why not? I'm not going anywhere. I've had a bellyful of clipped perfection lately – too much spared in the spare prose – let's fill those gaps.' He warmed to the subject shifting himself eagerly on the bed. 'And maybe you could find Montaigne's chapter on his illnesses, you know the bit where he goes on about his farting and the like . . .'

'Consolation?' Kitty asked drily.

'Christ no,' he denied. 'Commiseration. Commiseration, darling girl. It's all I can afford these days.'

Kitty clicked the door shut gently and chuckled for a moment on the landing. The stair carpet smelt dry and musty; she sometimes thought that the threads were held together by dust. Along the skirtings, yellowed paint bubbled and cracked, reminding her of the skin on untreated milk. Beyond the rain-streaked landing window, the magpies still cackled. The sound of her mother's highpitched humourless laugh drifting upstairs, sounded strangely similar.

November

Over a month had passed since Kitty had left Dublin. She did not intend to spend that long at home, but her father was enjoying her company so much she had called his cousin, her employer, and gave him little choice in the matter. She would return when she was sure that her father was over the worst and not before.

Dr Con was improving. He walked a little each day now, circling the overgrown gardens with his daughter. Although he read his newspaper every morning, Kitty still read novel extracts to him each afternoon and evening. It was less tiring for him, and besides it gave them the excuse to hide themselves away in the library beside a log fire, curled up like naughty children beneath a rug, in studious avoidance of the supplanted nurse.

Kitty's mother finally gave up all attempts at ministration when she saw that her daughter was determined not to return to Dublin. She could only glare – and retreat.

Danny was understanding at first, but when she did not return as promised with each passing week, Kitty detected a coldness in his voice. After three weeks, he would not take her calls, pretending to be out when she knew very well that he was standing by the phone, waving his hand at his flatmate. She was annoyed by what she considered his selfish disregard for her needs. So she wrote to him. A caustic note, containing barely veiled recriminations, but ending with an entreaty for him to come. For a weekend, just as they'd agreed before. He tore her letter into tiny pieces. Walked alone for hours, then returned to the flat half frozen from the cold, and called her. He would come.

It was evening when he slumped off the Dublin–Cork train, shouldering unseen adversaries out of his way. Kitty watched his brooding, pugilistic performance from the shadow of a nearby awning. He shuffled like a bagman, hands thrust deep within pockets of jeans that were too loose. He had dressed with intentional shabbiness, the gashes in his grey ribbed pullover showed an equally tattered check flannel shirt underneath. His sandy hair was tossed and stood on end in places. He was unshaven. Kitty smiled. She tried to hide the brightness of her eyes and fixed her face into a frown to meet his frown.

Danny's scowl increased when his eyes finally picked her out beneath the canopy. He lumbered forward, she had to admire his display of reluctance.

He dropped his duffel bag at Kitty's feet and kissed her gruffly on the cheek. His hands plunged back into his pockets, he lifted his shoulders, pursed his mouth and stared at passing strangers. The overhead lights refracted against the pale blue of his irises and intensified the cutting, shifting quality of his gaze. She had underestimated, as usual, his anger. He was desolate in his loneliness.

Instinctively, Kitty realized that he considered her lost to him. Lost to a world of casual conversation, drawing room parlance, chintz, real coffee and clothes with labels. In short, a world apart from him. She saw that he had always feared her visits home, afraid that when returned to him, she would find him somehow – distasteful. And as a child wilfully provokes a response it fears, he was doing everything possible to be distasteful.

His fear was petty and demeaning too, but looking at him that evening, seeing the naked terror and hostility in his eyes, the body racked and taut with a tension that manifested itself in twitches and tics and staccato taps on the floor, Kitty was touched immeasurably. She knew that if she so much as blinked in a way he considered offhand or dismissive, he would whirl about without a word, and leave her standing there. He would have suffered the loss of her rather than suffer real or imagined slights.

She resisted the urge to slap him into reality. Wing the back of her hand against his sullen face. But she realized, perhaps for the first time, despite the ease with which she could tell him that she loved him, that she was truly in love. It was, when all was said and done, as simple and as complex as that. Therefore, she would compromise. Compromise endlessly, if shamefully. Two years pretence at distance dissolved. It would never be so easy again – to tell him that she loved him.

'Want a coffee or a drink or something before we go?' she asked in a soft, emollient voice.

'No.'

'Are you sure?' she called after him. He was striding ahead into the car park.

Outside, he appeared to be looking for a car he could not possibly recognize. Kitty sidled up to him, she touched his tense shoulder and indicated the car with her head. He froze when he saw the large saloon. She pulled a face. Then, suddenly, awkwardly, he turned and pulled her to him. He groaned into her hair.

'I thought maybe you weren't coming back. I thought you'd changed your mind about London . . . about us . . .'

Kitty held him, stroking her hands up and down his back until she could feel him begin to relax. He cupped her face and stared down at her with a shy smile curving his lips. He took a deep breath and gently kissed her forehead. Kitty smiled reassuringly as she dragged him to the car. He was rigid with cold and she wryly observed that despite his shabby attire, he had not gone the full hog and brought the threadbare coat with him; neither had he brought the good wool coat she had bought. She wondered if there was any end to the little daily torments he inflicted upon himself.

They drove into blue-black darkness beyond the city, along narrow hedgerowed roads which snaked into dark unrelenting bends. Kitty turned the heating up full blast to warm him, and little beads of sweat glistened on her forehead. She had to stop the car to take off her coat. A third of moon, dusky yellow and veined, slipped through the clouds and promised a clear indigo night.

Danny talked about work at Coonan, Doyle and Ferguson's. He smiled ruefully when he told her that the partners had not exactly wept when he told them one afternoon, that he just might feel obliged to look for employment elsewhere if they continued to thrust the usual dross at him. Evidently they were blind to his potential.

Kitty spoke of her month with her father. His gradual but hopeful recovery. She did not go on about her lengthy evening talks with him. Danny could only absorb so much, after that he would see anything as a dismissal of himself. They were more than halfway there when he said:

'Pull in up there.'

Kitty drew the car up to a jog in the road which was the entrance to a section of State forestry. She nosed the car's front right up to the long wooden gate and turned to him expectantly.

'Now what?' she asked.

'Now turn the lights off.'

She complied. Pale, blanched light suffused the car's interior. Danny's expression was inscrutable. Kitty was not sure if she saw a smile or a grimace.

'Now?' she asked.

'Now get your jeans off,' Danny grinned broadly.

'God I love it when you're so masterful,' she laughed.

'Masterful my arse,' he said. 'I'm in agony.'

She was prepared for a certain roughness whenever Danny would reach across to pull her toward him. But he surprised her with gentleness. He glided his hip across and lowered her seat back with admirable dexterity. She was not in the mood for fumbling. Then, he hovered above her, balancing on one outstretched arm as he brought his head down to kiss her face with such exquisite tenderness, Kitty was unsure for a moment if she had begun to cry or not. He strummed her eyelids shut, stretching the soft skin toward the corners and pressed his lips against the tautened sheen of flesh. He brushed his full lips along her forehead in a slow, prolonged movement while his fingers tangled in her hair and pulled her head back further so that he could kiss her cheeks and chin and neck. His lips moved up to her lips and brushed teasingly but did not engage. He caught a tear from her cheek, balanced it on his forefinger with the same excruciating gentleness that had caused the tear and rubbed it along the contours of her mouth before his tongue delicately licked the salty moistness of it from her swollen lips.

Danny was never unsure when making love. There was an integrity in his unselfconscious groans, his sometimes thoughtless hands. If he was unsure, diffident, in all else in life, he possessed a confidence, a sense of certainty in lovemaking that countered Kitty's initial hesitancy. He moved his body in an easy language, a vocabulary his voice did not know.

He was slender, not skinny, he was too well formed for that. He possessed the body hair of a woman – underarm and pubic – though unlike most women, his lean curved legs were hairless. He did not work at any sport in particular but perhaps from the perpetual state of anxiety he endured, which caused the tensing and contracting of each muscle in turn, he had become resilient to the touch.

He smelt of sweat, soap and stale beer, faintly rancorous though not unpleasant. He smelt too of warm, dripping sex. He shuddered almost as he entered her, and withdrew to spill himself over her belly. They were not disappointed, knowing that the first urgent ejaculation spent, meant slow easy sex next time. He allowed his weight to press on top of Kitty and she wrapped her legs around him to wait. Then she got cramp in her left leg. She laughed. Sex in real life was never like the movies.

'Get off,' she said. 'I've got cramp. And I want a cigarette.'

'What happened to romance?' He smiled as he withdrew.

'You've had it.'

'What about you?' he asked, leaning across again, placing his hand between her thighs. She brushed it away.

'Later. When I'm ready. First, a cigarette.'

Kitty smoked three cigarettes in the car that night. Bedlam reigned at times as they twisted into awkward body knots and suffered cramps in feet and calves. When cars passed they shunted down and covered themselves with Kitty's coat, giggling together in the warm enveloping darkness. They read the details on Danny's packet of condoms and erupted into yet more laughter. The ribbed, ringed, lubricated, extra-safe, extra-sure rubbers made every promise Kitty remarked, bar the promise of a stiff dick to wear them.

There were also moments of intense gentleness on Danny's part. He apologized with caressing hands for his earlier surly performance. Kitty understood.

When there was not one drop of body secretion left between

70

them, that was not oozed into a condom or smeared across their bodies or embedded in the plush velour by hastily rubbing fingers, they prised themselves apart. And Kitty experienced a familiar sense of melancholy to find herself alone in her body once more.

Danny fell into a deep sleep as she drove the rest of the way home. She studied him from the corner of her eye as they passed through the lighted streets of small town after small town. He appeared so peaceful but moaned softly and shielded his eyes from the lights with the back of his arm, dropping it again when they continued into darkness. For the first time, Kitty wondered what sort of reception he might expect from Eleanor. The thought made her reach out protectively to stroke his head. He smiled in his sleep.

'Dan?' she whispered after a while.

'What – are we there . . . ?' He blinked rapidly and wriggled upright.

'No, not yet . . . I was just wondering if you'd given the notion of London any more thought over the last few weeks?' She spoke casually but darted him a quick sideways glance to check his reaction. The last time she had suggested that it might be a good idea for them to try living and working in London for a while, he had remained singularly unimpressed by the prospect.

'You don't want to go back to Dublin?' He rubbed his eyelids.

'Not especially, no. Well – at least not forever, you know?'

'I've thought about London aye.'

'And?'

He sighed and shrugged. Kitty twisted her mouth to the side – she should have waited a few days before broaching the subject.

'There's nothing keeping us in Dublin, I suppose,' he said, doubtfully.

Kitty smiled and dropped the subject. She had pushed as far as was needed, for the moment. They drove on in silence.

It was only as she turned into the driveway with bleary, drooping eyes that she began to hope her mother was in bed. But Eleanor was not in bed. She had expected them hours ago, and stood in the doorway hopping from one foot to the other from cold and anger. She glowered. Kitty grinned mechanically. Danny's startled gaze and tossed hair made him look for all the world like some dishevelled drunk she'd picked up on the way home.

Eleanor eyed him with that blank cold look that was infinitely more disparaging than plain lip-curled disdain. He shuffled to suit his part. He mumbled an incoherent greeting with an apology mixed up at the back of it. Eleanor's gaze left him and travelled to take in her daughter's wild knotted hair, the lipgloss smear across her cheek, the guilty smirk. They reeked of fresh sex as they bundled past her rigid figure. She firmly clicked the front door shut.

'You'll find blankets and sheets on top of his bed,' she spoke to Kitty, indicating Danny with an incline of permed head. He would remain unacknowledged by all but elliptical references, Kitty gathered from her tone.

'In the guest room, the blue,' Eleanor added to her daughter's quizzical glance. They had not discussed his visit. Kitty presented the details of when and how long only the day before, thrust them toward her mother as though on a broken and soiled platter. 'From the North?' Eleanor had said, adding, 'How dreary.' She had turned with a small triumphant smile playing on her scarlet lips.

In the kitchen Kitty made herself a hot chocolate. Danny wanted a drink.

'I think I need one,' he said. 'Herself doesn't think much of me, does she?'

'Never mind her,' Kitty responded gaily. 'She's always the same. Don't think for one minute that it's you.'

She went to fetch his drink from the living room cabinet. Eleanor was busy dusting the undusty figurines on the mantel above the dying fire.

'How long will you be?' she asked.

'I don't know – How long have we got?'

'Don't be so cheeky with me, my dear. I have to make sure you don't wake your poor father up when you go upstairs. Do you think you could bring yourself to make this fellow's – what's his name . . . ?'

'Danny. As you well know. Seeing as you knew he was from the North.'

'Ah yes, Daniel. Do you think you could see to Daniel's bed please? It's been a long night. Your father has only just fallen asleep. He waited up to meet this fellow but he had to give up in the end. You oughtn't to do that to him you know.'

Kitty deflected the barb just in time to turn her wince into a smile. She beamed. Slowly fixed the drink. Swirling the contents around the glass, she dipped her finger in and sucked.

'We're going for a walk actually.' She surprised herself.

'What do you mean – walk? At this hour of night? Don't be ridiculous. Really. I've had quite enough nonsense for one night. Go and fix this fellow's bed.' The round spots vied with the rouge on her cheeks.

'No. We need a walk. Don't wait up. I'll put the lights out,' Kitty stated simply, and left the room.

Danny had to be persuaded but not with great difficulty. He studied Kitty through sleepy satisfied eyes. The lust was still there. Kitty blew him a silent cheeky kiss. He laughed.

'She's going to call you Daniel you know – so be prepared,' Kitty said.

'Whatever,' he shrugged. 'Look, can't this walk wait until the morning? It's the wee hours already. We can't see anything in the bloody dark anyways.'

'We're going for a walk, just a short one, and that's that.'

They walked out into the cold night air with the aid of a dim torch. Kitty felt that they were in perfect communion as they stumbled past the house to enter the black avenue of trees; the closeness between them like a living palpable thing. Once, she looked back to see her mother standing in the lamplight of the living room. She appeared frozen, unmoving, as she watched their halting progress through unblinking eyes. It seemed to Kitty that just as their present closeness was almost tangible, so too was the halo of exclusion that seemed to surround her mother's solitary figure.

She shivered and hugged herself closer to Danny. She realized that the thrill of pleasure that coursed through her veins was quite vicious. That insidious pitilessness Eleanor invoked. But the enjoyment was all Kitty's own.

If he could have slept while walking, Danny would have snored.

Kitty picked out a cautious path with the wavering beam from the torch. She breathed in. She could smell the sour cider odour of fallen maggoty apples from the orchard, crushed acorns, black sloes spliced and rain-sodden upon the ground, wet leaf pulp and layered upon everything, the faint tang of salty sea. The scents of her childhood.

She wondered if Danny was finding the night air as rich and heady as she did and turned to ask him. He placed a finger to her lips and whispered:

'Shh. Don't talk. Don't talk. We're happy now.'

She sighed with contentment. The naked branches of the trees around them clicked and rustled in the breeze. An owl hooted, she saw its hooded dusky form illuminated by moonlight stealing out from behind the clouds, and suddenly a vague unease swelled inside her. She remembered something hazy and deep interred from childhood – she pulled on the memory, drew it out – yes, to see an owl in your garden meant a death in the family. That was it. A childish yarn. Told on walks from school to pass the time.

She thought of her father and his long patient wait for them. She gazed sideways at Danny, his face was white and stark in the moonlight. Behind, Eleanor's rigid figure remained by the window. And for a moment, Kitty felt a pang of bittersweet sadness as if, in a way, she were already bereft.

December

Ma O'Neill was kneading dough for brown cake. Her hands pounded the soft light brown mixture into a round thick cake. She cut a deep cross into it and slid the tray to one side, turning her attention to the other half of dough which lay on a bed of flour on the Formica-topped kitchen table. With her knuckles, she began.

Her brother watched in silence and replaced his cup onto the saucer with a grimace of irritation. He always insisted on a cup and saucer for tea. Mugs were fine for coffee. His sister's blue mug of untouched tea had a skin on the surface. She would drink it cold, later.

His blue eyes, trancelike, fixed on Ma O'Neill's hands as she turned the dough over to sprinkle a layer of flour dust over the top.

Slurping back the last mouthful, he wiped his mouth with the back of his hand, then shook a few drops from the hand onto the ground, curling his mouth down at the corners as though offended.

'They're not very pleased I can tell you,' he said, finally.

'Is that so.' It was not a question.

'Yes. By all accounts Fogarty was seen only yesterday swanning around the garage with not a trace of warning on him. How do you think that is?' He tried to put her on the spot but she was not having any of it. Apart from a flicker of the eyelids, she might not have heard him. He said:

'Eh?'

'It's not for me to say,' she said.

'Oh I know. I know that,' he said in a placatory tone. He was treading on eggshells. 'Still. All the same. Eamon said he dealt with him.'

'Aye. He did that alright.'

'Did what?'

'Said he dealt with him.'

Fr. Joe clicked his tongue in exasperation, reached for the empty cup, pointed its emptiness toward her and she reached for the teapot to fill him up.

'All the same,' he said. 'Any milk?'

She nodded toward the fridge but before he could get up she ran across the kitchen to fetch it. She poured with her eyebrows poised. He nodded, she lowered her brow and replaced the milk in the fridge.

'Look Agnes, what I'm trying to say is, what I'm trying to say is – it's not easy. I'm between a rock and a hard place here. You know that. The Blessed Mother knows I'm not supposed to be involved in any of this. Fr. Mulcahy took a big chance telling me about Fogarty. The least we might expect is a few answers.'

'Like what?'

'I don't know. How should I know for goodness sake?' He shrugged. 'Something at any rate. Some results.'

'Bruises or holes maybe?'

'Now now . . .'

'Look it. Eamon said he dealt with it. That's enough for me. It should be enough for you too. He has his ways.' She began to spread the dough with splayed fingers.

'Yes yes. But . . .'

'But what, Joe?' a voice said from the hallway. Eamon followed, shaking a wet umbrella onto the kitchen linoleum.

'Put that thing outside,' his mother ordered over her shoulder at the sound of wet drops pinging on the floor. Eamon hesitated, catching the priest's wary eye, then acceded to her command. Fr. Joe spoke to the space Eamon had vacated:

'Don't think I'm trying to interfere, Eamon,' he called. 'I was just saying to your mother here, that that that . . . it has been said, only been said mind you that – that . . . that.' He shrugged at empty space.

'That?' Eamon re-entered.

'Well. That . . .'

Eamon leaned across the table. His eyes spoke what his voice could not.

'You do your job, Father and I'll do mine.' He spoke as if to a recalcitrant child, firmly, gently, but with a hint of impatience.

The sound of the front door slamming shut caused the priest to jump and reach for his teacup.

'That'll be Monica,' Ma O'Neill said.

A short plump woman in her mid-thirties with a round childish face and grey, heavily lashed eyes, bounced into the kitchen. She was soaked to the bone, her dark curly hair matted against her crown and neck. She shook her head as a wet dog might, laughing with apparent glee as the drops flew around the kitchen. Her mother glared with disapproval.

'You'll catch your death,' she greeted her daughter.

Monica stared at the solemn faces in the room and stamped her feet on the ground. She was frozen. Her brother did not offer a greeting and turned his back to her on the pretext of fetching himself a mug.

'How are you doing Fr. Joe?' Monica addressed the priest, who did not like to be called Uncle. She settled herself into a chair, disregarding her wet clothes.

'I'm alright I suppose, Monica. I haven't seen you this long while. How's himself and the babbies?'

'Grand. All grand. Not such babbies anymore.' Monica eyed her mother's breadmaking for a second then felt the teapot. It was lukewarm.

'Stick on the kettle, Eamon,' Monica ordered.

'Get a towel, girl,' her mother said, and: 'On your way shove that into the oven. It should be hot enough by now.' She pointed to the finished cake on the table.

'Eamon, pass me a towel and shove that in the oven for Ma like a good lad would you?' Monica twisted her head around to address her scowling brother. Muttering something, he tossed a towel at her. It landed on her head. She squealed.

Ma O'Neill caught the tray and placed it in the oven herself without a word. A warming blast of hot air from the opened door suffused the small room. It was not cold in the kitchen but not entirely warm either.

'Just a social call, Father?' Monica asked. He hesitated, looked across at Eamon and nodded his head. Monica caught the look that passed between them and pursed her lips.

'I see,' she said, staring first at the priest and then at her brother, with a glint of amusement in her eyes. Her first instinct had proved correct. She had sensed something was up the moment she entered the kitchen. Fr. Joe was always meddling. Whatever it was this time, and she certainly did not care to know, Eamon was not best pleased and that pleased Monica enormously. She chuckled as she tousled her hair dry.

Oblivious to them all, Ma O'Neill began to cut triangles from the dough, lining them up on another baking tray. Her nose began to drip. She sniffed and put the back of her floury hand up against her nostril to stem the flow.

'Eamon,' she said.

He pulled a tissue from a box and reached over Monica's head to put it against his mother's nose. She blew hard once. He wiped and threw the tissue away.

'It's this weather,' she explained. 'Non-stop rain. It gets into your bones. A person could be dead before they knew what happened to them, and so they could.'

'Aye,' Fr. Joe agreed. He didn't see much point in hanging around now that the opportunity to speak alone with Eamon was gone. In truth, he was relieved. He had got his point across one way or the other. That was all that mattered. He got up to leave.

'I may as well be off then.' He slapped his thighs for car keys. His pale blue eyes searched for his sister's but she denied him. She remained busy. They shuffled their shoulders in goodbye.

When he had taken his bleached angular frame from their company, they all began to talk together. A babble of voices, saying nothing, filled the kitchen. Eamon wanted to know how his nephews were and why couldn't she bring them to the house more often, it wasn't as if they were monsters or anything, himself and his mother he meant, or was her home too shabby for them, was she ashamed of it now that she had found nirvana in suburban climes? He made a fresh pot of tea as he talked, and as he talked his sister said, 'That's right yeah, that's right yeah, pass me the sugarbowl, oh that's right yeah.' And Ma O'Neill placed her batch of scones into the lower rack in the oven, telling her daughter to remove the wet towel from the table, take off her wet shoes and would Eamon ever go out to the front room and make sure that the fire was alright and if it wasn't, to make sure that he used the logs from the bottom of the basket first because the top ones were still a wee bit damp. And there was only brown cake and scones with jam for tea and they could like it or lump it.

Trickles of condensation rolled down the inside of the back window as the kitchen warmed up. Rain splattered, driven by wind against the panes. Arrows of silver beads reflected the direction of the gale. A particularly strong gust howled and rattled down the chimney in the other room. The window trembled.

'Would you listen to that?' Ma said, in a blasé tone.

Monica pulled out a chair for her mother.

'Sit down will you, for two seconds and tell me about your one, what was it Mrs Neeson said? A doctor's daughter no less. Loaded I've no doubt. Trust our Dan.'

'Who told you?'

'Girlie Neeson phoned me.'

'Oh she did, did she? The cheek. I was going to come round myself to you tomorrow.'

'Amn't I always telling you to get a phone, Ma?' Monica said.

'No telephones in this house,' her mother replied. Eamon grunted into his tea in agreement. Monica half swivelled in her chair to face him – he was leaning against the dresser in his habitual stance.

'Afraid of the old tap dancing Eamon?' Monica asked sarcastically.

'Maybe.'

'Maybe if you didn't have reason to be afraid yous could have a phone like any other normal house.'

He eyed her with derision, the intense blackness of his pupils dilated and contracted but he said nothing. His mother addressed him:

'Eamon, take a look at the cake for me. It should be done.' She turned her attention to her daughter whose cheeks were tinged bright pink.

'Now so,' Ma said businesslike. 'Now so – she's only staying a couple of nights. We're putting her in Eamon's room. Danny's room is a sight. He'll sleep with Eamon, they can share the bed. It'll do. I've arranged for Dave McLoughlin to come in and give downstairs a lick of paint over the next few days. He'll do it cheap. The place needs it anyway. But I need some sort of decent bed cover . . . ?'

'You mean a duvet?'

'Whatever. And curtains. We need curtains. The yokeys in Eamon's room – you can see the threads in them. You're bound to have something useful. And maybe an electric blanket if you have one to spare, she's probably used to central heating.' She rose suddenly and opened a drawer by the oven. She pulled out her glasses and rummaged for something. A folded newspaper cutting was produced. 'I don't know what you think . . . What do you think of those things? Is it a good price? Should we get one, d'you think?' She flattened the page onto the table and pinned her glasses back with one finger.

Monica gravely read the advertisement about a giveaway sale at rockbottom prices, never to be repeated – of microwaves.

'What do you want with a microwave?' she asked incredulously.

'I'm the one asking you. Should we have one? Are they useful yokeys? Is it a good price do you think?' Ma eyed the advertisement.

'Ye-es. It's a good price I suppose. But I know you, Ma. You'd never use it. You'd be better off with a tumble dryer or a freezer.'

Ma shook her head.

'No room. But I could fit that yoke over there on top of that cupboard. There's a plug there and all for it. Your one might be used to them.'

Monica raised her palms in a noncommittal gesture.

'I don't know Ma . . .'

'You'd swear it was the bloody Queen of Sheba coming to visit to hear the pair of yous,' Eamon protested. He had had a bellyful.

'Ignore him,' Ma said, with a toss of her head, and, 'So you don't think we should get one?' she asked again of Monica.

For a moment her daughter sized the situation in her mind. She watched her mother's face out of the corner of her eye as she eagerly devoured for perhaps the hundredth time the text of the advertisement. Monica measured carefully and placed her thoughts upon the scales.

'We use ours all the time. They're fierce handy once you get used to them,' she offered in the end.

Her mother exhaled with satisfaction. She folded the piece of paper into a perfect square once more.

'We'll get it tomorrow so. Eamon can collect it on his way home. Eamon – remember you'll have to take the car tomorrow.'

Eamon wrenched his tie off.

'Ye're all bloody mad,' he hissed as he stalked out of the kitchen.

Monica clapped her hands together, sipped her tea and tapped out an exultant patter with her feet upon the floor.

'A Kitty, eh?' she said.

Ma O'Neill checked her scones and began to lay the table.

January

Kitty took a few deep breaths as soon as they got outside. The unmistakable smell of fresh paint was almost suffocating in the narrow hallway. There were other signs too, signalling that her visit had been well prepared for – fresh flowers and new curtains in her room, which was, apparently, Eamon's. Then there was the gleaming microwave, never used she gathered, observing the cellophane still around the glass platter within. The thought belatedly struck her that all this preparation had been in hand since before Christmas, when they had originally expected her visit. It never occurred to her when she casually postponed her trip until the New Year, that Danny's family might be so inconvenienced. Now, she apologized again to Danny, but he waved a hand and told her not to worry about it. His broad smile indicated that he was pleased with the way her first introduction to his family had gone. After tea and the initial greetings, he had suggested that they head out for a drink somewhere. As they marched away from the house, he said:

'Listen, it's me who should be sorry – I should have known that Ma would have them all dressed up to the nines, waiting to kiss the ring . . .' He broke into a laugh at the memory.

'And there I was in my slashed jeans and sweatshirt – you might have warned me,' Kitty said. 'I don't think Eamon thought much of my outfit . . . He doesn't say much, does he?'

'Nope. But Monica does enough talking for the pair of them.'

'I liked her,' Kitty said. 'She's going to take me around Belfast tomorrow for a tour, or so she says.'

'Well you can count me out,' Danny said in a droll voice.

It began to rain, cold, sleet-like drops soaked their coats in seconds. Danny broke into a run, propelling Kitty along by the elbow.

'Where are we going?' She panted, already out of breath.

'I don't know – we could go to the Snooker Hall, it's not far . . .'

Kitty ran a few steps to catch up with him. She knew very well that the Snooker Hall was his intended destination, he had mentioned it often enough in Dublin, but typically he had to pretend that the notion had just occurred to him. As they walked along the narrow street with its small identical bricked houses on either side, she smiled to herself. The first meeting with his family had been a reasonably successful, if strange, affair. Danny's anxious eyes belied the careless grunts he addressed to them. Eamon hardly took his eyes off the hole in her jeans, while Ma O'Neill asked a hundred questions about the train trip, life in Dublin, her father's state of health; then, like Monica, she did not wait for the answers. Kitty found herself opening and closing her mouth like a goldfish on display. And Monica, standing there with her two boys Paul and Kevin, eager to be friendly, but not too friendly, just in case. They tested her alright, sitting her down to tea immediately to check her table manners. She was the only one in the end who drank from a mug, insisting her preference, while they clinked delicate cups on saucers that clearly gleamed from a recent dusting.

'Dan?' She stopped him again, her smile broadening. 'Tell me something – does your mother always rap your knuckles with the back of a knife when you say "Jesus"?'

He glanced at her and they both laughed.

'Very embarrassing,' he said, shaking his head. 'Very embarrassing.'

'I'll have to remember to turn Jesuses into Jeecuses and Jeepers all weekend,' Kitty laughed. Rain streamed down her cheeks. She had to blink rapidly to expel drops from her eyes. He cupped her face in his hands and bent to kiss the top of her nose.

'I won't let her rap your knuckles,' he said softly.

'Aren't you the brave one,' she teased. 'She's fairly formidable ' if you don't mind me saying so.'

'Aye. And so she is,' he called over his shoulder, 'but you don't have anything to worry about – she likes you.'

'She does?' Kitty ran again to catch up. 'How can you tell?'

Danny inched her along by pressing his hand to the small of her back. He was chuckling.

'Well?' Kitty demanded.

'She . . .' He exploded into a full throated laugh. '. . . she didn't ask you first thing about your Protestant mother – if she didn't like you she'd have brought that up straight away – to let the rest of us know.'

'I see,' Kitty said doubtfully.

'No, you don't.' Danny grinned.

'I suppose not,' she sighed. 'That sort of thing wouldn't even occur to me to be honest, but it's different here, I imagine.'

'Aye.'

'Dan – wait up a sec – how come there aren't any photos of your father around? I looked because I wanted to see if you – well – resembled him more than your mother. You've only got her blue eyes . . .'

'Ma has a photo in her room. That's all. She doesn't like to put them around the house,' he replied.

'Why not?'

''Cause that's the way she is – forget it – C'mon, c'mon for God's sake.'

They crossed the street, avoiding as best they could swollen puddles lapping in crater-like potholes. The neon 'S' was missing from 'Snooker Hall'. They stepped into a dimly lit, smoky room with five snooker tables and a small tongue and groove bar counter at the back. Danny greeted a few young men his own age; Kitty fixed a smile on her lips as he introduced her but she found their overtly curious appraisals discomfiting. They did not seem to know what to say to her, so they ignored her while Danny fetched drinks. She tried some small talk with someone introduced as 'Donut', who flushed and hung his head. He wore a seventies' pale blue tank top over navy blue flares. Kitty bit her lip – she hated herself for making such observations.

'Why are you called Donut?' she tried, after a silence broken only by the click of the snooker balls.

'It's not Donut – it's Do Not,' the tall stringy fellow called Gerry said over his shoulder before he thrust his cue violently forward, ignoring her again. A roll-up clung to his upper lip.

'Do Not?' she said, the desperate smile making her cheeks ache. She wished that Danny would hurry up and rescue her but he was involved in some avid conversation or other with the elderly man behind the bar. The youth beside her, he was younger than Danny, no more than twenty she reckoned, scuffed at the floor with his shoes. He shot her a look, then hastily lowered his eyes again.

'Why Do Not?' she said directly to him.

'Why not Do Not?' Gerry said over his shoulder again, and a couple of his mates leaning on their cues sniggered loudly. Kitty flushed, she pursed her lips and folded her arms. She tapped a foot impatiently. Do Not cleared his throat.

'When I was younger like, in school it was, I said, "I do not know the answer" in a quiz once. And it, like, stuck. See?'

Kitty laughed too loudly. Do Not blushed miserably. By the time Danny returned with the drinks she had given up all effort at strained small talk. She watched Danny as he joked around with them, envying his apparent ease and lack of self-consciousness. She had never seen Danny so relaxed in company before. At first he did his best to include her in the meandering, joshing flow of the conversation, turning to her to explain who so and so was they were laughing about, but after a while he stopped. Several times, Kitty had to clamp her mouth tightly shut to suppress her yawns. She resented the barely concealed belligerent glances Gerry shot her whenever she made an effort to talk. Danny seemed oblivious to his friend's palpable hostility.

Finally, she addressed a question directly to Gerry in an effort to embarrass him into a polite response in front of his mates. He would surely have to keep up a reasonably polite facade after that she figured, but he glared at her disdainfully, then answered her question in a ludicrous parody of a posh English accent. Kitty blinked. Danny was just returning from the bar again.

'Awwfully sorry, old chap,' Gerry said to his opponent when he potted three in a row, in a voice just loud enough for Kitty to catch his words. Muted sniggering again. Kitty's cheeks were on fire.

'Excuse me,' she said, ignoring the glass Danny offered, 'why are you putting on that posh English accent around me?'

Evidently it was not good form to address one's persecutor directly. There was an embarrassed silence.

'Kitty?' Danny said with a perplexed frown.

'Excuu-uuse me . . .' Gerry said and they all laughed again. He was about to take a stroke when Kitty brushed past Danny and touched him lightly on the elbow. He froze and glared steadfastly ahead.

'No – excuse me,' she said pointedly. 'I don't know what the joke is – all this posh voice bit – after all, I'm the one who is *really* Irish here . . .'

The snooker cue fell onto the green baize. Do Not took a step backwards. Danny spluttered out a mouthful of lager and, still coughing, he slammed both glasses down before reaching for her. With his free hand he grabbed at their coats and propelled her toward the door without so much as a backward glance. Kitty turned once to find them all standing stock-still as if in a state of shock.

Outside, the rain had let up for a few minutes. Danny stalked ahead of Kitty, he still carried her coat. She called to him but he only increased his pace. Even at a distance she could hear his swearing. She stopped and lit a cigarette – there was little point in trying to talk to him when he was like that. A woman passed him by and cast him a horrified glance over her shoulder.

'Terrible, isn't it?' Kitty said to the woman and lifted her eyes to heaven. The woman muttered something about foul mouths and scurried by. Kitty shivered. It was freezing, she needed her coat.

'Ah Dan . . .' she called to him.

He stopped suddenly and waited for her to catch up with him. His head was down and he was still muttering. She reached for his arm but he yanked it away.

'I can't believe you said that,' he spat.

'Alright, alright – it was a stupid thing to say – I just didn't think . . .'

'Too damn right you didn't think . . .' he cut across her. 'I mean, take a look around you girl – where exactly do you think you are, for Christ's sake?'

'And that's supposed to give them an excuse for being so rude is it? Sorry, maybe you should have explained that to me before you took me there.'

'They didn't mean to be rude, they're just –' He waved a hand in exasperation. '– just shy – is all. I've known most of those lads all my life, they're not used to strangers . . .'

'Well maybe it's just as hard for "strangers" to get used to them,' she spat back.

He turned, still scowling and thrust the coat at her. She managed to grab it before he took a step backwards off the kerbside, and landed both feet into a deep pool of rainwater. There was a moment's silence while he gazed balefully downwards, then they began to laugh together. Danny's hand snaked out, encircled her wrist and hauled her into the puddle beside him.

'Truce?' she asked.

'Truce,' he agreed, draping her coat over her shoulders.

They squelched homeward. At the door, Danny stopped and tapped her arm.

'Listen,' he said. 'Don't mention anything about us going to London just yet, alright? I haven't told Ma . . .'

'Just as well you told me,' Kitty said. He was about to go in when she caught his sleeve. 'We're still going, aren't we Dan?'

'Oh aye.'

'I mean, I've started looking at jobs already . . .'

'Me too. Me too. It's the thing to do alright. Aye.'

Ma O'Neill was alone in the kitchen when they entered. She glanced up from her newspaper and peered over the rim of her glasses at them. Kitty noticed the woman's slight flush; she appeared to be uncomfortable in Kitty's presence and to alleviate her discomfort Kitty made an effort to chat idly about this and that. She quickly ran out of small talk when she realized that she would have to keep it up all night if necessary, because Ma O'Neill was not budging from her kitchen until everyone else was in bed. She declined Ma's offer of tea, and said she would head for her bed.

'Monica'll be round about ten or so in the morning to take you out for the day,' Ma reminded her, and Kitty's heart sank. A city tour was not quite what she had in mind for tomorrow, after the Snooker Hall debacle. She smiled wanly and bade them goodnight. Out of the corner of her eye she caught Danny's knowing grin, and she glowered at him.

*   *   *

As they set off next morning, at Monica's insistence without their bags for safety reasons, Kitty told Monica about the lads at the Snooker Hall the night before.

'Did you really say that?' Monica bawled on the bus. 'You're bloody lucky to be alive.'

Kitty squirmed and gazed out the window. They were heading into town, past the brick wall with its ubiquitous graffiti and skeins of barbed wire along the top. Past boarded-up shopfronts and rows of houses, many empty and windowless, stacked up like hollow, rotten teeth. Their bricked flanks offered elaborate murals of men holding rifles with intricate emblems entwined above their heads, and painted banners incorporating harps and shamrocks and the Republic's Tricolour. Everything was turned into a statement of identity. Her throwaway remark of the night before made her catch her breath.

In the centre of the city, Monica walked Kitty around the Victorian heart, showing her the City Hall and University, generally taking care to show her visitor as much of the unafflicted buildings as she could. Kitty came to understand that a certain degree of admiration was expected of her. But as Monica extolled the history of some edifice or other, Kitty's eyes would stray to the bombed-out shell of another directly behind. The people were very friendly. She found herself reluctantly making mental discernments – who was Catholic, who was Protestant, who was Nationalist and who was Loyalist. In the end, she had to tell herself to stop.

Monica took Kitty for a drink at the Crown Liquor Saloon, a pub restored by the National Trust. She smiled contentedly when Kitty admired the mosaic floor, the pillars carved into palm trees and its various snugs guarded by painstakingly hewn lions and griffins. It was a quixotic, strange place, all the stranger, Kitty felt, because of its location in the heart of a city where every building lay under the shadow of impermanence. Monica slugged back her large vodka and pulled out a small phial from her coat pocket. She swallowed two pills quickly.

'What are those?' Kitty asked.

'Smarties.'

'Smarties?'

'Valium,' Monica said, casually. 'Nine out of ten cats said their owners preferred them . . . Want one?'

Kitty demurred and they set off again, this time for the shops. Kitty had difficulty at times understanding the harsher Belfast accent. The words went by so fast, melting into one another like a pithy Glaswegian dialect. To her discomfiture, she had to get Monica to interpret several times.

On the way back, Kitty asked if they could alight early and walk through the Falls Road on their way home.

'Just like a Yank,' Monica said with an eyebrow raised, but she pressed the bell and they got off. Kitty felt a twinge of embarrassment again as if she were a tourist with a macabre interest in the barren, alien urbanscape of West Belfast. She coughed and said she just felt like a walk. They had walked about five or six miles already, but Monica was kind enough not to point that fact out. Her face softened and she awkwardly placed an arm around Kitty's shoulder as they stiffly walked up the street, pretending to be at ease. Monica adopted her high, gay guide voice once more.

That shop over there? There, there – the tobacconist's? – done over on average once a fortnight – and that one, see, the sweet-shop on the corner? Can't get insurance for love nor money, so they charge it up on the sweets. That house up there on the right, look, four doors up, the one with the yellow door – Jimmy Murphy's house – poor Jimmy had four cars, all red, all new – all gone – cycles to work now. Hoods were the problem. The real problem in Belfast. Young lads and not so young lads. Joyriding no-hopers brought up on crime; surviving on grabbing and glue and cider and the contents of old ladies' PVC handbags. Hoods,

Monica contended, waving her arm as they approached the grey bricked linear monstrosities of the Divis flats, hoods were the problem they didn't show on TV.

Kitty gazed around her in silence. She had never seen anything quite so hopeless. She thought she could smell the dank odour of stale piss wafting in the breeze from the outside corridors. Lines of washing strung up, limp and wet outside broken windows, boarded windows, smashed windows. The buildings were five storeys high except for one tower: over twenty storeys up to where the grey brick scraped the greyer sky. All around lay broken bottles, rubbish, car tyres. Soiled sanitary towels lay at her feet on a tuft of scrubby grass for no other reason, it appeared, than that someone had simply dumped them there. The usual political slogans were daubed on every blank accessible space. A child's tricycle, wheels missing, lay gaudy and yellow and solitary in their path. The sound of life going on ferried to them by the brisk efficient wind. Shouts, male and female, babies crying and dogs barking – large dogs, too large for such small spaces.

Kitty stood rigidly beside Monica and stared. To their right, huddled beside split bags of rubbish, a group of young boys, flimsily clothed, inhaled from a brown paper bag. Kitty could see the eyes of one boy, not older than eight or nine at most, roll back in his head as he passed the bag to his friend. They were oblivious to her gaze.

'Maybe this is what people will do, some anyways, if left to it,' Monica was saying. 'The truth is – I don't know. I've tried to keep out of it all my life – you know – making judgements . . . getting "involved" as we say here. Look at them . . .' She nodded toward the flats. 'Most of them aren't involved in anything but crime. Half the lads over fourteen will have had their knees done by now but still they go on – what else is there? You can see it in their eyes around the age of three, maybe three and a half – it's like a light goes out – it's as if they know it's not going to get any better . . . The Provos try to keep some sort of order here so that people won't turn to the cops, but they take no notice of them either. Ma and Da are pissed all the time and the sight of older brother Tommy with his thigh bone sticking out after encountering a Provo gun, aye and maybe his elbow too, isn't

going to stop young Jimmy from going down the same road . . .
Oh aye, it's crazy and so it is. But sure there you have it . . . The
spoils of war eh? The poor misbegotten gobshites.'

'What happens when a lad gets his knees done like you said?'
Kitty asked.

'He keeps his mouth shut, goes to the hospital, has it fixed up
as best they can and then claims compensation . . . He gets a nice
tidy sum in due course and then he pays a cut to the guys who
shot him in the first place.'

'I see.'

'Do you?'

'It's crazy alright.'

Monica lit a cigarette and cocked her head to the side, she
studied Kitty's face for a moment, in amusement.

'C'mon,' Monica said, linking her arm with Kitty's. 'Let's go.
I'm frozen stiff.'

Two boys, shaven-headed and dressed in flapping, oversized
basketball shirts, passed them by and stared insolently. The
younger, a small wiry eleven- or twelve-year-old, winked cheekily
at Kitty. She winked back. His chest puffed out within his flimsy
shirt and he gave her the fist in the crook of his elbow salute,
leering with his small glazed eyes. Monica and Kitty laughed
aloud. His grin broadened showing a row of badly rotted teeth.
He turned and swaggered on after his friend. Kitty observed the
way he held out the arm which wore a huge blackstrapped watch,
some sort of diver's equipment, nicked no doubt, but it was the
way he held the arm out, reverently and carefully, which attracted
her eye.

'Put your head down and don't look up,' Monica hissed. She
nudged Kitty forward with her elbow. Ahead of them, a group
of skinheads in their mid- to late-teens approached. They were
jostling amongst each other, and Kitty could not be sure if they
were noticed yet.

'Don't catch their eye. Just walk on. Don't say anything if they
stop us and just keep on walking if you can . . .' The fear in
Monica's voice made Kitty's flesh crawl.

They were almost up to the youths who were bawling obsceni-
ties and playfully cuffing one another across their prickly heads.

91

The smell of petrol fumes almost made Kitty choke. She desperately wanted to cough but that might draw attention. The youths fell silent as Monica and Kitty, with their heads down, began to pass them by. An acne-scarred face with huge raw lips thrust itself at the side of Kitty's head. It emitted a jeering, hoarse laugh, and Kitty thought she would pass out from the fumes which made her eyes water. She held her breath, walked stiffly on, and the head withdrew. They were well past before Monica peeked over her shoulder.

'Christ!' she exclaimed, and opened the palm of her hand. The remains of her scrunched-up cigarette fluttered off in the breeze, and a sizeable welt was rising where the tip had burned into flesh.

'Why did you do that?' Kitty examined the hand.

'I didn't want to draw their attention by stubbing it out in front of them – they'd stab you for less than a pack of fags . . . C'mon . . . c'mon. Here endeth the tour . . .'

Danny was out with Eamon when they got back to the house. Kitty saw him briefly after supper later in the evening when he breezed in on his way to the Snooker Hall. This time he did not ask her along. And the following day he made his excuses again, in spite of Kitty's silent glowers, when Monica suggested a trip to the country – in her husband's car – as she put it. He stood at the door trying to stifle his giggles by pulling on his nose, as Kitty glared at him from the front of the departing car. Ma O'Neill sat in the back at her own insistence in her good brown check coat and matching kangol beret; beside her sat Paul and Kevin, Monica's boys of nine and seven, all spruced up with shiny, squeaky haircuts slaked to the side. They drove past the small village of Ballylesson, and stopped to walk by the banks of a small stream which flowed into the Lagan. It was a clear, crisp day – the countryside was beautiful – it felt like Ireland again. Kitty began to relax and while she could not say that her stilted snatches of conversation with Ma O'Neill were exactly heartwarming, she did enjoy an immediate fondness for Monica's youngest, Kevin. She spent the rest of the day teasing him gently while he cast her liquid-eyed, shy smiles, and he held her hand briefly by the stream. She gave the hand a little squeeze as he smiled up at her before slipping it from her grip again. They passed three blue Army patrol jeeps on the way home which served as the only reminders of where they were.

Danny arrived home late again that night, but Kitty held her tongue, savouring instead, the prospect of the train ride back to Dublin the next day. By the time they were finally alone together seated across from each other on the train, Kitty had her speech so well practised that she was able to fulminate for the best part of an hour, without stopping for breath.

When she finally rendered herself speechless from sheer exhaustion, Danny gazed out the window and said:

'Are you finished?'

'Yes,' she said sourly.

'They really liked you,' he said, as if they had sat in silence for the past hour.

'Oh did they?' Kitty sneered. 'I didn't realize this was some sort of test.'

'Of course not.' He waved a hand dismissively. 'Still . . .'

'Oh shut up,' she cut across him. Their eyes locked, and she could not entirely conceal her gleam of pleasure. It was absurd, but she could not help but feel that she *had* passed some sort of test. Danny leaned back and closed his eyes.

November

Naked tree branches clacked and scratched against the windows and roof of the double-decker bus as it grunted up to the crest of Crouch Hill. From the top of the hill, Kitty looked down on the straggling streets of Crouch End which spread out in a hollow scoop until the land rose again and the mellow bricks of Alexandra Palace dominated the distant skyline. A white wintry sun had followed the morning's rain and cast the buildings below into incisive, angular shapes, their gables sharply illuminated in the frosty air. Kitty looked back toward Finsbury Park and the city-scape beyond. She found herself alone with her packages on the top deck. Diagonals of roofs glinted like battalions of spatulas where the sun slanted across their still wet slates. She pressed the bell and alighted two stops early in the middle of Crouch End Broadway.

She negotiated the clocktower which stood awkwardly at the intersection of several roads, causing pedestrians to stop and start several times before they could get to where they wanted to be. She went into the Off Licence, and deliberated over Spanish Cava or a more expensive French champagne which would be wasted if Danny did not come home in time for dinner. It was her birthday so she bought the champagne. Earlier that morning, she had chosen not to remind Danny, but asked him to come home on time, this once, as she was going to cook a special meal for them.

A card had arrived from her father of course, accompanied by a generous sterling bank draft, nothing from Eleanor and a few cards from old college friends – she was pleased that they had evidently gone to the trouble of finding her new address since she still hadn't found the time to keep in touch and let them know what was happening with her.

At lunchtime she considered asking a few of the secretaries out for a drink, but decided against. She did not know any of them very well and the prospect of strained conversation and a spurious intimacy was not inviting, so she worked through lunch as usual and left the office a couple of hours early in the afternoon. Her six month trial period was over, and with justification she expected to be promoted to Assistant Editor within a couple of months. She was pleased with her progress and she figured that as soon as she didn't have to prove herself at work quite so diligently she would make the time to catch up on her social life; but as she paid for the champagne she had an image of herself waddling from the shop like a sad Charlie Chaplin, all trembling sighs and fluttering shoulder shrugs. The ache of loneliness was quite exquisite; she had to catch her breath by the clocktower.

London was not anything like Dublin, they had quickly learned. Offices were strange places full of people who did not wish to intrude upon those who might gladly have been intruded upon. It was difficult getting to know anyone, and when Danny appeared to make little or no effort at all, Kitty followed suit. It was just easier that way; she was constantly exhausted. Travelling to work, for milk, for newspapers, to parks, took up vast quantities of time and energy. She tired so easily at first. There was so much to learn and while she tailored her colloquialisms, if not her accent, in order to make herself understood, she observed that Danny had almost entirely lapsed into that harsh, defensive Belfast dialect he hid behind. On top of everything else, they were learning to live with one another, discovering as each day passed, little irritating habits and personal regimes. Danny resented the amount of time she spent working while Kitty resented the fact that he chose to call Eamon at Monica's house from a phone box rather than use the phone in the flat. It was only a petty thing, but she felt his need for privacy shut her out. But then again, she told herself that the first few months were especially difficult for him while he searched for work. So when he found a pub south of the river in Elephant and Castle where some old Belfast acquaintances hung out, she was initially pleased for his sake. He went Wednesday nights at first, then Friday nights too, but the arguments only really started once he began to overnight occasionally; kipping down on some mate's floor and wandering in on Saturday morning looking wan and dishevelled as she remonstrated with him.

Still, things would resolve themselves in time, she thought, as she hunched her shoulders against the cold November wind and walked the distance to their flat. She pressed the soft parcel of meat against her chest and wondered if she would peel real apples for apple sauce or open a jar of readymade. It all depended on whether or not Danny would deign to come home on time to eat dinner with her; if so, she would not hesitate to open the jar, if not, martyrdom would be consummated by the useless peeling and stewing of apples. She smiled at her own duplicity, and asked herself if she would not in truth prefer to be alone for the evening. She could not find an answer to the question as she entered the front door.

It was cold and dark within. She placed her parcels upon the breakfast bar in the narrow kitchen and went from room to room switching on electric heaters and lights; she settled on a taped selection of adagios, and changed into jeans and sweatshirt to the melancholy strains of Albinoni. She wondered if she would cry now or later, and decided on later when the solitary meal was spread out upon the small foldaway table.

She stuffed the pork tenderloin and prepared the vegetables; set the table remembering to light the candle; she dimmed the harsh overhead bulbs which filled the room with such stark white light – and commenced her wait.

Her own meal was on her plate, her second glass of wine poured when she heard Danny come through the front door. He peered around the living room door.

'Am I late?' he said, shuffling out of his coat.

'Only about an hour or so – not bad for you.'

'Sorry. Bloody W7 bus – I had to wait for ages.'

'Sit down. I'll get your dinner out of the oven.'

'Kit? Is there something wrong? What have I done now?'

'Nothing.'

'Something. Look at the face on you. What's up?'

'Oh shut up and sit down.'

Kitty infused the act of rising with weariness, a sad sigh, a slight shake of the head. She hated the part – she loved the part. He was not late enough for her to be really acrimonious but not early enough to warrant full unequivocal smiles either, and besides, there was her birthday – which he had forgotten. There was that at least to look forward to. She returned, wearily, from the kitchen just as he spied the birthday cards on the mantel over the gas fire. He fisted his forehead dramatically. Kitty eyed him sullenly, silent reproach in her every gesture. She began to eat her meal, but a bittersweet lump swelled in her throat and she had to swallow past it.

'Oh Kitty. Your birthday. I completely forgot. God, I'm sorry.'

'It doesn't matter.' A sniff.

'Of course it matters.'

'Not to me.' She eyed his wince with satisfaction from under her lashes. 'Sit down – your dinner will freeze.'

He hesitated for a moment, evidently calculating in advance the quantities of blood which would be required. She was holding her tongue well so far which meant serious bleeding, copious bleeding, a brutal retribution. Behind her feigned weariness there was a shaft of steel glimmering behind her eyes, which promised death by a thousand cuts. He backed out of the room with his palms held out facing her.

'I'll be back in a sec. Two minutes. Just hang on . . .' He ran out hustling his coat on before she could protest.

Kitty slammed the food into her mouth and swilled the wine around her glass. She tried to draw on the strings of exquisite self-pity again, pulled at the shimmering threads, but they had spliced and frayed, and hot, real anger, got in the way.

When Danny returned, sheepishly offering a bunch of red roses, Kitty had finished her meal. She spat into the apple sauce and sat there quivering with righteous indignation.

'For me?' she asked dangerously.

'Well. Yes.' Gingerly offered again. She eyed him with disdain.

'You know what you can do with your roses – don't you?'

'Shove them up my ass?'

'Precisely.'

'I got you a card as well – here – take it. Please.'

'Shove it up after the roses.'

'Is this going to be an all night job?'

'What exactly do you mean?' She was hissing now, her eyes narrowed. Was he trying to be funny? That was really dumb. Incredibly, stupefyingly dumb. Inconceivably cretinous.

'You know what I mean. Can't I just apologize now and be done with it? We could try and enjoy the rest of the evening . . .'

Kitty stuck her tongue in her cheek and shook her head slowly. She lit a cigarette and flicked ash into the apple sauce. He tried the boyish look, eyebrows raised, hapless grin. Her teeth gritted. She sucked on the cigarette and hissed out the exhalation. And wondered behind the cloud of smoke, when this would all end in sex and if it would end in sex and how long should she prolong the charade and did it really matter, matter in the slightest, that he had forgotten her birthday and what was the hidden agenda tonight? She thought of Danny across the road in the callbox, and her face set rigidly.

Seeing the firm line of her jaw, Danny began to back away.

'I'm going to take a shower,' he said. First, he removed her adagio tape and clicked in an Elvis tape instead. Before he left the room, he cocked his head to the side and cast her a lopsided smile. He pointed at the tapedeck, and she understood what he was inviting her to remember. When she did not react he sighed heavily and left for the bathroom. Kitty fingered the roses on the table, burning holes in the plastic wrapper with the tip of her cigarette. His dinner congealed on the plate. She shook her head and tried to hold onto her anger, but his little trick had worked. She was remembering last July in West Cork with Danny. It was hard to believe that it really was only a matter of months ago. She couldn't suppress a chuckle at the memory of his face as he watched her eating mussels . . .

*   *   *

'If you eat another mussel like that – I'm going to come,' he had smiled. He was resting his elbows on the table, chin extended on the bridge of his hands.

Kitty threw her head back and laughed. Several people in the restaurant turned to stare. She lifted another mussel to her mouth, circled her tongue around the meat, licking the garlic first before she prised the orange plump mollusc free with her teeth. A thin stream of butter juice dribbled down her chin. She wiped it with the back of her hand, then licked the hand.

'I never saw anyone like those things the way you do,' Danny said. His face was a contortion of disgust, amusement and lust. His own plate of fresh crabmeat was already picked clean.

'Want one?' Kitty offered a dripping shell.

'No. You've spat all over them now.'

'Suit yourself.' She popped it into her mouth. 'You don't know what you're missing. Mmm. Mussels and brown cake with slabs of butter and cold, creamy Guinness. And the sun is shining. What more could a person possibly want?'

They were sitting in a steamfilled seafood restaurant, overlooking the square of the small town a few miles from Kitty's home. It had rained solidly, a mantle of cloud clinging peevishly to the ground, for the first two days of their visit, and Kitty had begun to think his coming with her was a very bad idea, but she was the one who had insisted, purchasing the ticket for him behind his back. They were confined to the house, Danny growling like a caged animal, especially when he had to endure another of Eleanor's corrosive glances. She maintained a regal silence at mealtimes, while Kitty's father chattered amiably, but with a hint of desperation at the back of his cheery tones. Danny appeared to be comfortable enough in his company, but spoke in the main when spoken to, and snatched his jacket to run outside on the rare occasions the rain let up. Kitty would watch him from the library window. Stalking down the avenue, shoulders hunched, hands buried deep in his jeans pockets. She tried to involve him in her evening conversations and reading sessions with her father, but though he nodded obligingly enough when addressed, he gazed wistfully through the streaming window at the mists outside. He only relaxed fully when they were alone together, splashing through the ceaseless rain. Away from the house, he would slip an arm around her shoulder and tenderly tuck a few straying curls inside the hood of her jacket.

Then just as Kitty had more or less made up her mind to cut

the visit short and return early to London – after all, Danny still had a job to get – the sun came out and they hopped into her father's car with a wave and a sigh of relief from him, to play the tourists. It seemed to Kitty in the long, hazy, sunfilled days that followed that she would never be this happy again. She found herself making mental snapshots, already storing memories. She wondered if Danny felt the same way but did not ask him in case she broke the spell.

He took to the countryside with enthusiasm, carrying a camera everywhere which made a lump rise in her throat. He was forever making her stop the car to take a picture of her by the ocean's edge here, beneath the shadow of a hill there, and she had to bite her lip to stop herself from mocking him gently, his pleasure was so pure and unaffected.

The day before, she had taken him up a winding track carved into a hill at the top of which, after a long trek across moorish grasses, a still, black lake lay in a horseshoe shaped socket; the remnant waters of a glacier. From this cirque the ice had slid and oozed itself down into the valley below. They stood and gazed from the shallow dipping shore before Kitty knelt and scooped water in the cup of her hands, offering it to him. Danny sipped and agreed that it was the best water he had ever tasted. She watched him as he wandered off alone toward the far side where the steep cliff-like rock plunged into dark waters beneath.

'Must be incredibly deep just there,' he shouted back to her, pointing to the place from where the cliff arms fanned out.

'Did you come here a lot?' he asked on his return to her.

'A bit,' she said, 'with my father. On Sunday afternoons, he would park the car over there see? Back there at the top of the hill and I would walk across alone.'

'Weren't you lonely?'

'Sometimes.'

He took several pictures and Kitty had to turn away to hide her smile. They drove down the tortuous road into the valley. Wild rhododendron bushes scraped against the side of the car. She took him to where the road ended beside a farmhouse. Dogs circled the car. A handful of houses spread out on the valley floor, some facing directly onto a sheer black rock.

'A person would have to be very strong in themselves to face that rock every morning of their lives,' she said.

'How could you forget it? How could you ever really leave it behind?' he wondered, echoing her thoughts.

She pointed out Eagle Rock to him, and they left the car to walk down the valley, dogs sniffing at their heels.

'No, don't stroke them,' she cautioned, 'or else they'll feel free to nip your ass. Sheepdogs are a terror for it . . .' But Danny was already on his haunches, clicking his tongue as he stroked a couple of nuzzling heads. They walked on and Kitty laughed when Danny yelped, thrusting his pelvis forward away from the pinching teeth behind. She shooed the animals away.

A couple of rooks with huge serrated wingspans circled overhead. Tiny waterfalls, residues of the recent rains, streamed down the gorge-like flank of rock to their left, glittering like chains of gold in the sunlight. Scattered along the rockface, stunted, leafless trees poked out their twisted limbs almost horizontally from every fissure as though they would not be denied a chance at life. Huge boulders, carried by the glacier until it weakened, were strewn around everywhere, chaotically tumbling over one another across the valley's bed. One was an almost perfect rectangle, smooth-topped like a table. Two smooth ovoid boulders lay one upon the other like whales copulating. Ferns burst out of every crevice like tiny fronded explosions.

Kitty and Danny still stood at the neck of the valley with high, deeply scored landcliffs behind and to the side of them, and the gradual descent through strata of grey rock, darkgreen fern pockets, solitary, ambushed trees and ropey, tanned straits of swaying grass, stretched out below them until the valley levelled out and melted into forest. Kitty swept aside a sheaf of long grass to reveal the tiny herbs and flowers hiding shyly at the base of the strawlike, husky spires. Mauve milkwort, blue skullcap, dull purple comfrey, forget-me-nots, daisies and buttercups. She plucked a bouquet for Danny to smell, and told him the different names and their alleged remedial properties. He nodded and listened with grave interest. He was allowing her, for a change, to tell him something. Encouraged, she could not then stop herself, but he listened and took his pictures and asked her questions until she sighed with contentment and finally rendered herself speechless.

She gazed at his profile from the corner of her eye. His eyes were hooded, lips curved in a dreamy smile. He looked up and caught her gaze. He smiled shyly. She knew that he wanted to say something, just as she did, to preserve the moment, but his smile widened and he shrugged helplessly. He reached out and drew her hand to his lips, she slid her palm along his cheek and he tilted his head in a reciprocal stroking movement into the shallow cup of her hand. For once she could feel what it must be like to be him, words sticking in great, cumbersome, unwieldy clusters at the back of her throat. She said:

'I wish I could believe in a God.'

'You mean to thank?' he responded.

She looked at him curiously.

'Yes. That's it.'

'Aye, he's handy for that alright.'

'You're so sure God's a he then?' she asked lightly. Danny's religion had more to do with habit than choice.

'Oh aye,' he said, glancing down at the zip of his jeans. 'To make you feel this good, God would have to have a dick.'

She put her arms around him and gently drew his head down to kiss his lips. He withdrew from her embrace slowly. His fists clenched involuntarily as his feet scuffed against grass. He smiled sheepishly at her and she wanted to tell him then, how strong and intense was this love she felt for him, how it sometimes felt like a palpitating, ever-present ache, deep within the pit of her stomach. But he was moving away from her, pointing to the rectangular slab of rock. She understood what was required, and posed as he took his picture. She was glad in a way that she had elected to be silent. He would have felt diminished by his inability to match her pretty speech.

They continued on further down the valley, walking along the erratic curves of a spare, fast-flowing stream which cut through the valley floor. The stream levelled in places, skimming over flat slabs of grey rock until it gained momentum again as the course dipped. Small bruised clouds bearing no malice, swept across the milky blue July sky. They stopped and watched the changing light fall into pockets of darkness below where the forestry fanned out into the distance, bordered by ash and drills of spruce until further in, the oaks dominated the heart of the woods. Kitty wondered about the last ice rock, the final ice cube dissolving into the sighing grasses to reveal all this – life after the ice. The sky beyond the oaks seemed to sag beneath its own great weight, it draped heavy and grainy, in moody orange-yellow bands along the cusps of the rising hills above the wooded plateau.

Later, on the drive home, Danny turned to her and mouthed 'thank you'. She did not say 'for what', but smiled, enjoying a delicious tremor of contentment. Danny flicked the car radio on to Elvis singing, *Love me tender, love me true*, and he rolled his eyes at such perfection. Danny loved Elvis. Kitty turned the volume up full pitch and pressed the accelerator to the floor, enjoying the turned heads and bemused frowns along the roadside as they whizzed by.

*   *   *

The other diners had left, leaving Kitty and Danny alone in the restaurant as they sat in amiable, food-stupefied silence, watching the teeming square outside. Kitty reached across the table and squeezed his hand. She observed the embarrassed clench of his free hand, but he forced himself to permit the hand within her grip to remain dormant. It was the first Friday of the month – Fair Day. Once a purely rural arena for the buying of animals and produce, it had grown over the years into a more eclectic bazaar with everything from aran sweaters to music cassettes on offer. Occasionally, relics from the past might still be seen. They watched two men, one capped the other hatted, in faded granite grey suits, haggle over a piece of rope. The seller, with his hat pushed back on his head and the vestiges of a cigarette butt clamped between his lips, showed the properties of the thick skein by tugging on it with both hands while his feet rooted it to the ground. The buyer followed suit. He asked a question out of the side of his mouth then withdrew, shaking his head slowly from side to side. The seller spat, shrugged then gazed away. The man with the cap crept up again, a disparaging expression on his face as he looked down at the rope. The other ignored him. The performance continued for some time with Danny saying 'he won't buy', and Kitty assuring him that he would. Finally the deal was struck with a spit and a handshake and the careful unravelling in cupped hand of a scrunched up wad of notes to reveal within the silver coins which paid for the rope.

Danny laughed and conceded defeat. Kitty knew that he was itching to produce the camera but he refrained; she presumed it was because he did not wish to appear like a stranger – she had felt like that herself so often in Belfast.

They were sleepy and a little drunk as Kitty swung the car into a wide arc in front of the house. Eleanor's red lips set formidably as they shuffled into the hallway. She stood at the dining room doorway and flourished a hand toward the dressed table inside.

'Excuse me,' she frosted, 'am I to understand you won't be eating this evening?'

'Sorry,' Kitty pulled her mouth down. 'We just didn't think. We ate earlier – in town.'

'I hope you didn't go to any trouble,' Danny offered soberly.

'I'm sorry?' Eleanor's voice was clipped. Kitty could see the warning little twist of fury knot her mother's features, but Danny continued to throw himself headfirst into the mire.

'I was just saying that I hope you didn't go to any trouble on our account, Mrs Fitzgerald.' So meek. So deferential. Kitty could barely contain her laugh.

'No more than the trouble I go to every evening, Daniel. No more than that,' Eleanor hissed. The top curls of the perm danced with rage. Kitty flipped back into childhood and heard the click of her bedroom door, her mother's voice calling icily up the stairs – 'And there you shall stay, my girl'. There were times she had thought that there she really would stay, and wondered how long it would take before her hair grew as long as Rapunzel's. But here was Danny. Not an obvious sort of prince for sure – but here all the same.

'I could eat again, what about you, Dan?' she heard herself say. She did not want the perfection of the past few days to evaporate because of Eleanor.

'What? Oh right enough. We'll eat so.' Then hesitantly to Eleanor, 'Will we?'

'Suit yourselves.' She turned and took her place at the dining table. Mussels for dinner. Kitty wanted to gag but she enthused heartily.

Danny, rare for him, stifled a giggle which was caught by Eleanor who began to fold her napkin into tiny triangles. Suddenly she scraped her chair back, the familiar sound making Kitty's teeth grind, and with a contemptuous look, Eleanor made a slow and rigid exit. Kitty's father was nowhere to be seen so they toyed with the food for a while and left to watch TV. Kitty felt a pang of guilt and went upstairs to find her mother.

Eleanor was sitting bolt upright on the side of her bed when Kitty entered. The curls were still bobbing up and down.

'I'm sorry,' Kitty offered.

'For what?' The snap in Eleanor's voice was like a whipflick, Kitty blinked.

'Well, for being so late for dinner. For not ringing to say we had – well – an extended lunch. I know you like to be told in advance . . .'

'Since when do you care about what I like?'

'That's it. I've said I'm sorry. That's it.' Kitty turned to go.

'I have such a headache.' Eleanor put her middle fingers to her temples and rubbed.

'Can I . . . Let me get you something . . . What is there, paracetamol? Aspirin? What do you usually take?'

'Paracetamol.'

'Where do you keep them – in the bathroom here?' Kitty rushed into the small en suite bathroom as Eleanor rose to her feet suddenly.

'No – wait!' she cried.

But Kitty in a frenzy of activity borne of acute embarrassment at having to endure this relative intimacy with her mother, the finding of tablets for her, the doing of something, anything, for her, was already flinging cabinets open in a desperate search. She opened the cabinet beneath the sink and the bottles tumbled out and rolled around her feet. They were all the same. Small, round, clear and empty. Vodka bottles. Some bore the dust of their long confinement; not disposed of because that would mean facing the bottles, counting them. Kitty's mouth dropped open, a bottle rolled and stopped at Eleanor's feet. She was standing at the door with her fists clenched by her sides. A slow flush suffused her cheeks. She would not meet Kitty's horrified gaze.

'Get out,' she hissed. 'Get out, get out, get ouuut . . .'

Kitty bent to pick up the bottle by her mother's feet but Eleanor lashed out and sent the bottle flying across the bathroom. It shattered into splinters by the toilet. Kitty was about to move toward the shards when her mother caught her by the shoulder, her nails dug into Kitty's flesh painfully.

'Just – get – out,' Eleanor said, catching Kitty's eye. Her cold glittering gaze made Kitty shudder involuntarily. She opened her mouth to say something but the red talons tightened their grip on her shoulder.

'I'm sorry,' Kitty muttered. 'I didn't know . . .'

There was a brief moment while Eleanor held her gaze when Kitty thought that they might clamber out the other side of this, bruised and shaken, yet hopeful; but Eleanor was shaking her head. Her mouth trembled as her hand slid down Kitty's arm dismissively.

'It's too late,' she said flatly and turned away.

'Don't say that – I didn't know – I never suspected . . . Daddy doesn't know I'm sure . . .' Kitty cried.

Eleanor whirled around, her eyes flashed in a way Kitty had not countenanced before, a fleeting pain in the dark pupils and something else – regret, maybe? Kitty could not tell.

'Do you want to know something?' Eleanor asked.

'What? What?'

'I – hate – you.' Eleanor enunciated slowly, a bitter little smile curving on her lips. Kitty gasped and waited for her to retract but when she did not, she realized that her mother had waited a lifetime, Kitty's lifetime, to say those words.

'Why? For Christ's sake why?'

Eleanor appeared to consider for a moment. She dropped her eyes and stared at her shoes.

'I don't know why,' she said, and sighed wearily. She gestured toward the door with her head. 'Now, get out.'

Kitty stood for a moment with her hand curled around the doorknob. But Eleanor was silent. Kitty swung the door open and fled down the stairs with her hand over her mouth.

In the living room Danny was laughing at some sitcom or other. He looked up.

'Is she alright now then? Did she accept your apology?'

'I don't think so.' Kitty slumped into a chair. 'I think we've gone beyond that,' she added quietly.

Danny gazed at her for a moment, waiting for her to expand but when she did not, he turned his attention to the screen again. Kitty waited until he was fully engrossed then yawned and stretched in an exaggerated manner. She rose and bent down to kiss his forehead.

'I think I'll have an early night,' she said, leaving the room.

In her bedroom she lay on the bed fully clothed for hours with her head resting on the cradle of her arms. She listened to the close of her father's bedroom door, and a couple of hours later, the pad of Danny's feet in the room beneath her.

A little while later she heard the creak of his feet on the stairway. Her door opened letting a crack of light into the darkened room.

'Are you awake?' Danny whispered.

'Yes.'

'What's the matter Kit? What did she say to you this time?' He sat on the bed beside her. She pulled her hand away from his, afraid that his gentleness would bring on the tears she had managed to suppress for the past few hours.

'Nothing. Just her usual crap. Forget it.'

Danny stretched out and lay beside her, pulling her rigid form against his. She resisted at first then gradually allowed her body to mould into the waiting curve he had made of his body. She sighed heavily. He leaned across and kissed her cheek.

'What is it? Mmm? What did she say?'

'She said – she just said – she just said that she hates me, that's all . . . Well, we all know that, so what's the big deal?'

'She really said that – I hate you – she said that?'

'Yes.'

'She's nuts of course – you do realize that?'

'Yes.'

'I mean that's bloody crazy. You're her family for Christ's sake. You don't hate your family. Not your own flesh and blood.'

'She does.'

'And do you hate her?' he asked softly.

Kitty had to think for a while.

'I thought I did. I think I do now. But I've been lying here thinking . . . I don't know . . . I mean, it's not like I didn't know or anything – but hearing her say it – well, there's no way back from that is there? But why? Why? What have I done that is so terrible?'

'I don't know Kit. I suppose hate just has a way of happening – like love. Who the hell knows why?'

She thought about that for a while. In some respects, it was easy for Danny, things either were or they were not, you loved or you hated, the lights were green or they were red, he did not acknowledge amber. She could not bring herself to tell him about the bottles, seeing in advance his shrug, the spread, upraised palms of his hands, as if to say, 'there you are then', as if it really was that simple. She could not find the words to explain how she had felt when Eleanor launched her devastating little missile; it was only at that moment that she realized that she had never really believed in Eleanor's hate. She had found excuses for it, diminished it, even at times pandered to it by deliberately taunting her mother. And now, did she really hate Eleanor, could she finally admit it as a verity, as Danny assumed she must? It was not that simple.

It was not hate she felt for Eleanor, the sad truth dawned on her, but love. Nothing like the easy, warm love she felt for her father, but love all the same. A twisted, tormented kind of love, a punishing love. She moaned and buried her head in the pillow.

'It's alright Kit, shh, it's alright. Don't worry about it. She hates you, you hate her, so what? What of it?' Danny crooned in her ear, misconstruing her distress. She opened her mouth to try to explain to him, then closed it again. He would never understand – it was not the revelation of her mother's hate which disturbed so greatly, it was the extent of her own impotent, superfluous love and the knowledge that much of what she had considered written on stone now proved far from runic. She was the one who was floundering, Danny was safe in his harbour of absolutes. She turned to him.

'Next week we'll be back in London and all this will be forgotten,' she said.

'Are you sure?'

'Of course I'm sure. It's always like this with her. Let's just forget it.'

'Kitty?' he said, 'yesterday – you know – that valley, the lake – it was the best day of my life. Honest to God. It was. Thank you.'

For a moment she didn't know what to say. She had to bluster to cover up.

'You'll remember you said that, won't you, the next night you feel inclined to spend the night out with your mates?'

'I'll remember,' he said gravely. 'I swear it.'

And he did remember for a while. They spent the following months doing up the flat while Danny searched for a job. Kitty was sure in her mind that it was all he needed to help him settle down. Once he was employed and the flat was finished, he would no longer feel the need to spend so much time in that pub with all his Belfast cronies. She figured that it was only important to him while he felt so insecure and entirely dependent on her.

When he did find a job, conveyancing again – but he said that it was just for a while – he insisted on paying her back for the months when she had supported him. Even for the ticket to Ireland in July which she tried to offer him as a present. She protested but he was adamant and she felt awful knowing that as he left the flat each morning he had the price of his tube fare and nothing else. He made a sandwich for himself in the evenings, wrapped it in foil and put it in the fridge for lunch the following day. Every time she opened the fridge and saw that silver triangle her heart would contract, but he would not take a penny from his wages until the debt as he saw it, was repaid. They splashed out on dinner and champagne in an expensive restaurant the week he finally agreed that he was absolved of his liability. He even insisted on returning all the money he had had to borrow from her in the early months, so he could go to the pub. And she thought that was a good sign. She did not have the heart to tell him that his money remained untouched in her bank account – it was her father's money and not her salary that had sustained them for the first few months and paid for all the pine-veneered furniture.

But gradually, from September onwards, Danny began to drift back toward that pub again. Kitty decided he was lonely so she determined to spend more of her evenings with him instead of working all the time. The end result was that she sat beside him in the pub more miserable than she would have been at home alone. She hated the place. Hated the interminable tube and bus ride to get there, hated the sour, dreggy smell of the blackened velour seats, the almost desperate animation on the faces of the men by the bar, the sluttish women with their bacardis and cokes and highpitched cackles, the hardfaced bony children who constantly approached the women with their hands out for the slot machines. It was just as it had been in the Snooker Hall that time in Belfast. For the most part, Kitty was ignored by Danny's tight little circle, everyone was an 'ey' except for Diarmuid. Seany and Tommy, Marky and Mikey were all labourers who hated London and could not wait to get back home, all deliberately brusque even offensive, to hide their shyness and feelings of inadequacy in the big city, and all with a glimmer of admiration in their eyes when they looked at Danny, the solicitor. To her intense irritation he basked in their admiration, coming to life in their company the way he did in Belfast. She stopped going after a while. And when he asked why, she told him the truth. She simply could not bear the place. He told her that was perfectly obvious and maybe if she just tried a little harder and stopped saying 'pardon' so, so obviously, every time they said anything to her . . . Her cheeks burned but she said it wasn't like that at all. Not at all . . .

*   *   *

The Elvis tape came to a finish, ejecting her from her reverie. He was already forgiven but she still had to play the game. She kept the scowl on her face but her eyes had softened.

Danny re-emerged with a towel draped around his waist. He turned the tape over and raked his wet hair, casting her a surreptitious glance through the spluttering candlelight to check the lie of the land now. She did not return his crooked smile.

'Danny?'

'Mmm?'

'You're quite happy that we came to London, aren't you?'

'Sure. Why do you ask?'

'I don't know – it's just that – well, sometimes I wonder if you only came because of me.'

'You had something to do with it aye.' He pulled his mouth down and shrugged.

'But you think it was the right thing to do?'

'Oh aye.'

'I mean, I wouldn't like to think that you just came for my sake.'

He smiled, and she realized that he knew he was forgiven without her enjoying the pleasure of saying so. She remembered to scowl again.

'Ah get away with you,' he smiled, and stretched languorously. His torso still shone wetly from the shower. Rivulets ran down his hairless chest from his dripping hair. He swayed unselfconsciously to the music. In the sepia candlelight his body appeared burnished, tightly packed into a slender frame, muscled, fatless and sinewy. He smiled over his shoulder, aware of her scrutiny. Kitty still remembered to glower but she could feel the tension ease from her body. His smile broadened and he swayed his hips in an exaggerated circle. Elvis was oozing sex into the song, squeezing the words out, uh-huhhing as if the effort was all too much for him – *'Well, he'd never been to Spain, but he kinda liked the music, he heard the ladies were insane, but they sure knew how to use it . . .'* Kitty hid her smile at the ridiculous lyrics, which never failed to sound sexy the way Elvis dripped them out. Danny sidled up to her, he extracted one rose from the bunch and offered it to her with a complicitous grin. She ignored him, sat back and lit another cigarette.

He drew the rose along his wet shoulders, down along the centre of his breastbone, the red velvety furls soaked up a few drops of moisture. He tilted her head back with the crook of his finger to face him. She sucked her cheeks in and stared blandly

111

with her eyebrows raised. He held the rose under his nose, inhaling the sweet scent of it, then blew gently across the delicate petal tips. His smile widened when he saw Kitty twist her mouth to the side to prevent her own smile. She shifted on her chair when he began to stroke the petals with such exquisite care it seemed as if the flower was opening in response. He kissed the outer petals and licked his tongue along the top of the thorn-free stem. Kitty caught her breath as he prised apart the centre of the rose to point the tip of his tongue into the very heart of its redness.

'Oh no,' she groaned.

He grinned and drew his tongue along the core, caressing the tightly packed petals, his tongue flicked faster and faster. Kitty laughed and shook her head. She leaned across and took the rose from him. They stood together. She pulled the towel from his waist and rubbed against him. He smelt of soap and rose petals.

He chuckled and buried his face in her hair. They swayed in time to the music. Gently, he guided her head down along his chest and abdomen.

'Guess who gets to blow out the birthday candle,' he said.

Later, sprawled across the bed, Kitty contemplated, through slitted sleepy eyes, the prospect of cleansing her body or just slipping into the lazy slumber which lay beyond the next eyeblink. She smiled, aware of Danny's scrutiny, his face inches from hers propped up on his elbow. His breath fanned her cheek. He gently traced a finger along her jawbone. He shifted and lay back with his head resting on his raised arms. She could picture the blue gaze aimed at the ceiling.

'Maybe we should just go away somewhere.' He spoke in a dreamy voice. 'America or Australia or Canada – we could go to Canada. Couldn't we? I mean, there's nothing to stop us – just – going, is there?'

Kitty blinked rapidly. London had been far enough. The very idea of Danny contemplating North America seemed somehow absurd. She turned to him.

'If that's what you want . . . What brought this notion on?'

'I don't know. Just a notion like you say. Forget it. There's nowhere far enough away in any case, is there?'

'Far enough away from what, Dan?'

She felt his shrug. She heaved herself upright.

'Don't mind me,' he was saying, but the depth of his sigh chilled her. 'Seeing you like this, you know, lying there with that smile on your face – I want it to be like that always and I can't help thinking . . .'

'Go on.'

'Oh, just that we might be better off away from it all. Look, I'm just being stupid. Stupid and sentimental. Life can't always be about lying on beds with smiles on our faces can it?'

'I suppose not.' Kitty felt something slipping away from her. Just slipping away. Skulking out into the night beyond the room, beyond the bed. Suddenly she felt old and tired and inexplicably sad. She shivered and turned toward Danny, but he had already turned on his side so she kissed his rigid back and pulled the duvet up around his shoulders. She slid out of bed and ran a bath, knowing that it would be hours now before she could sleep.

December

'One more for the road.' Monica laughed and leaned forward to refill Kitty's glass. The bottle of Paddy showed a gulf of over a third.

'What road?' Kitty responded, catching Monica's wrist to steady her liberal hand. 'Where are we going?'

'Where indeed.' Monica rolled her eyes comically and took a deep swig from her glass. Her face twisted into a grimace and she drank again. They had been drinking steadily for over an hour, seated across from each other at the kitchen table. Kitty eyed the kitchen clock.

'They'll be back soon.'

Monica waved a hand.

'Not for ages yet. Trust me. Ma expected you to go to Mass with them so she'll have arranged some visit or other to show you off. Besides, they have my lads with them so Eamon will want to take them for fish and chips after Saturday evening Mass. He always does – whenever he gets the chance that is.'

'I suppose I should have gone along really,' Kitty said doubtfully.

'Why should you? Just to please Ma? Not at all girl. She won't approve of you not going to Mass of course but she'll respect you for being honest . . . Don't look at me like that . . . She will really. She likes a strong spirit – like myself,' she added, doing her drink and grimace routine again. This sip almost drained her glass and her body shuddered. She splayed the fingers of her right hand and studied them. Kitty wondered if she was checking her nails or checking for the shakes. She hastily looked away as Monica caught her eye.

'What about Eamon,' Kitty asked, 'does he like a strong spirit too?'

Monica swirled the dregs in her glass for a moment.

'Ach Eamon,' she said quietly. 'Eamon Eamon Eamon. Who in the name of Christ knows what Eamon thinks or likes.'

'I don't think he likes me much,' Kitty cast out quickly, but eyed Monica intently over the rim of her raised glass.

'What gives you that idea?'

'I don't know really . . . Just – things. I don't think he likes the idea of us living together in London. Maybe he feels that I sort of forced Danny to go, you know?'

Monica stared droll-eyed at Kitty.

'Maybe,' she said.

Kitty shifted uncomfortably in her seat. She glanced at the kitchen clock again. 'God, Danny will be like a bear if they keep him out all night away from his beloved Snooker Hall . . .'

'Oooh – he'll be like a bear will he?' Monica spluttered. 'Oh teasy teasy. Isn't young love sweet, still playing little games . . . What are you now, twenty-five? Sure you're still only wains the pair of yous . . .' Kitty blushed and fixed her mouth into a pained smile. Monica went on, 'Wait until you're married since Jesus was a boy, like me. Then when the phone goes, it'll be . . . "It's Gerry. He's late. Fuck him."'

Kitty had to laugh. While Monica's tongue could be razor-like at times, she somehow managed to inflict the sharpest edge on herself. They had become immediate if slightly abashed friends in spite of an age gap of over ten years, since the first evening Kitty had walked into the O'Neill kitchen. Speaking on the phone every other weekend – at first they just tagged their conversation onto the end of Danny's call; he was quite happy to call Monica from the flat within Kitty's earshot, if not Eamon. Then they began to call each other direct, Monica reducing Kitty to tears of laughter as she regaled some trivial domestic trauma or other. But she was a good listener too, revelling in Kitty's work stories in a way that Danny did not. Sometimes, Kitty made things up just to amuse Monica who was hungry for any information at all. Her own life was so boring, she said. Kitty did not have the heart to disabuse her of the notion that somehow Kitty's office was a magical exciting place.

Calling Monica on Friday nights while Danny was out at the

pub became a habit Kitty slipped into with pleasure. Sometimes Monica would take her by surprise with the seriousness of her tone. She would elicit opinions from Kitty who made them up as she went along, expecting the usual mercurial interruption until she realized that Monica was listening intently in preparation for debate and then Kitty would be forced to backtrack and sidestep as Monica parried ruthlessly, as if in a way, she was aware of Kitty's disingenuousness and wished to punish her for it. There were times she left Kitty feeling drained and exhausted; the school swot, moreover a pretentious school swot, to Monica's capricious, prank-playing schoolgirl. And then having backed Kitty into a corner on some point or other, Monica would lose interest as easily as she gained it, leaving Kitty exasperated and frustrated having spent the better part of an hour on the phone espousing some theory she did not hold true in the first place. It was strangely like a love affair, Kitty concluded once, they excited one another.

'Ach, don't you worry your head about our Dan,' Monica was saying. 'He's with Eamon, isn't he?'

'You don't appear to worship at the shrine of St Eamon like Danny,' Kitty probed lightly again.

'No. I don't,' Monica responded. She drained the last drop from her glass and refilled it. Her deep sigh and wriggle on her chair told Kitty that the subject was closed. A sly smile formed on Monica's lips, her long dark eyelashes cast spiky shadows on her cheeks as she kept her gaze averted.

'So are we allowed to ask or not?' She pulled deeply on her cigarette and raised her eyes to peer at Kitty through a cloud of smoke.

'Ask what?'

'You know – the big question – to be or not to be. Well, will it be?'

'What are you talking about? Will it be what?'

'Marriage, you dozy cow. You and our Dan. We're all waiting to hear. Ma's gone through three rosary beads the past year what with the two of yous "living in sin" and all.' Monica spluttered a wheezy cough in amusement past the cigarette butt clamped between her lips.

116

'God, does she go on about that?' Kitty asked in dismay.

'Never mentions it to tell the truth, I'm just kidding on. I suppose she pretends like yous were just in London together, but not together together if you get my meaning. It's easier that way most likely . . . But you haven't answered my question . . .'

Kitty pulled a face and lit a cigarette.

'It's not an issue right now Monica.' She cringed inwardly at the prim note in her own voice, 'We're happy enough the way we are – for now.'

Monica knew when she was being told to mind her own business. She refilled her glass and cast Kitty an amused look. Kitty wondered how it was that they were all so adept at these silent conversations which had her digging her nails into the palms of her hands. She laughed uneasily.

'Maybe you should ask that brother of yours the same question.' Kitty tentatively offered Monica the interpretation she assumed Monica had come to, namely that it was Danny who was reluctant in his laddish fashion, to get married, and not her. She had to conceal her blush again when Monica's shrewd gaze told her that she was being condescending again. Sometimes, Kitty felt that she was in a hopeless no-win situation, she was invariably either condescending or blissfully ignorant. She felt a stab of anger and ground her cigarette out.

Monica reached across and touched her gently on the arm.

'A wee drop?' she said, with the bottle poised.

'Oh why not?' Kitty held her glass out.

They sipped in silence for a while.

'He's quite happy you know,' Monica said.

'Who?'

'Our Dan. In London. He's quite happy.'

Kitty sighed heavily. There was just no stepping ahead of Monica. By now her head was spinning slightly. She decided to throw caution to the wind. It was too exhausting this parry and retreat, parry and retreat.

'You know damn well that he's not, Monica. I can see it on Eamon's face too, every time he looks at me, like he's accusing me or something. The way he puts his arm around Danny's shoulder before they go out and Dan stands there lapping it up

117

like someone home for a cure. Please don't insult my intelligence, you know as well as I do that he's not settled. Where do you think he is for Christ's sake every Friday night when we phone each other?'

'Well, the pub, I suppose. But you never seem to mind.'

'I didn't – at first. But it's different now. It's – It's as if he's only happy when he's there, surrounded by all his Belfast mates. Labourers to a man . . .'

'. . . I see.' Monica sat back with her eyes hooded again.

'No you don't,' Kitty splurted out. 'You're judging me again.'

When Monica raised her eyes, they had lost their usual self-protective glaze of amusement. She looked genuinely sympathetic. Kitty immediately regretted her honesty, she wished she could take the words back; in London she spent her time avoiding the truth. She felt another spasm of anger toward Monica for making her say the words that said there was a problem. A hard little laugh gurgled in her throat and she widened her eyes.

'Ah it'll pass,' she said.

'It's hard you know, Kit,' Monica was saying in a quiet voice, 'to let a place like this behind. There are so many memories, most of them bad, admittedly, but they sort of bind you to a place somehow; they make a person what he is in a way. I know it's hard for you to understand. Just be patient. It'll be alright. Dan loves you very much, even a fool like me can tell that much. It'll work out in the end. Believe me . . .'

'But what exactly is there to leave behind, Monica?' Kitty cried. 'I'm not blind – I can see for myself what it's like here . . . The place is falling apart. Walk out the door there and what do you see? Soldiers on every corner, young lads with guns as big as themselves, barbed wire and bricks and graffiti everywhere . . . It's just so hopeless for Christ's sake. The faces, the streets, those bloody flats we passed last time . . . Danny never even talks about the place. He *never* talks about it. What's there to miss I ask you, apart from family maybe – but really, what exactly is there to miss?' She stopped, flushed and breathless. Monica's face was impassive. Two bright red spots had settled on her plump cheeks. She ran a hand through her curls and hissed an intake of breath, drawing it out slowly between her gritted teeth.

118

'I'm sure you're right,' she said after a while, with a slight twist to her lips. 'Aye. I'm sure you're right.'

Kitty's heart sank. They were back in the land of unspoken dialogue again. She had unintentionally caused offence for perhaps the tenth time since they arrived yesterday, beginning earlier in the morning when she came down to the breakfast table in her more than modest candlewick dressing gown which scraped the floor when she walked, yet Eamon's offended glance and his hasty scuttle out the door suggested that modesty had less to do with the volume of clothing she wore and more to do with its connotations. Bedroom attire was strictly for bedrooms. She would not make that mistake again. But so many other mistakes yawned out there ahead of her. No matter how carefully she trod, there was always something. Even when she feigned an interest in the politics of the surrounding area, asking questions because she thought they might consider her an unfeeling, disinterested beast if she did not, there was that closed, over-polite expression on their faces as they responded curtly and succinctly, just as Danny used to do when they were in Dublin. It was as if the pain of their community had to be held in reverential awe without them ever having to communicate that pain to an outsider. She got the message alright. And while it was a temptation sometimes to feign a greater degree of interest, she felt that would be too dishonest. In any case, she suspected that they knew the truth: that she could not wait to see the back of the place from the moment she arrived.

'It's good of you to come – for Danny's sake,' Monica said with a hint of sarcasm, as if she were reading Kitty's thoughts.

Kitty licked her lips. She opened her mouth to say something, then closed it again. Fuck them, she thought crossly. Monica lit another cigarette and sucked furiously, her eyes darting from side to side. Kitty watched her appear to race her cigarette and whiskey; sip, pull on the filter, sip again, unconsciously measuring the remains in her glass against the remains of her cigarette, managing to finish both at the same time to repeat the whole performance a few minutes later. After a broody silence during which Kitty squirmed and wriggled on her chair, forcing herself not to be the one to talk first, Monica sighed and wiping an eyelid with her thumb, she said:

'You see what you see and good luck to you.' Her face creased into a smile and she leaned forward. 'Good fucking luck to you, girl, is what I say. You're right. You're perfectly right . . . There's nothing here for anyone in this Godforsaken hole . . .'

'. . . I didn't mean . . .' Kitty tried to interject but Monica had risen to her feet and was obviously warming to her subject.

Suddenly Monica crashed her glass onto the table, the contents slopped over the rim. She stretched her arms expansively.

'Christ! I wish I could go to London . . .' She stopped and wagged a finger at Kitty who was about to interrupt. 'No, I don't mean to visit. I want to go there. Just go. I want to go anywhere. London would do – for a start. Then New York maybe. Yes, I can see me in New York. I'd have it eaten in two days . . . But I'm bloody stuck here aren't I? Stuck here in dreary old Belfast with a dreary old husband and this dreary old life . . . I tell you, girl – I'm wasted . . .' Monica picked up her glass and began to circle the table, Kitty had to turn her head to follow. Monica took an exaggerated swig from her glass, and encouraged by Kitty's laughing reaction she whirled about again in a frenzy. 'Look at me. Just look at me. I'm a dying breed. The last twentieth-century woman . . . I eat too much, I drink too much, I smoke too much – and – I fart in bed . . . No. Don't laugh. It's too tragic for that. No one appreciates that I'll soon be extinct. Wiped out like the dodo. Replaced by pert-breasted aerobics teachers, parking their pert red Ford Fiestas at the supermarket – Oh yes – We have them in Belfast too. And how did I get like this? Hmm? Because I did what was expected of me . . . Eamon and Danny were expected to go to college, expected to have careers while I – and I don't mind telling you this – I – who have twice the brains of the two of them put together, was expected to get married. It's an ancient story, isn't it? You wouldn't think that it still goes on in the civilized world but sure as everyone keeps telling us, we're fairly uncivilized up here anyways. *And* you listen to your mother. Two through college was hard enough – three would be out of the question. I can hardly blame her. She did her best. No, don't talk – I'm not finished yet!' Monica stopped in mid-flow to light a cigarette. She took a sip of whiskey then began to pace again with the cigarette clamped between her clenched jaw, her eyes squinched against the smoke. Kitty's head began to spin and she began to hiccough.

'So what did I do?' Monica continued. 'I popped the fourth man I could find between my legs, small and bald this time, I stirred him about – put him on gas mark three and what happens? Out pops another small bald thing nine months later – looking remarkably similar, I can tell you. But sure haven't I two lovely boys? That's what everyone says to me. Haven't you two lovely boys, Monica? Oh aye. I have. I have that. And a lovely soft old coot of a husband who'd do anything for me – the poor eedjit. I want too much, Ma says. Everybody wants too much according to her. She wanted though – for her two fine sons. If you knew the half of what that woman did to put them through college, no mean feat around here I can tell you – she had two cleaning jobs going at one time and she worked nights at the hospital . . . Oh yes indeedy. But sure haven't I two lovely boys – what more could I possibly want?' She paused for breath, striking a pose in the middle of the room, the top of her shoe worried a splinter of peeled-back linoleum. Kitty cleared her throat.

'London isn't all that great, Monica – maybe I make it sound better than it is . . .' It sounded feeble so she stopped herself. Monica was staring down at the cracked floor.

'Ah fuck it,' she said and swooped down onto her haunches, catching the cigarette between her teeth. She pulled with two hands at the linoleum splinter, it curled free leaving a wide arc of concrete floor in view. She was up again then, staring at the offensive sliver in her hand. Her eyes were blinking rapidly, and Kitty shifted awkwardly in her chair and looked away. Suddenly Monica began to laugh. A loud, rippling, infectious laugh that caught Kitty unawares so that she too was holding her stomach and rocking to and fro before she knew what was happening. Monica leaped forward and sent Kitty's glass whizzing across the table, catching Kitty's shoulders in a fierce grip, forcing her upright as she squeezed the air from her lungs in a tight, lunging bear hug. Kitty hiccoughed as Monica extended her arm and whirled her around the kitchen in a frenzied waltz.

'Time for some diddledididy I'd say,' Monica gasped and ran to the radio. Kitty reeled to the table.

'What?'

'Diddledididy music. You know how it goes – here we are.' The old-fashioned transistor radio belted out a jig. Kitty backed away with her hands raised as Monica approached with her eyes half closed and her arm extended waltz fashion again.

'Monica . . .' Kitty protested, laughing.

'C'mon. C'mon . . .' Monica caught her around the waist and whirled her around the room shouting 'yeeh-hah' at every turn. She took a quick swig from the bottle, another yeeh-hah, and hopped on top of the table. There, she hitched her skirt up beyond her waist showing her plain white knickers and wobbling thighs above her black pop-socks. She appeared to forget what sort of dance she was supposed to be doing, and began to shake her breasts, leaning forward like a belly dancer for better effect. Kitty had to cross her legs; she was dangerously close to wetting herself. But she could not move toward the toilet.

Monica pirouetted around and around, faster as the music quickened feverishly. Her brow was sweaty, the grey eyes closed as if she was caught in the throes of some inescapable passion. She pounded the table with her feet. Hitched her skirt higher still. Her laugh came in gasps and splutters.

Then as the music rose for a crashing close, Monica mounted her final onslaught on the trembling table, slamming her feet down harder and harder until the table finally succumbed, and almost with an audible wheezy sigh, it clattered to the ground, legs buckled inwards, sending Monica splaying onto her back with her two pop-socked legs spread in a 'V' in the air above her. It was to that vision and the sight of Kitty bent over with her hand between her legs, convulsed, that Ma O'Neill, Eamon, Danny and Monica's boys, entered.

An icy silence shivered around the room as Ma O'Neill slammed her hand onto the radio and turned to survey the wreckage of her kitchen. Her jaw remained firmly clamped as a dazed and shamefaced Monica tried to heave herself up onto her elbows. The expression on her face like a guilty schoolgirl had Kitty snorting into her free hand once more; she was silenced by a sharded

122

glance from Ma. Eamon surveyed the scene through slitted eyes under a furrowed brow. Only Danny and then the boys laughed. The latter ran to their redfaced mother and helped haul her from the debris. She stood rubbing the back of her head with her skirt still clinging to her waist. Kitty snorted again. And when Danny asked:

'Had a good time then, girls?' She ran blindly for the toilet unsure if she would have time to urinate before she vomited. She did both at once, and neither within spitting distance of the toilet bowl so she had to endure the further ignominy of slinking back to the silent kitchen to request a mop.

*   *   *

It was afternoon when Kitty stumbled downstairs, fully clothed, with her head in her hands. She took a deep breath and entered the kitchen with a shamefaced smile. Ma O'Neill was clearing away soup bowls from the new makeshift trestle table in front of Eamon and Danny. Kitty quickly noticed that the split linoleum had been covered by brown masking tape. She groaned inwardly and racked her brains for an appropriate apology.

'How's the head?' Danny asked with a beam.

'Not too good,' she said drawing back a chair beside him.

'Soup?' Ma asked with her back to them.

'Em. No thanks. I'll just have a cup of tea – if that's alright . . .' Kitty desperately tried to catch Danny's eye but he was too busy suppressing his smirk. Tentatively she turned her gaze in Eamon's direction but he was sitting straightbacked staring at his splayed fingers on the table, his mouth compressed into a tight, unyielding moue. Kitty hopped to her feet so fast, she had to sway for a second to steady herself.

'Anyone else for tea?' She forced her voice to be cheery.

'Sit down. Sit down girl,' Ma urged over her shoulder, 'I'll make the tea.'

Kitty sat again.

'Thanks . . . Emm . . . About the table and stuff – I'm really sorry. Please let me pay for a new one, it's the least I can do.'

There was an icy silence for a few moments. Kitty grimaced.

123

'And why should you do that?' Ma was saying, busy scalding the teapot. 'Sure, it was Monica's fault. That old thing was on its last legs anyways. 'Twas only fit for the scrapheap. Don't say another word about it – Here's your tea, drink it up now like a good girl – d'you like it weak or strong? ... One second now and I'll get the sugarbowl.'

'I don't know how you can say that about the table Ma,' Eamon interjected. 'It was the only thing left going back to Da's time, you said so yourself not a week past.'

'Eamon,' Ma barked.

'No, no,' Eamon continued in a reasonable voice, the splayed fingers opened and closed on the tabletop. 'I don't see why Monica should get away with it just like that.'

Kitty's top lip billowed out over the rim of her mug. She cast an innocent smile toward Eamon, aware that as far as he was concerned the blame rested squarely on her shoulders and not Monica at all. He caught her eye and she sipped and smiled again.

'So what do you want to do – shoot her?' Danny asked, exploding into laughter.

Kitty was about to join him when she caught the frozen expression on Eamon's face. Hastily, she turned her snort into a cough.

'Not funny,' Eamon was saying. He stuck his tongue in the side of his mouth and stared down again at his fingers as if he was noticing them for the first time. 'Not funny.'

'Ah hush up the lot of yous,' Ma said blandly. She turned to Kitty. 'So what are your plans for the rest of the day Kitty?'

'Well I don't know ... What are you doing Dan?'

'There's this competition – it's an annual thing before Christmas – at the Snooker Hall. Somebody put my name down ... so I thought I'd go along for a while if that's alright with you ... I mean, you can come too if you like but you'd probably be bored out of your mind.' He rubbed a finger along the tip of his nose and cast her a furtive look. Kitty wanted to say that it was not alright with her, it was very much not alright with her but she could see Eamon studying her reaction from the corner of his eye. For some inexplicable reason she did not want to give him the satisfaction of an argument.

124

'Fine,' she said. 'What about later?'

'We'll meet back here around teatime and take it from there,' Danny suggested. 'Alright?'

'Fine,' she said again with her mouth twisted to the side.

'Eamon,' Ma said, 'go over the road to the phone box there and give our Monica a ring will you? Tell her if she's finishing her Christmas shopping, to call here on her way for Kitty.'

'It's alright really,' Kitty protested. 'I'm quite happy to read my book by the fire. Honest.'

'Monica won't be going anywheres today Ma – not with the head she'll have on her,' Eamon said reasonably.

'Call her.' It was as if there was buckshot in the order. Kitty jumped involuntarily. And Eamon rose with a weary sigh.

The remainder of the afternoon was spent accompanying an even more reluctant, ashen-faced Monica through the pedestrianised Belfast shopping centre. Trawling their way from shop to shop, they queued up endlessly to have their bags inspected at doorways. The city centre in the early twilight was a lively place, festively lit and bustling with Christmas shoppers. They could have been in the heart of any affluent city. A thought occurred to Kitty a bit late in the day which she put down to the stupefied state of her mind. They were waiting listlessly in yet another queue when she said:

'Monica – what about bombs?'

'What about them?'

'I mean . . . How likely do you think . . .'

'Oh quite likely,' Monica said blandly. She looked like she was about to vomit. 'Do you care?' she added.

Kitty shook her head. At that particular moment she could not have cared less. Suddenly Monica grabbed her by the arm and hauled her out of the line.

'Fuck this for a game of soldiers – c'mon – let's get a cure someplace.'

'I don't think I could . . .' Kitty began, but Monica was already hauling her into the nearest pub doorway.

It was dimly lit inside and thronging with people. Monica shoved her way up to the bar and ordered a large vodka. Kitty insisted on a coke. The thought of alcohol made her stomach heave. She knew her face had taken on a decidedly green pallor. As Monica sipped in dour silence, Kitty found a phone and called her father. Yes, she was having a nice time, and yes she would be there in a couple of days time and no she hadn't wasted her money on an expensive present for him . . . As she listened to his familiar voice with that little crackle of excitement at the back of it at the prospect of her homecoming, she leaned her head against the wall and began to feel soothed for the first time that day. She wished she could somehow melt herself into the receiver and ooze her liquefied form through the cable to solidify once more beside him like a genie. She kept pressing coins into the slots even though there was nothing left to say and she could barely hear him in any case with the crush of bodies all around. Just to prolong the contact she asked if Eleanor wanted a word. After a pause her father returned and said that Eleanor was up to her eyes in baking. A special cake for her daughter, he added to soften the rejection.

'I can't wait to see you,' Kitty whispered hoarsely.

'Ah my darling girl,' he responded.

It was ridiculous she knew, but she had to choke back the tears. She said goodbye and replaced the receiver before she upset him by blubbering into it.

Back by the bar, Monica was on her second double. Her cheeks had taken on a slight flush again. She rolled her eyes at Kitty's approach.

'Another coke?' she asked.

'No no. I'm fine.' Kitty looked at her watch. 'It's gone six, will we head away so?'

'Two secs, I'll just throw this down.'

But she had another after that and it was past seven when Kitty bade her goodbye at the O'Neills' front door.

'I won't come in,' Monica said, pulling her mouth down at the corners. 'Eamon will shoot me over that bloody table . . .'

'That's what Dan . . .' Kitty laughed but Monica was already speeding up the street.

Inside, Danny and Eamon had their coats on and looked as if they were just about to go out.

'Kit,' Danny exclaimed, 'you're back. I thought maybe you and

Monica were going to make a night of it so Eamon said he'd come along with me to this pub down the Falls.'

Kitty felt a little vindictive pang at the obviously disappointed expression clouding Eamon's features. He recovered instantly and offered her a stiff smile.

'Are you going to stop in for the night or what?' he asked.

The thought of going out again and moreover to another pub made Kitty blench. But she gritted her teeth and returned Eamon's smile with all her teeth on display.

'Ah sure, why not,' she said. 'It's Christmas isn't it?'

'Great. We'll all go.' Danny put his arm around her shoulders. But Eamon began to shunt out of his coat.

'Let the two of yous go – I haven't much interest really. I was only going along to keep you company.'

'You're sure?' Danny asked over his shoulder.

As Eamon closed the door behind them Kitty had the distinct feeling that his eyes were making two laser impressions on her back. She shivered involuntarily.

Danny was in splendid form, he had won his match. He told her about it as they walked along. Kitty had to keep her head down, her neck felt too weak to support it. Saliva seemed to gush from apertures in the fleshy insides of her cheeks. She kept swallowing. Her stomach had evolved a language all its own – it pinged and gurgled, rolled and rumbled.

'Stop,' she had to say weakly. She stood for a moment, bent forwards with her hands resting on her knees. 'I think I'm going to be . . .' Only a thin line of yellow drool splattered onto the pavement. She remembered that she hadn't eaten all day, and dry heaved again.

Danny stood behind her stroking her back. But she caught his suppressed snort. She tried to cast him a baleful look over her shoulder.

'Sorry,' he said. 'I always want to laugh when somebody's sick. Sorry. Will we go back?'

Breathing deeply, Kitty slowly straightened her spine. She felt a little better. She kicked backwards with the heel of her boot catching him on the shin. He howled obligingly.

'No. Let's go on,' she said. Anything was preferable to another night of watching everything she said and skirting around Eamon in the kitchen.

As they walked along the Falls Road, Kitty counted at least six patrol jeeps which passed them by. The grey street with its bricked surveillance towers looked like one long garrison. A sudden shower drenched them in minutes. Kitty pulled her coat up over her head, but she was soaked by the time they stopped at a shabby looking pub with slits for windows. Beyond the tattooed bouncers who let them past with a jerk of their heads, they entered a dark, thrumming interior. They found an empty table and Kitty slumped gratefully onto a chair. Danny went to the bar, Kitty said she would try a Bloody Mary – it might help – and peanuts, lots of peanuts. She observed him at the counter, looking around him but evidently whomever he hoped to encounter there had not arrived yet. While he waited for his pint of Guinness he chatted amiably with the man beside him. At one point, he threw his head back and laughed that full-throated, easy laugh she only heard in Belfast. Deep grooves cut into his cheeks, the blue eyes sparkled, even his teeth seemed to gleam whiter than usual. He caught her gaze and winked. She thought how handsome he was. How incredibly handsome. By the time he returned with the drinks she wanted him so badly she felt slightly breathless. She told him this in a whisper, enjoying the complicitous smile curving on his lips. Under the table, he squeezed her hand. His eyes continued to sweep the room.

'Who were you hoping to meet?' Kitty asked.

'Just a lad I used to go to school with – he's been away for a while and someone told me that he hangs out here sometimes.'

'Away? Where away?' She sipped the Bloody Mary, it tasted surprisingly good.

'Does it matter?'

'Christ – I'm just making conversation.'

'Sorry. In the Maze actually,' Danny said, poking his ear with a finger.

Kitty opened her mouth to question him further but he was looking around again, then he groaned and turned to the side in an exaggerated attempt to avoid the elderly woman who had spotted him. The short, heavily wrinkled woman approached, swaying slightly.

'Danny O'Neill, is that you?' the voice slurred.

'Mrs McGlashen. Yes. It's me. Long time no see. How's it going?' Danny grimaced to Kitty.

'Could be worse I suppose. Could be a hell of a lot better too.' The woman had bloodshot eyes under which folds of skin jiggled as she spoke. Her large mouth stabled huge, yellowed teeth which vindicated Kitty's first impression of a haggard Shetland pony.

She hovered above a stool beside Danny for a moment with her hands clutching her knees until she sank down with a sigh.

'Who's your one?' This of Kitty.

'My – My uh girlfriend,' Danny replied.

'Oh aye?' The eyes slitted suspiciously. 'Where from – round here?'

'No. County Cork. South.'

The woman visibly warmed to a newly constructed image of Kitty. She reached over and clasped her hand in a drunken lets-be-friends grip. Kitty smiled coldly.

'Isn't she a little beauty. You're a lucky lad is all I can say. Wha'? What's your name, pet?'

'Kitty.'

'Kitty. Ah that's nice. Kitty . . .' She appeared to muse on that for a second then tipping her head back she began to sing in a croaky voice, '. . . I'll take you home again Kathleen . . . How does the rest of it go? Sure nobody ever knows that . . . I'll take you home again Kathlee-een. Wha'?'

Danny and Kitty winced together.

'Three times last month,' the woman was saying, 'three fucking – exchhuse my language – but three fucking times – the little fucker done me in. I know it was him. He knows I know it was him. Jesus Christ the whole fucking world knows that I know and he knows that I know it was him. Wha'? Wha'? This time he took the bloody till and all. Bad enough the booze and fags and whatever bit of cash is lying about – not much these days I can tell you – but this time the little fucker – pardon my – ah fuck it the little fucker – took the till, the receipt pad, Jesus Christ he even took the toilet paper from the bog. Imagine that eh?'

'Mrs McGlashen here owns an off-licence, it's forever being done over by the same lad – Denis Leahy is his name – everyone knows but nobody can catch him at it,' Danny explained in a hushed voice to Kitty.

'Exhhactly. Exhhactly.' The woman nodded.

'I'm very sorry Mrs McGlashen. I don't know what to say to you. Maybe a dog might be the answer,' Danny said, throwing Kitty a wink.

'A dog?' Mrs McGlashen was not taken with the idea. 'A bloody dog you say? A dog my arse – sure they'd take the fucking dog and all and so they would. Bastards. No. You'll have to have a word with Eamon for me. I've been on the lookout for him. Tell him that. Tell him I want to see him. I don't want to trouble your mother at the house. You know yourself. Just tell him Maggie McGlashen wants a word. Alright?'

Danny flushed and glanced quickly at Kitty. A slow pink rose up from his neck and suffused his cheeks. The blue eyes glared coldly at the woman who licked her lips coyly and wriggled her body in preparation for more. Danny raised his hands to his head and ruffled the dark wet waves in a motion as though washing the woman from his hair. He hissed:

'Get away with you. Go on now.'

'Something will have to be done. Sshomething. Something serious. And that little fucker's brother got the silver cross and all – you'd think it would make him think twice but oh no, not at all, they're only laughing. Only laughing. The little fuckers . . . And I'll tell you something else for nothing – that young Fogarty lad – he's one of the worst these days . . . You tell your Eamon that from me . . . You'd think . . .'

'. . . Mrs McGlashen.' Danny cut across her.

'. . . You'd think,' the woman continued, encouraged by his cautionary tone, 'that he'd have had enough by now. Didn't his father only die in his arms. And his poor mother trying to run that garage all by herself. Sure who'd have any truck with her now after what her husband done? Wha'? But only laughing they are, mark my words. Time was when you could reason with them, a good shoe up the arse and so on, but not any more. You couldn't shoot the fuckers enough I tell you. Now so, you tell Eamon that I wants to see him and today before tomorrow d'you hear. Don't forget mind . . .' Mrs McGlashen rose in a huff to stagger imperiously toward the bar.

Danny glowered silently. Kitty waited, watching him through narrowed slitted eyes as he reached for his pint and took a deep swig. He wiped the top of his lip with his hand. For a second Kitty had the impression that he really intended to let the incident pass without comment. Her insides twisted uncomfortably again – was she really that uninquisitive, that unfeeling?

'What was that all about?' She finally broke the silence.

'Don't mind her. Big mouth. Stupid big bloody trap that woman's got. And everyone knows it.'

'She's upset you though.'

'I'll live.'

'What's a silver cross – some sort of award?' she asked.

'You could say that.' Danny pulled his mouth down at the corners, he sounded bitter. He pointed to his elbows, then his knees. 'Back of the knees, back of the elbows job – that's the silver cross – sometimes the base of the spine too.'

'You mean bullets?'

'Of course I mean bullets. Kitty, sometimes I think you're living in another world . . .'

They both had to smile. Kitty lit a cigarette and spluttered as the smoke caught in the back of her throat. She rubbed her eyes.

'Why did that woman want Eamon's help?' The question was out – quickly – on a casual smoke ring. Kitty's mouth opened and closed, making more rings. She thoughtfully followed their progress up toward the ceiling.

Danny half swivelled in his chair so that his body if not his voice might appear to be withdrawing from the conversation. Kitty waited. She scraped her hair back tightly from her face, held it in a winch, turning it over her index finger until it pulled at the base of her skull. With her free hand she gently touched Danny's arm.

'Go on,' she said quietly.

'Ah Kitty can't we just drop it?'

'No.'

Danny hissed out a sigh. He looked over his shoulder and tried to remove his arm from Kitty's grip but her fingers encircled persistently.

'You can't shut me out forever you know,' she said. 'Alright, I admit I haven't exactly shown the greatest interest – but . . .' She stopped and shrugged, remembering her mother's empty bottles. She still hadn't told Danny. Maybe they were both a little guilty of the same crime of concealment. 'But I do want to know, Dan. Even Monica tells me more than you do.'

'Monica? What has Monica told you?'

'Nothing about Eamon if that's what you mean. Just stuff. About your childhood, about this –' She waved an arm in the air. '– this – place.'

'What – place?'

'Belfast.'

'Oh Belfast.'

'Come on Danny – stop messing. Why was that woman going on about Eamon?'

Danny sighed heavily. He sucked his top lip and would not meet her eye. She gave his arm another gentle squeeze.

'Eamon's involved, Kitty.' He finally expelled the words.

It was her turn to choose her words carefully. Images of balaclava'd men in fatigues, clutching rifles in one hand, balls of semtex in the other, shot through her brain. She released his arm and sat back.

'In what way?' she said quietly.

'We can't talk here,' he hissed.

Kitty glanced around.

'There's nobody listening for God's sake.'

'There's always *somebody* listening,' he countered. 'You really don't have a clue do you?'

'How could I?' she retorted bitterly. 'You never tell me anything.'

Danny drained his pint and rose.

'C'mon. Let's go.'

'Where?'

'For a walk.'

She followed him out. It was raining again but not heavily, just a fine powdery drizzle. It felt good against her inflamed cheeks.

'Well?' she said, once they had crossed the road from the pub.

Danny stopped by a boarded-up shop. He leant back against the barricade.

'It's complicated,' he said with a sigh. His feet scuffed the pavement. 'I don't go on about here because I don't expect you to understand – no, no, wait a sec, let me finish – I don't mean that in the way you think; it's just that, well, you'd have to be brought up here really to know what it's like. You've been here – what – two times – twice – and you think you understand. You see a few patrol jeeps, a few bombed-out buildings and you think: Right – that's that – that's Belfast. Like I go to West Cork and I see a big fancy car and a big fancy house and I say to myself: Well, that's Kitty's life, that's what she's used to. You know?' He paused to look at her. Kitty nodded her head soberly. She had underestimated him again, she realized with a pang of regret.

'Go on,' she said quietly.

'Eamon.' He stopped to clear his throat. 'Eamon's very involved in the community round here. People look up to him. They come to him with – with problems they might be having.'

'Like Mrs McGlashen?'

'Well yes. They don't have anyone else to turn to – they can't go to the cops, it's just not done that way, so we have to look out for our own . . . Eamon and others, they sort of keep an eye on things, on the local hoods. It's the only way.'

'. . . And that includes awarding the silver cross from time to time?' Kitty interjected bitterly. Danny twisted his mouth to the side and nodded.

'Aye.' He shrugged. 'You see? You'd have to live here – to understand.'

He was right she conceded. She would never understand. She recalled her walk last year around the Divis flats with Monica. The young glue-sniffers on the first stage of their evolution into the more menacing teenage skinheads; a hopelessly predestined progression briefly interrupted from time to time by a bullet in the thighbone. The few sips of Bloody Mary eructated in her throat. It stung when she swallowed. Danny was opening his mouth to speak but she raised her hand.

'You don't have to say it,' she said wearily. 'I've no intention of mentioning it to Eamon or Monica either . . . To tell you the truth, I just want to go home.' By home she meant West Cork.

As they walked back toward the house, Danny continued to talk. It was as if his tongue had been unleashed from some self-imposed fetters, and now he felt obliged to make the sordid reality more palatable by offering little morsels from his childhood. Another time she would have savoured the tasty little titbits but her feet dragged as they walked and she listened desultorily, imagining ahead the train trip and her father's lopsided welcoming grin. Just one more night and she would be leaving this Godforsaken place behind.

*   *   *

Kitty ordered coffee and bumped her way up from the buffet carriage to her seat near the front. She sipped the scalding liquid, dark and tasteless, and stared out the window. There was nothing to see as it was early morning, rainy and black, so her eyes fixed on her own reflection on the grimy pane. She could see the dark circles beneath her eyes quite clearly. It had been a relatively sleepless night. Her skin appeared abnormally pale in the strange light of the train's interior. She wondered if she had reached an age when make-up would help but then the thought of her mother's polyfilla'd beige sponges strewn across her dressing table changed her mind. She rummaged in her bag and pulled out a small round jar of lipgloss; with her little finger she smoothed on a dollop, smacked her lips at her reflection then wiped it off again with the back of her hand. She read for a few moments then tossed the book aside with a sigh. Sleep hovered tantalisingly just out of reach.

A long tedious day of travelling stretched ahead, it would be evening before her second train trundled into Cork station. Still, at least she was moving. At least she was leaving.

She thought of Danny's face as he had waved her goodbye in the crepuscular morning light, his anxious eyes searching her face for evidence that she might now find him distasteful, his grin too broad, too contrived and uneasy. And her own reciprocal cheesy

134

smile, the teeth chattering in her head from the cold. They would be back in London, neutral territory, when they met again and everything would be alright, she told herself. She sipped the foul coffee, then shook her head. Try as she might, she could not entirely expunge an image of civic-minded Eamon with a gun in his hand directed at some unfortunate youngster. Perhaps he only gave the orders. She hoped that might be true. She could not help but wonder what other 'community' activities he indulged in. And – she tried to block the thought – had Danny been involved too? The notion made her shiver. Their departure to London took on a whole new complexion. She determined that in time she would help Danny to sever the umbilical cord that bound him to Belfast – and to Eamon.

The train picked up speed. Trees and farmhouses emerged from their shroud of rain beyond the window. A weak sun battled with the rain clouds. Kitty thought about Danny's idle chatter about his boyhood as they had walked to his house the night before. If nothing else, at least she now had a few new mental snapshots to store away; an image of him following his considerably older brother around, padding after him with dove eyes full of wonder and admiration; a picture of him with his cowboy suit on fire, careering around the kitchen while Ma threw a bucket of water on him; kneeling in his school shorts every evening while they said their decade of the rosary . . . Her head began to nod in time with the train.

Drifting on the edges of sleep, she smiled, remembering one of his anecdotes about Eamon. She understood what Danny was trying to do alright – humanizing and thus trivialising Eamon to vitiate the damage done by his earlier revelation. It was a story Monica had told and retold Danny much to Eamon's invariable discomfort. Danny hadn't even been born – Eamon was about ten, maybe less, Monica around four or five. They were at the kitchen table and Eamon's hand was down the front of his shorts. Ma was glaring, observed by Monica, unnoticed by Eamon. Hand twiddling, spooning egg from its shell with the other. Ma coughing loudly, not wishing to mention it or notice it. And Eamon still not noticing Ma noticing. Monica leaping with fright as Ma finally thumped her fist onto the table and reached for the large

135

orange-handled scissors – snapping them open and shut inches away from Eamon's crotch. No warning. No explanation. No rudimentary discourse on basic table etiquette – Danny laughed, just – 'Touch it again and I'll cut it off.'

Kitty snorted. She would keep this image handy for the next time her skin crawled under Eamon's discomfiting scrutiny. Perhaps it was not such a bad thing after all, to have learned, albeit in such an accidental manner, about his extra-curricular activities. Danny wouldn't have to feel so defensive about his past any longer, maybe it was the beginning of a whole new commitment to their lives together. It might prove to be the catalyst in jolting Danny into an acceptance that one part of his life was over and it was finally time to move on. Her initial disgust and repugnance faded a little; she began to feel quite hopeful. She had boyhood images to fall back on now, the minutiae that helped to bond people together once the initial rose-tinting passion dissolved. She yawned and stretched, cognizant of the fact that the point of no return was reached once a woman began to imagine her lover as a boy.

July

'Kitty? Kitty, dear – I'm so sorry. Your father . . . Daddy died a little while ago. I'm so very sorry, dear.' There was a choking sound and Eleanor's voice cut off. Kitty stared at the humming phone.

'Mother? Mother?' Silence.

Kitty stood for minutes holding the phone. She replaced the receiver slowly and continued to stare – when it did not ring again she went to the wardrobe and stared inside, looking for something black to wear. She pulled out an old suit – it was navy blue. She draped it across the bed and searched for shoes. A violent pain shuddered through the pit of her stomach. She pressed her hands against her abdomen until it abated then went to the bathroom to run a bath. She poured in bubble bath, remembered baby oil.

While the bath filled she went along the corridor to the kitchen, opened the fridge, peered inside, left the door open, went to the stereo and put on some concerto or other – just noise. Her legs suddenly felt too weak to carry her weight so she crawled back to the bathroom and opened the window there, back to the kitchen again to find a candle; she found a stub which she lit and carried to the bathroom, undressed and heaved herself over the side of the bath. She lay back, then remembered to turn the flowing taps off.

She concentrated on breathing. Something she had never noticed before, how each breath could evolve into an expedition, a little adventure embarked upon – soon she was panting.

A summer wind swept through the open window. The candle stub flickered, and the bathroom was suffused with the scent of fragrant wax. The evening hum of the city reverberated outside.

People going home. Driving, busing, tubing home. Not knowing. Not knowing. She panted harder.

A flight. She jumped up from the bath and ran dripping to the phone in the bedroom. She forgot to breathe and had to concentrate on that for a moment. Breathing had become something to remember, she would not forget so easily again. The number of Aer Lingus came to her without an effort, easier than breathing. The woman said that all the flights were full, this evening and all of tomorrow – height of the season and so on – maybe tomorrow evening if she put her on a wait list. Kitty heard her own voice, high and shrill, it said:

'But this is an emergency.' The woman on the line waited. Kitty blinked and replaced the receiver.

Danny arrived home a couple of hours later. He found her huddled in a corner in the darkened room, still naked and shivering. She said she was just breathing and waiting for the phone to ring. She mentioned Eleanor and he quickly dialled the number. Eleanor told him that she had been trying to ring Kitty again for the past few hours but there had been no reply. A flight had been arranged for the morning.

Gently, stroking her body as though she were in physical pain, Danny lifted her onto the bed. He wrapped the sheets around her and placed a cold compress on her forehead. She grabbed his hand and would not allow him to prise free. He spoke soothingly to her – nothing words – 'there theres' and her name – Kitty Kitty Kitty. She stared at him through the darkness, blankly, like an animal stupefied by pain. She was hyperventilating badly, and he had to force her to breathe into a paper bag from time to time. He kissed her face and brushed her tangled hair with his fingers. He offered tea – coffee – a drink? She held his hand tighter and kept repeating over and over again that she had a flight booked for next week anyway. Her voice sounded dull and leaden, as if she were astonished by her own optimism.

Throughout the night she moaned slightly, awake but feverish. When she grew overheated he ran from the room despite her protests and soaked a cloth in cooling water to dab over her body, and when she trembled from the cold again, he wrapped himself around her and blew warm air onto her cheek.

Finally, as the sky paled into the dark velvet blue of first light, she drifted into a fitful sleep. Danny closed his eyes too, but remained alert in case she hyperventilated in her sleep.

*　　*　　*

Kitty's intended stroll turned into a fast, brisk stride along the level pathway beside the pond. She had walked through Hampstead Heath every evening after work since her return to dusty kerbside trees and bone dry pavements. London was besieged by drought and withering roses.

In West Cork throughout the days before the funeral and just after, the rain had been pitiless. She barely remembered those days now, the handshaking rituals, the endless pots of tea, her mother's glazed eyes. It all seemed a foggy distant memory from someone else's past. But the day of the funeral itself remained ruthlessly clear. Standing by the open graveside with the rain plunging down all around and the pungent odour of sticky wet peeled-back earth in her nostrils, it was as though his death, his absence, her cognizance of that fact, had only just then dawned on her.

She had uttered a cry and looked across the open grave toward her mother. Eleanor's right cheek had been scarred with lipstick, lumpy mascara streaming from glittering eyes which held Kitty's gaze. Kitty instinctively made a move forward but Eleanor had raised a hand almost imperceptibly and halted her. When Kitty looked again, Eleanor's eyes had recovered their blandness. Their eyes did not meet again until a few days later when they stood at the departure gate together. Kitty could not stop crying, and Eleanor, make-up firmly in place, had cast her one last bitter look before striding away, heels clickety-clacking across the tiled airport floor.

It was still unbelievably warm for late evening, dry air caught in the back of her throat like sediment. Her eyes sought out an empty bench. All along the pond, elderly men and women stooped forward like rows of question marks, contemplating dormant hands, lifeless on their laps. Strange how they neared the end in the pastel shades of their infancy – a few of the women did look for all the world like heat-frazzled babies with their lower lips protruding almost petulantly as if about to cry and their wispy hair matted to their crowns. By this time usually they would be long gone from their benches, but for the past few evenings, they had lingered on, rendered helpless and immobile by the flat, dead heat of the evening sun.

Up ahead, Kitty spotted an elderly man who usually cast her an endearing smile. She walked past him slowly, waiting for him to lift his head; she had her smile ready, but his chin remained firmly pinioned to his chest. She was not surprised to find, a few moments later, that her cheeks were wet again. This happened recurrently without warning gulps or sobs; she would touch her cheeks and find that she had been silently weeping for an indeterminate length of time.

In a strange way it felt as though the arid, heaving metropolis itself was responsible for her loss. Everyone and everything seemed harder somehow, dehydrated and brittle with all life and animation sucked out, leaving behind just the hollow empty husks.

Yesterday, a woman had beaten her child mercilessly in the supermarket aisle while people who would have once stopped to click their tongues in disapproval, passed by without so much as a flicker in their eyes. A woman at the checkout inadvertently touched Kitty's fingers, just a brush, when handing her the change, and Kitty stood, unable to move while tears ran down her cheeks and the queue behind her shuffled and lifted their shoulders in discomfort.

Later, sitting with Danny in their usual restaurant, a drift of cigar smoke crept up insidiously on her and she blundered her way to the toilets. When she returned, swollen eyed and puff-faced, Danny was shrugging helplessly, shovelling lasagne into his mouth.

She found to her surprise, that she could still work as diligently as ever. For the eight hours or so she spent in the office, she somehow managed to cast off the cloud which immediately settled again once the double glass doors swung behind her in the evenings. Her colleagues were sympathetic at first, passing her sheafs of paper with sympathetic glances and speaking to her in hushed tones – it occurred to her that they had considered her aloof and unapproachable before – moreover, it occurred to her that she had unconsciously encouraged that impression. And so, surprised by their kindness she agreed to join them one evening in the nearby pub, but they could no more constantly remember her loss than she could momentarily forget it. She made her excuses and left and immediately regretted her abrupt departure when she returned home to the empty flat. That was the first night since her return, that Danny stayed out all night again.

In a way she did understand. Danny who had not known true grief for his father, who had grieved in his way only for the imagined, seemed quite unable to cope with her grieving for the real. Sometimes, she would catch him gazing at her, a little puzzled frown creasing his forehead and when she tried to articulate to him how she was feeling, she could see him physically back away from the pain in her eyes.

She tried to put it into concrete terms so that he might comprehend a little better. Dealing in the abstract, the purely emotive was never Danny's strong suit. She explained to him how she could not yet disassociate her father from being a tissued, tendoned living person. She told Danny how she could not erase from her mind an image of him, rotting in the ground, hair and nails still growing while his face grew ever greyer and more prune-like with every passing day. The memory of his hands was clearest of all. She could see the white flatness of them, the little dark hairs curled above the knuckles and the pink pads of his palms even when the memory of his face seemed murky and irresolute. Her father was rotting beneath the shovelled earth, flaccid flesh melting from his bones. All alone without his cigars. And Danny nodded, but she knew he was uncomfortable; he was, after all, from a household which subjugated emotion to a degree whence not even a solitary photograph of his father was permitted as a reminder. As if, in a fashion – death could be ignored by unacknowledgement.

Furthermore, she saw to her sadness that her every effort to explain this hollow emptiness inside her, instead of drawing Danny closer, pushed him further away. He could not compete with such feelings and therefore he felt threatened. He felt as diminished by her grief as she felt by his lack of comprehension.

Beyond the ponds she turned and followed a pathway up to the right. Stretched out below in the distance, the contours of the city lay wrapped in heat haze. The sky looked dirty and dusty. On either side of the path once luxurious tracts of grass now bore scabby patches of brown dry earth. Even the curled, yellow-tinged leaves on the beeches appeared to be weighed down by a layer of dust, the branches sagging, listless and heavy. Several joggers passed her by, sweating and gasping profusely, and she could only wonder at their tenacity. Somebody's dog, a sweet little mongrel with tiny toy-like whirring legs and enormous liquid eyes, almost tripped her up as it ran after a stick. Its owner, a tall steel-haired woman approached Kitty with a concerned expression.

'Are you alright, dear? I am sorry.'

'I'm fine thanks,' Kitty reassured her. 'Is he yours?'

'Yes. He's an absolute darling but very boisterous for such a little thing.'

'He's lovely.' Kitty knelt and beckoned to the animal. It bounced up to her and settled its head in her lap with such trusting familiarity she felt a lump rise in her throat.

'Are you sure you're alright, dear?'

Kitty could not answer. She swallowed and rose with her hand covering her face; suddenly she needed to see Danny so desperately it was like a physical ache. Abruptly she hurried off, leaving the woman behind with an arm still extended, curled around empty space.

She ran the mile or so back to the entrance to Kenwood, pausing for breaths along the way. The bus journey seemed to take forever, then a fifteen minute run through the backstreets of Highgate down to Crouch End – she was panting and covered in a film of sweat by the time she rammed the key into the lock of the communal front door.

He was on the phone and jumped with fright when she barged in, slamming the door shut behind her. He placed his hand over the receiver and cast her a puzzled look. She realized that he must think that something terrible had happened to her.

'Nothing – nothing,' she gasped, waving a hand.

She had to stand with her feet apart for balance, the top half of her body bent forward with her hands on her knees, to catch her breath.

'Listen, I have to go now, see you tomorrow – Yes yes, alright so.' Danny said quickly into the phone. He replaced the receiver and went to Kitty.

'What is it? What's the matter?' He tried to put his arms around her but she could not straighten yet so he had to stand there awkwardly with his hands outstretched in an abortive embrace. Kitty reached out and tugged at his trouser leg, pulled him nearer and laid her cheek against his thigh. Gradually, he helped her to stand up. She leant back against the door.

'I think,' she gasped, 'I thought that I was going to – I don't know – die, or something if you weren't here.'

'What's the matter?' he asked again.

She laughed bitterly.

'I think I'm losing my mind – that's the matter.'

'Kitty?'

'Jesus.'

'Kitty – what happened?'

'Nothing. Nothing at all.'

'Then – why . . . ?'

'. . . Why am I standing here gasping for breath, looking like some wild, half-demented creature . . . ?'

'Well – yes.'

'I thought – I was afraid, no terrified – that you wouldn't be here. That's all . . .' She broke off and shrugged helplessly.

His face clouded over and he took a little step backwards.

'But I am. I am here.'

'I know.'

'You ought to see a doctor or something. I don't know.' He scraped the fingers of both hands through his hair.

'Why? Because I had a panic attack – for Christ's sake what's so strange about that? Listen, it was quite likely that you wouldn't be here . . .'

'. . . And that's enough to justify this – this . . .' He waved a hand in exasperation.

'This what Dan?'

'This . . . you . . . look at you, look at the state you've got yourself into, for Christ's sake.'

He turned away from her then, wrapping his arms tightly around his waist. She could tell from the hunched shoulders and the downward droop of his head that he felt he was being wronged again.

'Danny?'

'What?'

'Look at me.'

He turned slowly .

'What?'

'Just be patient, alright?'

He nodded but she could tell from the stiffness of the shoulders still, that he had something to tell her and instinctively she knew that the something was eating him up with guilt – all the telltale signs were there, the lack of eye contact, the defensive shoulders raised, the foot endlessly scuffing at the frayed carpet threads. His own guilt was the reason for his gruffness.

'Whatever it is – I don't want to hear it,' she said. Brushing past him on her way to the stereo, she banged in the first cassette to hand. Elvis. She clicked it out again and slammed in Beethoven's 'Corialan', turning the volume up to almost full blast. 'I don't want to hear it Dan . . .' she shouted over her shoulder.

When he did not respond she whirled around.

'What is it this time? You have to meet some "mate" or other tonight? Is that it? There's some extraordinary shareholders meeting at the pub tonight . . . ?'

'Kitty.'

'Am I asking too much of you – is that it?'

The music behind her was so loud she couldn't hear herself think. She swung around and tore at the cassette flap with her fingernails, the tape ejected spiralling out its brown shiny gut. Pulling at it with her claws she swept the entire deck from the table.

'Take it easy,' Danny was saying.

'Take it easy?' she screamed. 'You take it easy.'

She scrabbled through her bag for her cigarettes, but her hands were shaking so badly she couldn't get a match to strike. She threw the box to the ground and stood staring down at the scattered matchsticks, the cigarette clamped between her teeth. Danny bent and picked up a match and the box, gently prised the cigarette from her mouth and lit it for her. She looked at the gust of smoke blowing through his lips as he coughed, and handed the cigarette to her. She inhaled so deeply her lips stuck to the filter, and her fingers travelled up the length of it, singeing on the tip.

'Shit.'

'Kitty?'

'I told you – I don't want to hear. Just go. Go on – get out of here . . .' She stumbled toward him and pushed him backwards with her outstretched arm. He retreated a step but dodged her second attempt to shove him.

'I'm not going to the pub – I'm not meeting any mates,' he said quietly.

'Ah what do I care,' she said bitterly. She went to the window turning her back to him.

'I know it's a bad time,' he began. Her eyes slitted. 'And I wouldn't go if I didn't have to – you have to believe me Kit . . .'

'Go? Go where?'

'Home. Belfast. I have to go.'

'You have to go.' Her head nodded as if to a refrain.

'Aye. Tomorrow.'

'Tomorrow he says. Tomorrow, just like that – For how long?'

'Just a few days.'

'I see.'

'Kitty I . . .'

'. . . Shut up. Please shut up.'

'Don't you want to know why?'

'You *are* going? I mean – no matter what I say – no matter how much I might ask you not to go, you are going?'

He did not respond, but she caught the slight tilt of his head forwards from the corner of her eye. She sighed heavily.

'In that case I don't think I want to know why. You couldn't possibly give me a good enough reason.'

'It's Eamon . . .' he began, but cut off when she visibly shuddered and closed her eyes.

145

'How could I guess?' she rasped. 'And what about work, when are you going to tell them?'

'They know already.'

'So you've had this arranged for a while. I see. Tell me something, I'm curious – just when were you going to tell me? In the morning before I left for work, or were you going to leave a little note for me to find tomorrow evening?'

'I've been trying to tell you all week but you've been acting so strangely – you know – weird . . . I didn't know how to tell you, to be honest. I am sorry. I really am. I've made a mess of this I know, but I promise I'll make it up to you when I get back . . .' His voice trailed off.

'You're good at promises, aren't you Dan?'

'I know how this must look – but . . . but I promised Eamon too. I gave him my word that I'd come. He's been mixed up with these school trips for ages now – every year they take a whole bunch of deprived kids, you know, kids who might have lost a parent or been injured themselves because of, well, as a result of – what's going on . . . They take them on a trip somewheres during the school holidays, and the thing is, the thing is, Eamon says that Ma hasn't been too good. There's something wrong with her insides, she's been in a lot of pain – here – down low in her stomach and she has to go in for tests but Eamon will be away. And Monica is already away in France with the boys . . . so . . . So I promised.' With his shoulders up so high they almost grazed his ears, he shrugged and thrust his hands deep into his pockets, waiting for her reaction. Kitty could only shake her head in disbelief. She stubbed out the cigarette end on the carpet, grinding it with a rotating foot over and over again.

'So you can be there for Eamon but not for me,' she said quietly, and turned to face him.

'It's not just Eamon,' he protested. 'It's Ma. She's been in dreadful pain Eamon said. They didn't want to tell Monica before she went away in case she cancelled her holiday. The boys . . .' His voice trailed off again.

'Aren't you lucky to be part of such a caring – such a close family.' Kitty's mouth twisted bitterly to the side. 'Look how you all stand by one another in your time of need. I'm impressed. I really am.'

'Oh Kit.'

'Don't you "oh Kit" me.'

His expression turned dark and angry then.

'Wait up just a wee second here – Listen – you were the one going off on your own to see your father earlier this month, did I complain when you didn't so much as ask me to go with you, eh? No no, hold on a minute . . . And I didn't like it when you spent a whole month away from Dublin that time when your father had his stroke, remember? I don't remember delivering any ultimatums though. If I remember right, you just did whatever it suited you to do at the time – you didn't give a shit about landing your last boss in it either, did you?'

'That was different,' her voice choked. 'Besides, my father's dead now.'

'And maybe my mother will be dead soon too, Kit. Can't you look at it that way? I can't let her go into hospital all by herself. No one to visit her or be with her when she finds out whatever it is that's wrong . . .'

She tried hard not to concede the points he was wrenching from her but it was too late. As if he knew that he had managed to gain a foothold, Danny moved across the room and tentatively placed his arms around her rigid body.

'The time will pass quick enough,' he murmured soothingly in her ear. 'Look it – come with me if you like.'

'You'd better go and pack,' she said, shuffling out of his stiff embrace.

He was about to entreat further but she stopped him.

'Go on,' she urged. 'I can't think straight right now. All I know is – I don't want to go to Belfast.'

'Alright,' he said gently, withdrawing.

She stood by the window lighting cigarette after cigarette, listening to the sound of him fumbling around the bedroom looking for jeans, socks, underwear. She heard the definitive birrrpp of the suitcase zipper, then the flow of bathwater, the kettle boiling for his accompanying coffee. He asked if she wanted some and she did not turn, but shook her head.

Outside, the light was finally fading. Car headlights swept past down below. She watched people enter and leave the Pakistani corner shop. The wind through the open window carried smells of fish and chips and vinegar, petrol and city smog, and other indistinguishable food odours – tandoori, she detected for a moment, then it was gone. She gazed around the shadowy room, the walls a tired and gloomy yellow; they had spent hours agonizing over the choice of colour, as if it mattered. Her plants were dying she noticed, then lit another cigarette. She was about to play some music when she remembered her earlier destruction. Danny was having a good scrub, she could hear the constant lap of water. Her head drooped.

Belfast again. Always bloody Belfast. And Eamon. She wanted to spit. Something was nagging at the back of her mind, she had to grope to draw it out. Of course it was understandable that Danny should want to be with his mother when she needed him. If anything, it was commendable. Of course she didn't want him to go through what she was going through now. In her heart she could confess to a rational guilt. She had neglected her father in the last few years, despite his illness, despite a facade of phone calls and irregular visits; it was true that once she was satisfied that he was out of danger she had transferred all her attentions to Danny again. She had not meant to be negligent at best, cruel at worst, it had just happened that way. She should not now deny Danny his honest response to his family's needs. And yet she continued to feel aggrieved, not so much by Danny as by Eamon and his role in all of this. He had no compunction about wrenching Danny from her at this time.

She threw the cigarette butt down to join the others strewn around her feet. Suddenly she felt weary beyond measure. She had to close her eyes, just for a minute. A late July moon, ripe except for a tiny sliver shaved from its left side, hung above the sweltering metropolis. If she strained her neck she could see beyond the rooftops of the immediate houses, down to the golden, pulsating, connect-the-dot streetlights of the outstretched city. Somehow tonight, it did not appear as grand and estranging as it usually did; the horizontal regular rows appeared strangely vulnerable in their endlessness, as though they lay self-importantly

148

twinkling beneath an indifferent moon which would long outlast them. For the first time since they came, she felt part of London; just another anonymous participant staring out a window.

She did not want to leave the window but the need to close her eyes was overwhelming. She fell on the sofa, curled up and immediately drifted into deep sleep.

She awoke to arms encircling, bearing her up gently.

'What?' she asked, still half asleep.

'Shh. Stay asleep. Don't wake up,' Danny was urging in a whisper as he carried her to bed.

The scent of him so close to her, soapy and somehow buttery, the touch of his hand on her forehead, warm and fluttering somewhere above her eyelids reminded her of a blanket she insisted on holding to her face every night as a child. She breathed him in and slipped into sleep again.

When she reluctantly dragged herself from deep sleep in the morning to the sound of the insistent bedside alarm clock, he was gone. There was a note by the clock. She stared blankly at it for a moment then sank back into the pillows. There was no need to read it. She already knew its contents.

She went to the kitchen and made coffee. The next few days stretched ahead like an eternity. Her work would do little to fill the void. For a minute she considered calling in sick, but what would she do all alone in the flat for the day? No, that was not a viable answer.

She realized sadly that there was no one here for her to call, to say 'come over', to make the slightest break in the solitariness of the next few days. She had somehow managed to cut herself off from everyone but Danny, while he still had his family, his pub, a life apart from her. Without meaning to, she had become the very thing, the type of emotionally dependent, obsessive woman she had once despised. She made toast and went to survey the destruction of the previous night. Standing with the toast clamped between her teeth, she dialled her mother's number. Eleanor answered crisply.

'Hi. It's only me.' Kitty forced a friendly voice as though she phoned her mother every other day.

'Kitty. How are you, dear?'

'I'm – fine . . . And you?'

'As good as can be expected I suppose.'

'I still can't believe he's . . .'

'. . . Yes. Me too.'

There was a long silence. Kitty listened to her mother breathing. She thought she heard a slight choking sound, but when Eleanor spoke again her voice was as dry and crisp as ever.

'Did you want something dear?'

'I just wanted to say – to say –' Kitty realized she was blabbering but she could not stop her voice from going on. '– that – that I'm sorry – I know you think that I took him away from you . . .'

'What are you talking about?' Eleanor's voice was glacial.

'Daddy,' Kitty spluttered. 'I'm sorry for taking him away from you. I am. Sorry.'

She could hear Eleanor's gasp on the other side.

'I don't know what you're on about,' Eleanor barked. 'You sound half hysterical. Pull yourself together Kitty, I'm not in the mood for this nonsense.'

Kitty closed her eyes and took a deep breath. She held it until she felt slightly less lightheaded. She cleared her throat.

'Listen, I was wondering if maybe – Well I was thinking about coming over for a few days or so – if that would be alright with you . . . I mean would it? Would it be alright with you?'

'It's not a good time, dear – I've got decorators in.'

Kitty winced. Decorators in – he was dead a matter of weeks.

'Please,' she forced herself. 'Please let me come home . . . I – I need to come home right now.'

'With or without that Northern boy?'

'Without – I mean, just me. I want to come alone.'

'I see.' A deliberate pause. 'So that relationship has finally hit the rocks, has it?'

'No. It's not like that – I . . .'

'. . . Listen Kitty dear, if you're wondering about money – there is none; just the house which is falling down, as you know. I've got that, naturally, and whatever little bit I get from the life assurance policy . . .'

'You – you bitch!' Kitty shrieked. 'Of course it's not money, it

150

never even crossed my mind. I just wanted to come home. That's all. What's so strange about that?'

'Ah that's more like it,' Eleanor said smoothly. 'Still throwing tantrums to get your own way . . . By all means come home, dear, if you need to so badly – but please don't ask me to pretend that you're welcome . . .'

A peculiar feeling of relief took hold of Kitty as she listened to the barely concealed hatred in Eleanor's voice. It was as if she was finally able to let go of Eleanor, as if she no longer had to bear the responsibility for her mother's lack of love.

'You're a very sick woman,' she said gently. 'You'd like me to tell you now that I hate you, that I've always hated you . . . but I'm not going to say that. I'm not going to tell you either that I love you – but I don't hate you. Do you hear me, Mother? I don't hate you. I wish I could. Goodbye.'

Eleanor did not respond, and Kitty clicked the receiver into place again, visualizing as she did so, a constricted little smile on her mother's painted lips. She stood and stared down at the phone for a few long minutes, sickeningly aware that she would not see her home again, at least not in Eleanor's lifetime. The dry toast churned in her stomach and she ran to the bathroom with a hand to her mouth. Doubled over the toilet bowl with rivulets of sweat streaming down her forehead and little masticated bits of undigested brown pulp floating on the water's surface, the face her mind conjured up, lips drawn back in a smug little smile, brown eyes gazing at her mockingly, did not belong to her mother but to Eamon.

*   *   *

The following day was cloudy. A constipated sky hung low and heavy, sagging over the rooftops. It was unbearably humid. At work, Kitty had to wash her hands several times during the day to rid them of their clamminess. Everyone wished it would rain. Later that night as she lay hot and sleepless in bed, the first flash of lightning finally signalled the breaking of the summer storm. A few fat drops crackled on the pavements below followed by hissing torrents of rain and long growls of thunder which shook

151

the room. The storm continued unabated for the next two days. She brought manuscripts to work on home with her each evening but left them to gather dust on the coffee table while she stood by the window gazing out at the opaque drifts sweeping across the city below. It was as though the streets, the dust-clogged bricks, the grimy pavements, even the wilting, defeated kerbside trees, all surrendered themselves with a wheezy sigh to the deluge. On the third day, Kitty went to work reeling from lack of sleep. Even when she did manage a couple of hours, her sleep was punctuated by such vivid dreams of her father that she forced herself to stay awake. In the dreams she kept saying to him 'but you're dead,' and he kept saying 'am I?' with a little ironical smile on his lips and that perplexed frown which was so familiar. And for seconds when she awakened again, she would believe that he was alive until the visceral truth kicked in and hurt like a physical pain. Then long hours stretched ahead in the darkness as she wallowed in a self-pity that was at once exquisite and repellent.

*　　*　　*

Danny called her at work from a phone box on his third day away. He sounded happy. His mother was alright, it was nothing serious. Kitty feigned relief. In truth, she had all but forgotten the reason for his abrupt departure. He would return tomorrow evening and was she alright – and were they having the same thunderstorms there as in Belfast? Kitty deeply resented the cheeriness in his voice. He might have made an attempt not to sound as if he were having such a good time.

By the time she heard his key turn in the lock the following evening, she had worked herself into a frenzy of anger. She reasoned with herself, told herself that she was just suffering from lack of sleep, the dreams, loneliness – there was no point in taking it out on Danny; but there was no one else to take it out on. Besides, it was easier to be angry than to grieve. She bit her lip when he appeared at the doorway. He looked so happy happy happy. She felt like the only girl in the class not asked to the birthday party. He kissed the top of her head and slumped onto a chair.

'So your mother is alright?' She closed her eyes and willed herself to stop; there was still time. Evidently, he had not detected the flinty edge to her voice because he was smiling and undoing his shoelaces. His hair was matted to his scalp and dripped in streams down his cheeks; tiny drops impaled themselves on the spikes of his unshaven jaw. A barely visible mesh of crepe-like lines in the bruised circles under his eyes suggested that he too had had some difficulty sleeping. She felt a brief pang of satisfaction.

'Aye. Thank God,' he said. 'And yourself?'

She swallowed her bile for a second. Savouring the bitter taste in her mouth.

'What do you think?' she asked frostily.

'Ah Kit – you're not still sore at me, are you? I didn't want to go – really I didn't, but it couldn't be helped.' He spread his fingertips in a motion that reminded her of Eamon, and her last tenuous hold on her temper fell away. Her mouth opened and she let out a string of recriminations, accusations and expletives that had him visibly shielding himself with his outstretched palms. He looked miserable when she finally ceased; her body trembled uncontrollably. He gazed at her, stupefied, then shook his head.

'If you go on like this, you'll make yourself sick,' he said.

'What do you care?'

He stood then and went to the window, fingers pulling at his lower lip. Kitty gazed at the bony wings of his shoulder blades sticking out so defensively. He looked drained – strung out. For the first time, it dawned on her what the worry about his mother must have cost him. The terror and sense of helplessness that she had experienced when her father had his first stroke came back to her. Her anger evaporated and she suddenly felt sick with remorse. But there was something else there too, tingeing the edges of her remorse, a horrible realization that he could be content in Belfast away from her while she could never be content in Belfast with him. She could not keep him, unhappy, in London forever. And she saw too, quite clearly, that she had been doing precisely that. While he was in London or for that matter, Dublin, she exercised a power over him. She could make him feel happy, or miserable; worthy or worthless – just as her mother had wielded power over her husband.

153

The thought was too depressing for words. She slumped forward, holding her head in her hands. Danny turned and gazed at her in the silence for a few moments.

'Kit?'

'What?'

'I'm sorry.'

'Me too.'

'Friends?' he said, with his head tilted to the side.

She did not answer but cast him a relieved smile. He came and knelt in front of her, resting his drenched head on her knees. She idly stroked his hair and closed her eyes as an intense weariness took over her mind and body, bringing with it a merciful release from her thoughts.

December

The book slid down her lap and fell to the floor. Kitty awoke with a start. Gusts of black smoke swathed the small front room, belching down from the chimney flue, harried by temperamental, impulsive December winds. She was alone. The room was womb-like in the foggy light. The air hung pungently in drifts that clung to her clothes. She looked around at the faded floral curtains, the assortment of chairs, random as the rest of the furniture, with their limp and lumpy cushions. The fire leaped and spluttered with every gust of wind. Kitty poked at it half-heartedly then sank back into her chair again.

She had fallen asleep after dinner, which they always ate at midday. In the dark post-Christmas afternoon Ma had left to attend to some church meeting or other. Eamon had simply left, and Danny attended to the wash-up. Apart from Christmas day, two days past, Monica had not been around. Kitty missed her. Still, there was something uniquely warm about the household this time, something refuge-like, hushed and reverential, some-thing seductive – like this glutinous room. Despite Eamon's sullen silent appraisals, the nervous jarring quality of her own home, borne of the endless testy skirting around her mother, was some-how dulled at the edges here. She did not feel, entirely, an intruder. And on a few occasions she had had the pleasure of receiving Ma's full, blue-eyed smile, a smile that sloughed years and split a handsome face, childishly, guilelessly open. On such rare occasions, Kitty could see where Monica came from.

It was entirely probable, she conceded, that she felt more relaxed this visit because it was not a hurried stopgap on her way to somewhere else. There was nowhere else to go to this Christ-mas, apart from a cold and empty flat in London. Danny had offered to stay there with her if that was what she wanted, but she knew he would have been deeply disappointed not to go home for Christmas. So she agreed to go with him, if only to keep the tacit peace which had existed between them for the past few months. Since his return from Belfast in the summer, they had both made an extra, if unspoken, effort to avoid conflict. Danny did not go to the pub quite so much and she stopped accusing him of neglect. She worked in the living room quite contentedly most evenings while Danny prepared the dinner, using every pot in the kitchen – the agreement being that she washed up. His culinary efforts were admirable, if not innovative. He stuck to the recipe book rigidly and bought a stopwatch so that he could time everything. It made her smile when she heard the loud 'Shite' when he invariably allowed the broccoli twenty seconds more than the book stated. Kitty had tentatively suggested that they might take a look at flats for first-time buyers at the weekends. She expected resistance, and in a way she was only testing – but he seemed to think that it might be a good idea. With Belfast receding into the background once again, she had felt sufficiently confident to spend Christmas there. Her own mother had sent a Christmas card to the flat, signed, With Very Best Wishes – Eleanor. Kitty had not sent a card in response.

In some respects she was quite relieved not to be at home. Every room, every chair, would have reminded her of her father, and Eleanor's hostility would have compounded her sense of loss. She yawned and stretched again. Really, it was quite pleasant when there was no one about.

The door opened. Danny's tentative head showed around it. Kitty smiled.

'It's alright. I'm awake.'

He perched on the arm of her chair leaning forward to pick up her fallen book.

'*Cousin Bette* – Balzac,' he said, examining the cover. 'Any good?'

'Very.'

'I never knew anyone to read as much as you do. Except maybe Eamon,' he added, surprising her. He threw the book onto a nearby table and kissed the top of her head.

Kitty reached back to kiss his mouth. She pulled him down on top of her pressing her palms against his buttocks. There was no such thing, as in her house, as slipping into one another's room in the dead of night. She stretched languorously and pushed her groin upwards.

'Are we alone?' she whispered.

'Aye,' he grunted, 'for now.'

'Could we . . .' She pulled on his belt. 'Could we d'you think . . .' She began to unbutton her jeans.

'We'll have to be quick,' Danny was saying, thumb-thrusting his jeans down to his knees. Like him, Kitty left her jeans around her knees. They struggled to get at each other, panting and red-faced with the crude effort. Kitty sank back further so that her head lay wedged between the back and seat of the chair, Danny rested his hands on the arms, muscles bulging from the strain. Wriggling and writhing, a crevice was found and Danny plunged hopefully.

'Wrong one,' Kitty laughed, squeezing her hand between her legs to guide him from his stuck position between her buttocks.

'Jesus!' Danny panted.

'Now, now,' she reprimanded, slicing the back of his hand with a karate chop. 'No taking the name of the Lord in vain in this house.'

'I'm . . . God . . . I'm not taking it in vain . . .' he spluttered, prodding the tight chasm again. The tip of his penis sank into somewhere soft and familiar. He sighed with relief. Kitty shunted down to take him in. Their eyes met and they erupted into laughter. His arms could take the strain no longer and he collapsed in a heap on top of her. Kitty was cupping his face, her forehead pressed against his, when the door suddenly swung open.

Eamon took a long look at Danny's naked buttocks, apparently unsure for a moment if he was really seeing what he was seeing.

'Oh Jesus Christ Almighty,' they heard as he retreated down the hallway toward the kitchen.

'Oh shit.' Kitty pushed Danny off and leapt to her feet, pulling her jeans up.

'Shit piss fuck,' Danny snorted.

Kitty sat for a while with her hand over her mouth staring into the fire once Danny had sped off to the kitchen to sort his brother out. They were whispering furiously when she entered with her shirt-tail hanging out and her hair sticking out at an angle to one side. She put her palms to her scarlet cheeks and glanced cautiously over at Eamon, but he would not meet her eyes. He appeared to be suffering his own excruciation of embarrassment. Kitty hopped from one foot to the other while she glared at Danny to do something, to say something.

Danny shrugged helplessly. But she sensed something else behind his confusion too. He was showing off to his older brother. She frowned furiously at him.

Eamon did not seem to know quite what to do with himself. He made a show of putting the kettle on. Placing mugs out. A sugar bowl. In the silence, his eyes met Kitty's once – she almost reeled in shock. There was so much hatred there, and she sensed also, that it was all directed at her. But more than that, and infinitely more disturbing, was that other quality at the back of the arid, caustic gaze. In that brief moment when he had looked in her direction and met her eyes, Kitty had detected the lust there too.

It seemed to Kitty that his head gave an almost imperceptible nod as their eyes locked for that split second. She had the feeling that she was now standing on entirely new territory. She watched him check his tea for sweetness with the fastidious expression of an old woman on his face. Then sighing out his satisfaction and casting a last curious glance toward Danny, Eamon left the kitchen. He deliberately swerved to avoid her though she stood feet away, and as the door clicked shut, Kitty immediately exhaled with relief. She realized that she had been holding her breath.

'Well, what did you say to him?' she demanded.

'What could I say? What was there to say?'

'Did you tell him we just sort of got carried away and it won't happen again?'

Danny's expression confirmed to her that she was stating the obvious. She nodded and cradled the hot mug in her hands. That look. She opened her mouth to try to explain it to Danny but words eluded her. She shivered.

'I know you're feeling humiliated – but it's as good as forgotten.

Honestly.' Danny misunderstood her apprehension and ruffled her hair. He drained his tea and stood up checking his jeans pockets for money. He pulled out a few crumpled notes. 'Listen – you don't mind if I go out for an hour or so do you?' he said.

'You're joking,' she said.

'I won't be long . . .'

'I don't believe you sometimes . . .' She could only shake her head in amazement. There were times when his insensitivity, his blind indifference, took her breath away. She opened her mouth to protest more forcefully.

'Just a quick game . . . or two . . . you know.' He backed out slyly. Giving her the lopsided smile. The bashful blue stare from under raised brows. Usually it worked.

'If you go out tonight – I promise you'll be sorry – Danny . . . Dan . . .'

But he was gone. Gone to that Godawful Snooker Hall. Every evening as regular as an old man to his local, Danny slunk off amid cheesy grins and backward shuffles. She was supposed to be amused, and sometimes she could participate in the jaded routine but not that evening. She scraped a chair back and slumped into it.

An occasional thud carried from upstairs – Eamon's room, or rather Eamon in Danny's room. She was still in Eamon's room of course. She had scoured it well on her last visit; flame-cheeked at her own sneakiness she went through every drawer, even tried the back panels on the wardrobe, in an effort to fix something into place behind the sour sullen glances and biscuit dry conversations. She was looking for nothing in particular, a book, a letter, a condom packet – but the search of the room did not reveal a thing. It was so entirely devoid of anything personal that she had had the curious and disturbing notion that he had anticipated her sneakiness.

He watched her all the time, Kitty knew. It would not be obvious to another but she sensed his eyes on her. He blushed easily when she darted him sidelong looks to let him know that she was aware of his secretive appraisals. Sometimes she quite enjoyed his discomfiture.

Kitty poured herself another mug of tea. She steepled her

fingers and sat with her elbows on the table, the triangular construction tapping gently against her mouth. She noticed the ticking of the kitchen clock and, once aware of it, she was unable to ignore it. The difficulty after its constancy for a few minutes, was in the telling if the clock intruded on the silence or the silence intruded on the ticking of the clock. She realized that the warm, steamy, confabulatory O'Neill kitchen, while presenting her with a heady antidote for the frostbite of her mother's parlour, also offered its own quietude, just a gentle, persistent ticking behind the easy chat, the clink of china and the hiss of steam.

She sipped, allowing the tea to trickle down her throat in hot little spurts. She decided that the time had come to push a little harder.

The door opened. Eamon looked around. She noted his flushed face on seeing her alone.

'Danny out?' he asked, about to withdraw.

'Yes,' she said and lifted the teapot. 'Look, a fresh cup of tea here if you want it . . .'

He considered for a moment, then as if she had challenged him, he strode into the kitchen, swinging the door behind him. Kitty poured a mug for him. He leaned against the dresser, not agreeing to commit to the act of sitting down. Kitty held the silence for as long as she could, but it was too heavy – too cumbersome. She could not wield it with the ease of an O'Neill. She said brightly:

'I'm sorry about earlier on. It was really stupid of us. Sorry to put you in such an embarrassing position . . .' She tried the humble, self-effacing smile, the one that shouldered infinite culpability, the one that usually appeased Danny.

'Me – in an embarrassing position . . . ?' He raised an eyebrow then stared down at the tops of his shoes for a moment before looking up to glare directly at her crimson face. For a moment Kitty thought that he might actually spit to the side. She held his gaze for as long as she could, which was not long. She racked her brains for something to say that would place them on an even keel once more. She flashed him a wide-eyed glance she hoped was laced with a sprinkling of irony, a touch of indulgent humour – young lovers will be young lovers, ha ha, we'll all laugh about this one day – and he blenched. She realized that he thought she was mocking him; she was making this whole silly episode worse every time she looked at him, so she trained her eyes to the crack in the floor. She opened her mouth to say something conciliatory – and said:

'What do you and Danny talk about all through the night?' Invisible clawing talons followed her words even as she spoke, but it was too late. She was more nervous, considerably more nervous than she had realized. Now, all she could do as he stared at her in disbelief, was shrug and stare at him in disbelief herself. Her jaw swung open and she greedily sucked in a mouthful of air.

'Did you just ask me what do myself and Dan talk about in bed at night?' he was saying slowly. 'Is that what you just asked me?'

'It was a joke. Well . . . a sort of a joke. What I meant – What I mean is – Danny isn't exactly the talkative type is he? Well – he's not. Not with me anyway. It's just funny that's all – the way he chats away for hours to you every night . . . Look forget it. For God's sake, forget that I ever said it. It was a stupid thing to ask. I don't know what I was thinking about. I'm tired. Actually I think I've a cold or something coming on . . .' She pulled at her nose as if it might be dripping.

'Maybe something is troubling you?'

'Like what?'

'How should I know? You tell me, my lady.' He shifted his position against the dresser. She could see that he was beginning to enjoy himself and she had the impression that Eamon might enjoy himself greatly at another's expense, once he had gained the upper hand. Furthermore, she could now admit to herself, in a sweat of self-recrimination, that she had enjoyed to an extent and yes, even encouraged, by means of a bending from the waist here – a leisurely stretch there, his stealthy, scorch-eyed admiration.

'What could possibly be troubling me?' She cast him a frozen look. She wondered if perhaps Danny had told him about the night they met the McGlashen woman.

'Did you ask our Dan what we talk about?'

The possessive pronoun bothered her as it sometimes did when Ma used it.

'Of course not. It's not an issue. It only just crossed my mind there. Can't you just drop it – please?'

'You have lovely eyes.' He tilted his head to the side.

'What?'

'Your eyes . . . they're lovely. I bet they don't miss much. Just like your ears . . . So tell me, what did you hear?'

'About what?'

'About – anything.' He smiled. The wide lips parted revealing perfectly white even teeth.

'Anything . . . ?' Kitty whispered.

In slow motion he signalled the three monkeys placing his hands with overlapping fingers, before his eyes, ears and finally a finger to his lips. The brown eyes glinted with amusement. Kitty involuntarily shuddered. Then as easily as he had entrapped her, with a last sideways glance, he released her – and poured himself some fresh tea.

'I think I'll go and watch TV or something,' Kitty said, rising. Eamon smiled affably. He sat on the chair she had vacated.

'Aye, you go and do that,' he said.

*   *   *

Kitty stared in bemusement at the microwave in the corner. A film of dust skimmed the top – forgotten as it was until each time she visited. Ma O'Neill was baking again. The kitchen was warm and cosy, the air heavy with the perfume of sweet dough. It was early evening. Kitty was just back from Monica's house.

'Was our Dan with yous at all?' Ma asked.

'He came round for lunch – then he left to help some mate of his prepare a CV or some such thing.'

'Oh that's our Dan for you,' Ma said smugly.

Kitty stuck her tongue in her cheek. This family was becoming more and more civic-minded by the day. She ignored Ma's quizzical glance. Kitty knew that the woman could sense that there was something the matter, but she was damned if she was going to engage in a conversation with Ma O'Neill after her heated

162

exchange with Monica earlier. The memory made her cheeks burn.

The morning had passed pleasantly enough with Kitty playing in Monica's living room with Paul and Kevin. Then Danny arrived for lunch and told Monica about the episode with Eamon the night before and Monica nearly wet herself laughing. Kitty had glared at Danny and spent the rest of the afternoon trying to get Monica off the subject. But Monica wanted all the gory details. She kept snorting into her hand at the thought of Eamon's face.

'Oh stop it,' Kitty snapped at one point, 'it's not that funny . . .'

'Indeed then it is,' Monica spluttered back.

She was fixing two mugs of instant coffee, pouring a large shot of whiskey into both of them. Kitty had had quite enough. She could not hold her tongue a second longer.

'Monica,' she said in a quiet voice. 'I know about Eamon.'

'What about Eamon?' Monica kept her head down and stirred the coffees.

'I think you know what I mean.'

'I'm not sure that I do.'

Kitty sighed and spread her hands on the table.

'Dan told me, Monica – a long time ago – about Eamon's involvement.'

'Did he now?'

'Oh stop playing games with me Monica,' Kitty snapped, and Monica's head jerked upright. 'You might have told me yourself . . .' She broke off and waited for Monica to respond, but she was engrossed in stirring the coffees again.

Finally, Monica gave her a crooked smile and said:

'Well well.'

'Well well,' Kitty rasped. 'Is that it? Just – well well?'

'I don't know what else to say,' Monica shrugged and sipped.

'You might try saying you're sorry for not telling me yourself. God knows you had plenty of opportunities.'

'I didn't think it was my place . . . It was right that our Dan should be the one to tell you. Don't you think?'

'Maybe.'

'Besides,' Monica looked up sharply, 'it's got nothing to do

with the pair of yous has it? I mean, you've known this for some time now from what you tell me, and it doesn't seem to have bothered you much one way or the other – Eh? – So how come it's a big deal all of a sudden? You're just embarrassed about last night is all. Try to look on the funny side of it, there's a girl . . .'
She reached across and gave Kitty's hand a little squeeze but did not meet her eyes, Kitty observed.

'Listen – I told Dan that I wouldn't mention it to you or Eamon,' Kitty interrupted, trying to soften the edgy note that had crept into her voice, 'so how can you know if it's been bothering me or not?' She smiled but it felt insincere on her lips, so she frowned instead.

Monica sighed wearily and drained her mug in one swig.

'Do you *really* want to know how I know?'

'Yeah.' Kitty nodded her head. 'I have to say, Monica, I'm just a bit sick of being treated like some sort of imbecile or something, like I couldn't possibly understand because I don't belong here . . . So go on, tell me. Tell me how you can stand there and categorically say that I'm not bothered?' She broke off and bit her lip. While they had often skirted around each other in the past, it had always been with a measure of flirtation, a mutual camaraderie; but this time Kitty could sense a shaft of cold, honest anger between them that would not be forgotten so easily. Monica was chewing on her lower lip, evidently monitoring her response in advance.

'Monica?' Kitty persisted.

'Because – because it's perfectly clear – to me – to anyone – that you don't give a shit. You couldn't care less about Eamon. You couldn't care less what he does or doesn't do – you only care that it might affect you and Dan in some way . . .' The words were out in a rush. Kitty's mouth opened wide to protest as Monica hurriedly splashed more whiskey into her mug. She sipped, grimaced, then shrugged helplessly. 'Sorry,' she added.

Kitty's mouth closed. The words to protest, to deny, simply would not come. She felt as if Monica had punched her in the stomach. Monica looked at her from under the canopy of her long dark lashes. She smiled contritely.

'Sorry,' she said again. 'Look it, Kitty, don't get me wrong here

– I'm not for one minute saying that you should give a shit, why should you for Christ's sake? Look, all I'm trying to say is – well – just don't confuse things. Is all. That I'm saying. You know?'

'No. I don't know,' Kitty said frostily. 'Maybe you can explain?'

'Ah Kitty.' Monica patted her hand, and Kitty had to force herself from instinctively snatching it away. 'Let's not fall out over this. Eh? Come on, have another drop . . . Let's just forget it . . .' But Kitty's flat blank gaze urged her to continue. 'Look, when I say about confusing things – I only mean – just don't confuse any feelings you might have about Eamon himself as opposed to what he does. That's all. God knows he's not an easy man to like. And I'm his sister saying that. I know it's not much fun for you around here. But sure, it's only for a few wee days of the year, isn't it? Then, you're back in London again, the pair of yous, and you have Dan all to yourself – you know?'

Kitty shot her a look but there was no trace of irony or sarcasm in Monica's expression. Instead, her eyes appeared distinctly watery and bloodshot around the whites. She pulled her mouth down at the corners in a childish, conciliatory way, and Kitty realized that these were not the first whiskeys of the day. An image of her mother and the empty bottles came into her mind followed by a clear picture of her father's empty room, shutters closed, bed stripped, and beneath it, lying side by side, his red and black tartan slippers. She scraped back her chair and stood.

'I think I'll head away now, Monica. No no – there's no need for you to get up. I'll see you tomorrow, alright?'

She left quickly, stopping to say goodbye to Paul and Kevin in the front living room on her way. Kevin was playing with the Transformer she'd brought for him, and cast her a blistering smile which made her catch her breath sharply.

Now as she sat in the O'Neill kitchen with the yellow walls sweating condensation and the kettle whistling yet more steam into the air, she realized to her surprise that she had never really been alone with Ma O'Neill before. Her own sense of unease was clearly reciprocated; she observed the tight, shy smile on the elderly woman's lips, the intense focusing of the blue eyes on the white shell of an egg as she deftly cracked it with one hand into her waiting mixture. Kitty further realized that she had spent the

165

best part of the last fifteen minutes yawning, though she did not really feel tired. It was something she did in her mother's company too, when she felt overwhelmed or intimidated. It was as if she had to fight for her portion of air. She batted the back of her hand against her open mouth and said casually:

'I haven't seen Eamon all day . . .'

'He'll be at practice now,' Ma said, glancing at the clock.

'Practice?'

'The Choral cum what have yous Society, aye. They're not anywheres near ready this year he says . . . He'll be home for his tea any minute now.'

She smiled helplessly at Kitty then lifted one batch of scones from the oven and placed another batch inside. Kitty said:

'Is there something I can do to help?'

'Good heavens no. It's all but done now. Not at all. Sit yourself down there now and take your ease. Would you like another cup of tea?'

Kitty shook her head to a third cup. Her bladder was swollen enough already. Ma coughed and cleared her throat, placed a hand to her chest, patted it, then a self-deprecatory smile before her hand churned the mixture once more. Kitty waited. She was beginning to interpret the peculiar little rituals of this family. Things – observations, statements, questions – had to be preceded by coughs and nose pulls and that certain giveaway – the nifty foot shuffle. Ma stabbed a finger toward a newspaper beside Kitty.

'There's a job in it that's right up our Dan's street.'

'Is there – which one?' Kitty asked lightly. It was a local paper. The advertisement was circled. She couldn't follow its exact requirements but essentially it was something to do with the handling of civil claims in the region. She blinked, smiled sweetly and firmly placed it back on the table again.

'Eamon knows that crowd,' Ma was saying. Her hand beat faster and faster, the bowl was clamped to her side with the other hand. A couple of beads of sweat glistened on her brow. 'It was him that saw it in the first place. He was wondering if yous might be interested 'cause he could put a word in the right place . . . if ah . . . if that was the case.'

Kitty merely nodded. She did not trust herself to speak. This

166

was so obviously contrived between them all, it would not have surprised her in the least to learn that Danny had already attended an interview. Ma's mixture had long submitted itself into a creamy smooth batter but she continued to whisk, lifting gobs with the wooden spoon and plopping them back in with a flick of her wrist. Kitty could have sworn the ear facing her had reddened with the strain of waiting for her response. She tapped her fingernails on the table for a few seconds.

'We'll have to see,' she said finally, through gritted teeth.

'It's just a thought . . .' Ma said. She began to ladle the mixture into a deep, greased tin. 'Madeira,' she added to a spot on the wall above Kitty's head.

'I might go for a breath of fresh air,' Kitty said, rising.

'Aye. You do that. Tea'll be ready in a minute. You might even meet Eamon on your travels.'

Kitty nodded absently and did not add that she had precisely that intention in mind. She blundered from the kitchen with an inward sigh of relief. She pulled her coat on and hissed, bracing herself against the surge of cold, crisp air beyond the hallway. Along the street, somebody, a woman, appeared to recognize her and nodded a greeting. Kitty nodded in return. She stopped at the corner of the street and cupped her hands around a match to light a cigarette. She had already figured in advance from which direction Eamon would approach, she knew that he was on foot because his white car was parked in its usual place across the road. Even as she waited she saw his broad shoulders hunched against the wind, heading in her direction. She inhaled deeply and tapped a foot on the pavement. Out of the corner of her eye she thought for a moment that she had seen a shadow, small and thin, flickering within an alleyway behind her back. She turned quickly and stamped her foot at the enquiring cat, which hesitated, back arched, then sped away into the darkness.

Her hands were trembling. There was still time to simply say hello and pass him by as though she were just taking a walk. She had to close her eyes and breathe in deeply to fight the temptation. But then she thought of Danny, and remembered why she was standing here, in the freezing cold, with buckling legs, watching a man approach with whom the very idea of confrontation made a slow, agonizing death by strychnine seem the lesser of two evils.

He was standing in front of her, staring for a moment from behind his raised coat collar as if checking her identity. She pulled on her cigarette and fixed her face into a smile of recognition. He did not return her smile.

'Hello, Eamon.'

'Hello yourself.'

'I thought I might catch you.'

'Aye?'

'At least I hoped I might.'

'Well – you've caught me . . .'

He took a step nearer and Kitty experienced that same sensation she sometimes felt in the O'Neill kitchen. It was as though her breathing space was violated – she blew a stream of smoke directly at him to see if she could make him retreat a little, but he merely blinked and stood there waiting with his hands scrunched around his collar. Slowly, his face creased into a wide, generous smile.

'I wanted to have a word with you.' Kitty flinched inwardly at the high, reedy note in her voice.

The smile remained fixed on his lips. He raised his brows and made a tiny spreading gesture with his forefingers, urging her to continue.

Kitty cleared her throat. The new insolent look in his eyes still persisted from last night. Before, his glances had always been covert and cursory; she wondered how long she would have to endure this somehow – anatomical – study. Her fists clenched.

'About last night . . .' she began.

'What about it?' he cut across her. 'You've already apologised.'

'I know – but I kind of got the impression that you . . . that you . . .' Her hands flailed uselessly in the air.

'That I what?' he said thoughtfully, pulling at his full lower lip with a thumb and forefinger.

'Well. I just thought we should talk . . .'

'Uh-huh.' His eyes did not flicker from hers for an instant. 'What's the matter, eh? What's really bothering you – afraid you haven't got our Dan as tightly tied up in your knickers as you thought you had, mmm?'

'What's that supposed to mean?'

'You know.'

'No, I don't know.' She had to steady her voice. 'Tell me.'

'I've seen your type before – you think you can own people.'

'Oh for Christ's sake.' Kitty spat out her cigarette, 'You've been watching too many old Bogart movies – who do you think you are?'

He simply smiled and tilted his head slightly.

'You do have fine Fenian eyes I'll say that for you,' he said.

'What? What are you talking about now?'

'Only that some might be inclined to trust you. But I wouldn't. Not as far as I could throw you, my little princess.'

Kitty gasped audibly. He was too slippery, too unpredictable, and she was floundering badly, suddenly aware that they had unconsciously begun to circle each other. She backed away, but he sidestepped her and she almost stumbled off the pavement. A slight drizzle clung in beads to the wool of his grey overcoat.

'Tell me something,' he was saying, affably enough but his eyes pinned her, 'if everything is so rosy in the garden – what's the little princess so worried about? Could it be, I ask myself, that she's losing her grip?'

'You mean on Danny? I wasn't aware that I had a "grip". Stupid of me I know, but here I was thinking that we loved each other . . . But I don't think you can understand that, Eamon, can you? And if you call me a princess again I'll knee you in the balls.' She observed his deep flush with satisfaction. A dull ruddy flush that crept slowly up from his neck and stayed on his cheeks as he returned her gaze. She watched him visibly compose himself, knowing that she had scored a bitter little victory for the moment. She had tapped into something, a seam that she would exploit if necessary.

'Listen.' He was stony-faced now. 'I'm a wee bit confused here – feel free to enlighten me won't you? But if the two of yous are so in love, how come you are here bugging me now eh? What are you so worried about that you can't ask your lov-er?' He said the word as though it caused the bile to rise in his throat.

'I think you know,' she said quietly.

He moved so quickly she had to jerk her head back as his

169

clenched jaw thrust toward her face. She could feel his cold breath on her cheeks.

'Why don't you just spit it out – say it right out – whatever it is that's troubling you. Mmm?'

That was too naked – he was asking her to step over the line, seducing her into his territory. She had no time to calculate in advance the long-term effects of stepping bravely, and perhaps blindly, onto his turf. He waited, a knowing little smile etched on his lips.

'Danny.' She shrugged. 'I want you to leave him alone, that's all I want. He's all I want.'

He stepped back, thrusting his hands deeply into his pockets.

'I thought you had him,' he said.

'Yes. Yes but . . .'

'. . . But nothing,' he raised a hand to cut across her. 'You've got your prince, now off with yous and live happily ever after. Mind your step and stick to the dance floor you know or you might find those dainty glass slippers of yours covered in all sorts of shit, and that would be a shame . . .'

'. . . Look I don't know what you're playing at – looking for jobs here for Danny, insisting that he phones you from a phone box, sending for him whenever you feel like it, but I want it to stop, do you hear me? I don't like people –' She waved a hand in the air. '– people – manipulating things behind my back. Alright? That's all I wanted to say.' She knew it was a mistake but she could not stop herself, 'You couldn't keep Danny forever you know. He's not your little boy . . .'

'. . . No, he's your little boy – I thought you'd established that,' he spat. She saw that he was trembling. Quivering fingers, raw with cold, tugged at his collar again. His voice through the cloth was muffled and so low she had to strain to hear him.

'If it means so much to you I'll phone the flat from now on, alright?'

'Look, I'm sorry,' she began, now that she could afford a little magnanimity again. 'I know Dan means a lot to you . . .' She would have gone on with a spiel that was already beginning to feel poisonous in her mouth, but he was glaring past her over her shoulder. She quickly turned.

170

A young lad of about twelve or thirteen stood shivering directly behind her. He must have crept out of the shadowy alleyway behind. He had a childish face, younger looking than his years, she surmised. Eamon appeared to be transfixed by the freckled, dark-eyed apparition.

'What . . . Who . . .' Kitty looked at each of them in confusion, but they ignored her. She fixed her gaze again on the boy. He had a hard face, she saw now. Bony with slitted eyes and a mouth curled down into a sneer. It was as if the taut white skin stretched like over-rolled pastry across a skull that threatened to break through. He did not look her way but kept his eyes trained on Eamon. When he moved past her to approach Eamon, she saw that he walked with a distinct limp.

Eamon had fixed his expression into a bland mask of indifference, but she saw the shifting, nervous quality in his eyes. He kept his arms up in front of his torso, the hands idly flipping the corners of his collar up and down. The boy opened his mouth, he had to swallow hard. Kitty might not have been there.

'They done my legs, you cunt,' the boy finally spat at Eamon.

'I heard,' Eamon said. His eyes darted over quickly toward Kitty.

'Both of 'em.'

'Aye.' Eamon nodded.

'I can't run no more,' the boy whined plaintively.

'You should have thought of that,' Eamon said brusquely, and stretched out an arm in Kitty's direction to draw her away from this exchange. The boy slowly turned and gazed at her, a cloudiness evaporating in his squinched-up brown eyes, she realized, as he hissed an intake of breath, that he was in great pain.

Eamon was evidently caught in a dilemma. Kitty sensed that he wanted to say something to the boy – he was biting his tongue not wishing to speak in front of her. The boy sensed his discomfort too because he turned to her and pointed down at his thighs.

'The cunts done me legs,' he said to Kitty.

'Right, that's enough,' Eamon barked. 'Get away home with you now. Your poor mother . . .'

'. . . My mother?' the boy screeched. 'You're talking to me about *my* mother? After what you done?'

Eamon advanced and the boy retreated slightly, but only to put Kitty between himself and Eamon.

'Look, Liam.' Eamon's tone was reasonable, the teacher addressing an overwrought pupil. 'Liam, whatever has happened to you – you've only got yourself to blame . . . Listen to me now, there's a good lad – you were lucky. Now, now, hear me out . . . You were lucky, from what I heard, far enough away from the knees . . .' He nodded his head and widened his eyes as if encouraging Liam to agree with him. 'Flesh only eh? You'll be running in no time. And who do you think you can thank for that. Eh, Liam? You've gone a wee bit astray is all, lad. Once you've got your head together you'll be fine. Believe me. Now stay out of trouble for God's sake. Stay on the right side of the tracks and I'll continue to keep my eye out for you. Fairer than that I can't say. Look, look at me, Liam – I'm on your side – don't keep hanging around here like this. I'm a patient man but . . .' Eamon let his hands drop to his sides. His expression was benevolent. The gentle tone of his voice appeared to affect the boy and it seemed to Kitty that he crumpled before her eyes; just a flimsy construction of brittle sticks held together by a fake leather jacket. His head hung limply, a drooping sickly growth protruding out above the twigs. She had never seen anything quite so piteous.

'Are you alright?' she whispered. When she moved toward him he flinched and stepped backwards. He was crying. Fat, rolling tears plopped onto the ground around his sneakers. He wiped the back of his wrist under his dripping nose. But it was his shoulders, the unbearable concave boniness of them heaving up and down that caused her to expel a loud breath and glance away. Eamon looked up at the starless sky, his mouth set into a rigid line while his hands rubbed endlessly together in front of him.

'We . . .' the boy spluttered, '. . . we – was going to America.'

'Maybe you can still go to America,' Kitty offered gently, knowing that she sounded ridiculous, but she felt compelled to say something, anything, that might console him. He looked up, his eyes slowly focusing on her. There was something terrible living in the dark pupils.

'How?' he choked.

'Maybe when you're older . . .'

The boy bit into his lower lip so fiercely she thought she could see a speck of blood. She quickly reached out and stroked the bony cheek. This time he did not flinch, he just stood there gazing back at her with a hungry look in his eyes, feeding on her pity. For a brief moment it was as though Eamon had disappeared altogether. There was only her and the boy.

'My Da . . .' he said, as if that was all that was required to make her understand. Kitty shook her head slightly, then she followed the path of his brown eyes until they rested on Eamon's rigid figure. The boy lifted his head once, then dropped it again.

'Liam . . .' Eamon said.

'My Da,' the boy repeated.

'Eamon? Eamon is your Da – is that it, Liam? Is that what you're trying to tell me?'

Eamon hissed and moved toward them. The boy dodged him but his eyes did not waver from Kitty's.

'My Da,' he screamed suddenly. 'He – him – that fucking cunt there – he killed my Da . . . He sent them . . . The bastards. The bastards!' He threw his head back and bellowed up at the sky wrapped in a freezing fog above them. A car swished past, the occupant staring straight ahead, oblivious to them.

'C'mon Kitty, let's go, he's hysterical.' Eamon had her by the elbow. She shook him off and reached toward the boy again.

'Let me go!' she cried out to Eamon but the boy was limping backwards.

'In my arms – in my own two fucking arms.' He held out his bony hands, staring at them as he stumbled back toward the alleyway.

Kitty could not move; Eamon had pinned her to him by the waist.

'Let's go,' he hissed in her ear. 'Let's go – Now.'

Kitty struggled, but his grip tightened. He was propelling her along the street. She looked around instinctively for someone to call out to, but there was nobody around. The street was deserted. And when she glanced back toward the alleyway the boy was gone.

173

At the door, Eamon finally relinquished his hold.

'Get a grip on yourself,' he barked.

'Oh fuck off,' she said, rushing through the opened door and into the kitchen beyond.

Danny and his mother looked up quickly when she tore through the doorway. Danny jumped to his feet. She stood there panting for a moment staring blankly ahead.

'Kit!' Danny cried. 'What is it? What's the matter?'

She opened her mouth to speak but something in the casual way that Ma raised her mug to her mouth stopped her in her tracks. Eamon stood closely behind her.

'The Fogarty lad again,' she heard him say. Ma nodded and sipped.

'What? What about him?' Danny was saying.

Kitty slowly turned to face Eamon. Fogarty – that was the name of the lad the McGlashen woman had been talking about in the pub . . . She wanted to be sick.

'Get – out – of – my – way,' she said. He looked toward his mother then stepped to the side.

'Kitty – where are you going?' Danny was about to move after her but his mother's hand had encircled his wrist.

'To bed. I'm going to bed.'

'Let her be. Let her be. She's upset.' Ma's hushed voice drifted out into the hallway behind her. Kitty ran upstairs and slammed the bedroom door so forcefully the window rattled in its frame for a long time afterwards.

She fell on the bed and listened in the darkness to their muted voices in the kitchen. Danny was shouting something at Eamon who argued for a while then banged his way through the hallway and out the front door. Kitty could hear Ma's voice droning on to Danny. She wanted the night to pass, just fade away and tomorrow she would leave. She could not shake the boy's face from her mind. The memory made her want to retch.

The front door opened and closed quietly again and she realized that Danny had gone out. His insensitivity was nothing new, but somehow this time she was truly shocked. It was not just insensitivity this time, it was callous, it was perverse. She turned her head and began to cry quietly into the pillow.

Some time later, she heard the door again, and the sound of Danny's feet running up the stairs. She could sense his hand hesitating on the doorknob for a second before he gently prised the door open. She sat up quickly. He put a finger to his lips and sat beside her, she could just make out his silhouette in the darkness.

'Are you alright?' he asked.

'What do you think?'

She heard something rattle. Danny's hand closed over hers, he placed something in her curled palm.

'Here,' he urged, 'swallow these. I got them from Monica. Valium. It will help you sleep.'

'I don't want them.' But she felt a sense of shame at her relief that he had not gone to the Snooker Hall after all.

'You've had a big shock I know, Kit.' He stood and scuffed the carpet with the top of his shoes. 'I . . .'

'. . . I don't want to discuss it,' she interjected.

'Eamon told me what happened,' he persisted.

'Did he? Did he indeed?'

'You've got to understand . . .'

'. . . Oh I understand alright. Believe me, I do understand.'

'It's not as simple as – as the boy made out.' He sat beside her again, slumping forward with his head in his hands. She felt that unbearable pity creep up on her again. It was insidious, and she turned on her side away from him.

'I'm not lying here thinking that it's "simple",' she said quietly.

'Kitty,' he began, drawing his hands down his face, 'Kit – I'm not saying if what the boy thinks is right or wrong – you can make your own mind up on that – what I am saying – what I want to say is – is . . .' He turned and leaned across to whisper in her ear. His hand stroked her wet cheeks in an upward motion with his knuckles until his fingers enmeshed in her hair. She wanted to brush him away, but the soothing, fanning quality of his breath on her cheek and the scent of him was so familiar, so comforting, she could not bring herself to do it.

'. . . Is this . . .' he was whispering. 'That's here. All that shit – it's here, Kitty. It has nothing to do with us. You and me. We won't come here again if that makes you feel a bit better – at least not together. Alright? Alright Kit?'

'You –' She felt a huge sob escape her lips, 'You didn't see his eyes, Dan . . .'

'Shhh. I know. I know Kit. I'm sorry. Really, I am. It should never have happened.'

'What – What should never have happened?'

'You meeting that lad like that.'

'Not to mention Eamon murdering his father, I suppose?'

'You don't know that.'

'He told me. The boy told me. Why should he lie?'

Danny sighed heavily. He rubbed his palms along his thighs.

'Did he say that, Kitty – did he say that he actually *saw* Eamon . . . do it?'

'He said that Eamon had "sent" the bastards who did it. That sounds clear enough to me . . . I'm not in the mood for wordgames, Dan. You know as well as I do that it's the truth. Don't you?'

'Maybe.' Danny hung his head. 'I did tell you about Eamon though. I mean you didn't think the reality would be pretty, did you? I'm not making excuses or anything for him – but, like I said before, you'd have to live here to understand . . . Eamon does a lot of good work for this community. Sure – laugh if you want to – but there are a lot of old dears out there tonight who can sleep a little bit easier in their beds because of the likes of our Eamon.'

'And what about the little boys crying in their beds for their fathers because of the likes of "your" Eamon? It's too easy to justify, Danny. I can't believe you don't see it that way. I can't believe you could be so blind.'

'Kitty – just wait up a second here – Believe me, I do understand your natural reaction. I'd feel the same way myself if I saw that lad, or listened to him. I'm sure I would. But you have to understand that what's blindness to one person can be seeing clearly to another. Sure, that's simplifying it, I know, but let me tell you something . . . just listen, please . . . That Fogarty lad's father was a tout – an informer – he knew what he was doing, he took his chances, maybe he should have thought about his son a bit more . . . and the consequences. Everyone living here is playing some sort of balancing act, every day. It's the way it is.

That lad would be in his grave by now if it weren't for Eamon – he's looked out for him, kept an eye on him. You won't believe this but Eamon cares about Liam Fogarty. He wants to see that the lad turns out alright . . .'

'. . . Alright?' Kitty shrieked incredulously.

'Aye. Alright. He's been running around with the wrong people. Older lads. A bad lot. I tell you, if Eamon wasn't looking out for him . . .' He stopped and shrugged.

'And how do you know all of this?' Kitty whispered.

'Ma's just told me.'

'I see.'

'Kitty – look . . .'

'No. Stop Dan. I think I've had enough for one night . . . I don't know where my brain's been. Maybe Monica's right and I don't give a shit . . .' She broke off into a deep sigh. 'I don't know. I don't know what to think. Just let me alone for a while, okay?'

'I'd rather stay with you for a while.'

'No – please. Just go. We can talk in the morning. Right now I feel like my head is going to burst.'

He hesitated for a moment then leaned forward to kiss her cheek. She did not move. He clicked the door shut behind him and she listened to his movements in the room next door, the thunk-thunk of his shoes hitting the floor, flick of the lightswitch, the creaking of his bed, a toss, a turn, until he was comfortable – then, silence.

A silence that was only punctuated hours later by the sound of Eamon's return and low murmurs from the kitchen. A little while later she heard the creak of floorboards outside the door, Eamon first, Ma soon after. Ma O'Neill gave a little cough on the landing and for a second, Kitty experienced an overwhelming compulsion to rush from the room with her head down, aimed at the woman's soft underbelly. The thought gave her a moment's satisfaction.

She lay for further hours listening to the sound of Danny and Eamon breathing next door and the sound, or so it seemed, of sleep winging past her ears on its way to somebody else. Already, she realized, she was transferring her pity, her protective response from the boy to Danny. She almost smiled at the thought – if he

177

did not need her so much, she might not need him at all. But, she decided, she had always known that. And all the analyses in the world, revisions, deductions and additions, would not make a blind bit of difference to her feelings for him – not even a pain in a boy's eyes that was so hot and immediate, she felt that it had seared her too. Not even that. She thought her heart must be a lumpen, leaden thing. She felt ashamed.

It was still pitch black when she creaked her way down the stairs to the living room. She stoked a few barely flickering embers in the fire and threw some turf on, blowing the embers into life with her breath. She found her book and settled down beside the fire; it cast just enough light for her to read without switching on a lamp. Within moments her eyelids were heavy, stinging when upper eyelash corresponded with lower lash. She curled up on the lumpy sofa and stared into the dancing flames through slitted eyes.

The room was sweltering when she awoke. A crack of watery morning light sliced through a gap where the curtains should have met. She was bathed in sweat, her mouth felt desert dry. Then she saw Eamon sprawled on a chair in the gloomy recess beside the fire. He was unshaven, the collar of his shirt standing up on one side, a lock of pewter hair grazed his forehead. Kitty had never seen him less than immaculately presented before, and his shabbiness was as disquieting as his presence. When he noticed her movement she thought she saw the full pink lips draw back into an uneasy smile. His eyes were lost in the shadows, but two glints of orange light reflected the dying embers of the fire.

'Awake?' he asked softly.

It was only then she noticed the drifts of smoke around him.

'I didn't know you smoked,' she said.

'I don't . . . At least I haven't for years. Filthy habit. I took one of yours. I hope you don't mind.'

Kitty peered through the gloom. He was holding the cigarette high in the air, tip pointing upwards, as a woman would. When he pulled on it his lips pursed too much and too low down on the filter.

'No. I don't mind.'

'I couldn't sleep either,' he shrugged.

'Your conscience troubling you?'

He sucked deeply on the cigarette. She could not see his face clearly.

'My conscience is content with itself,' he said. 'Not as the conscience of an angel, or a horse, but as the conscience of a man.'

'Shakespeare?' she asked, surprised.

'No. Montaigne.'

Kitty had to suppress a bitter laugh. Montaigne. How many nights had she sat reading Montaigne to her father? She shook her head.

'There's a lot you don't know about me,' he was saying.

'I'm not sure that I'd want to.'

'That's fair enough – you've got guts, I'll give you that.'

'And fine Fenian eyes?'

'Yes. And fine Fenian eyes.'

'Quite the charmer, aren't you – when you want to be.'

'So I've been told.'

Kitty shifted up on the sofa.

'What do you want from me? Why are you sitting there?'

'Who says I want anything?' He sounded offended.

'Oh you want something alright.'

'I just want to talk to you – that's all.' He leaned forward so that she could see his face; dark shadows like bruises scored the soft flesh beneath his eyes.

'That boy . . .' he began.

'. . . I don't want to discuss him.'

'Just listen to me for a second – please –' He raised a hand to prevent her leaving. She sank back. 'Believe me, I do understand how – how disturbing your encounter with him might have been . . .'

Kitty snorted but he ignored her.

'But you can't know the damage his father did,' he continued, 'to a lot of good people . . . If you think I'm some sort of a monster, then you're entitled to think that.'

Kitty felt an eerie calm descend on her. She continued to stare into the fire while he watched her keenly. She shook her head slowly. He was afraid, she realized. Afraid of her response to last night.

'You're worried, aren't you?' she said slowly. 'You don't really give a shit about what I might think – you're just worried about what I might say . . .'

He emerged from the shadows again. Their eyes locked.

'Aye,' he said. 'That I am. Don't misunderstand – you could talk to anyone you like and nothing, do you hear me, nothing will happen to me . . . Are you following me? Eh? But the boy – he's vulnerable. He's on shaky ground. If anyone was to talk to him – well, there's no knowing what he might say – Are you following all this? . . . Good. And if the boy talks – he'll be seeing his Da a lot quicker than he thought. Eh? And I like him. Oh aye, smile if you want . . . Do you understand me now? Are you sure?'

Kitty wanted to be violently sick. She could feel a dry retch creeping up her throat. The hate she felt for this man felt like a sickness. She wished she could just close her eyes, open them, and he would be gone. Gone forever from their lives.

'Get out,' she said.

He rose slowly rubbing his hands along his thighs. He moved toward the door.

'Wait . . .' She could not bring herself to admit the intimacy of saying his name aloud.

'Aye?' He paused with his hand curling around the doorknob. He kept his back to her.

'This is how it happens,' she said, 'how innocent people get mixed up in your bloody war – like that boy last night.'

'There are no innocents,' he said stiffly.

'One more thing – just answer me this – the boy, as long as I live I don't think I'll ever forget his eyes. What was in them . . . What – What did you see . . . ?'

His hand tightened around the knob, he glanced back over his shoulder and shrugged.

'My own – I suppose,' he said and quickly left the room.

The scrunched-up butt of his cigarette still smouldered in the ashtray. She reached across and stubbed it out.

March

She sat up in bed staring around – terrified – then realized that it was her own scream which had woken her. She checked the bedside clock – three in the morning. Instinctively, she reached out an arm toward Danny's side of the bed but it groped at empty space. Then Kitty remembered.

She swung her legs to the side of the bed and sat with her head caught between her hands, elbows resting on her spread knees. It was that dream again, the one that had plagued her for the last few months. It never changed, never offered anything new in the slightest which might have made it more decipherable. She lay down again with a groan, lit a cigarette and watched the plumes of blue-grey smoke spiral up toward the ceiling. The cigarette was clamped between her lips; she inhaled and exhaled, a long drooping quiver of ash threatening to fall with every breath. When it did cleave in two, the top half drifting down, she ignored the spread ashes and blinked. She did not want to switch the light on.

The dream was so clear, if she closed her eyes she could still see the images – stark and precise like a reel of high definition film.

She was in a darkened room. A vast room lit only by the white, flat light of a full moon outside. The nuns stood outside the window looking in, with milkpails in their hands. The clattering sound they made cut through the otherwise silent night. Danny knelt above her bathed in shadowy moonlight, like a subject in a Caravaggio painting, arms outstretched – crosslike. Kitty's limbs entwined around his hips. It was as though she were impaled by him as she lay on the crisp white sheet, arms extended above her head. He did not move or look down at her. The milk buckets rattled. She glanced toward the window. The nuns were still watching. Danny did not move. She pressed him into her with her heels but he did not plunge, he remained impassive with his head thrown back, the sinewy lines of his neck thrown into relief. The nuns whispered. Kitty strained but could not hear them.

A face by the window, blank at first and featureless, slowly settled into the honed, sharp-nosed countenance of Sr Aquinas. She was silently mouthing something. Then she smiled beatifically at Kitty, who stared again toward Danny. The light on him was solid and did not flicker. In the dream, yet outside the dream, she remarked how real he appeared. And how beautiful. 'This is a dream,' she said to Aquinas.

Aquinas, the nun who had found Kitty's books, the reading list prescribed by her father the doctor which went far beyond the constrained ambits of Aquinas's English curriculum. Aquinas of the bleach-dipped fingernails filed to razor sharp points, of the shiny nose, compressed lips and tight-stretched skin which attested to soap each morning and soap each night. She had suggested that perhaps *Lady Chatterley's Lover* and *Lolita* might wait until after Kitty was married, then flushed in misery when Kitty had laughed and agreed that it was true – the books were not suitable for nuns.

The nun's pointed face faded for a moment; Kitty had to concentrate on bringing her back, forming her from the nothingness outside. And there she was again, her breath fanning out in soft pulsating clouds against the latticed windowpanes. She was mouthing something again. What was she saying?

'Maybe it's too big for you.' That was it. And Kitty laughed back – 'No. No. It fits.' Then she remembered the occasion when she had first heard those words.

They had been discussing theology. Saints and sinners, the language of saints and sinners; frail, wretched, humble – both sides. That evening Kitty had been unnecessarily cruel as she plucked at the skeins of a lifetime's vocation; savagely, heedlessly, until she had unravelled the simple tenets of the nun's beliefs to her own satisfaction without positing a single viewpoint herself. And it was then, as she closed her eyes to the pain she had so casually inflicted, that Aquinas had turned to her and said quietly – 'Maybe it's too big for you . . .'

She wanted to say that she was truly sorry but Aquinas was fading again. And Danny too, above her, had begun to change. The clear contours of his torso wavered in the dim light, the outstretched arms seemed to attenuate, the wiry body to cave in upon itself until the head, still Danny's, loomed large and grotesque over a thin and bony frame. Then, the head too began to metamorphose: it shuddered for a moment on its frail neck, the wavy thick hair replaced by a shining, dark cap beneath which a splattering of freckles erupted across the bridge of a stubby nose, the widened, dark, staring eyes, no longer Danny's suddenly looked down at her – it was the boy.

Now, she stubbed her cigarette out and stooped along the narrow corridor of the flat to the kitchen, drank a glass of water and went into the living room. She turned a lamp on by the new stereo and searched for some soothing music. Settling on Brahms, she threw herself down on the sofa and pulled the cushions to her. Her head ached.

Outside it was raining. She stared at the window, registering each individual trickle down the panes. The flats opposite looked as if she were viewing them through a prism; every raindrop held a miniature streetlight. Through slitted eyes the beads shone like tiny glittering gems. She opened her eyes wide again and focused on one rivulet. It descended slowly at first from the top pane, gathering tributaries on the way down until it hovered, swollen and expectant about midway through the journey then plunged the rest of the way so quickly she missed the home run and felt curiously disappointed.

The sound of the violins was a bittersweet and mellow cadence, rising and falling in time with her breathing. As she listened and tried to expel the memory of the dream and all the other disparate thoughts that had tumbled one over the other within her head for the past few sleepless nights, she felt that she would not be surprised in the slightest, to learn that the world had ended, and she alone had survived. A desert of time stretched ahead, until Danny's return.

She recalled their fight three days ago when he insisted that he was going home for Easter. It was only one fight amongst the many they had endured since their return from Belfast after Christmas, but it was the worst. She had refused to go with him and begged him, this once, not to go.

'Look, if you won't come with me, why don't you go home too for Christ's sake?' He was shouting by that time, riffling his fingers through his hair with exasperation.

'Because – I can't,' she screamed in response. 'You know bloody well that I can't. She won't have me.'

'She's your mother. Your mother, Kitty . . . Fuck it . . . I can't stand this . . . You say you can't go home – you won't come with me – What do you want? What – do – you – want – from – me?'

She was crying then. They were both worn out from the ongoing battles since December. Eamon, true to his word, had begun to call Danny at the flat and every time Kitty answered she was so cold and monosyllabic, Danny took issue with her rudeness as he perceived it. When Eamon sent a couple of cuttings from the local newspaper advertising jobs suitable for Danny, she exploded and ripped them up before he could even read them. Her work was suffering too. A fortnight past, she had been called in for a 'chat' but she knew that she was in trouble. Danny suggested that maybe it was a good thing, maybe it was time for them to move on. She understood that 'on' meant 'back' in his vocabulary – back to Belfast. His family had begun to take the shape of some dark, inexorable magnet. Even her weekly telephone chats with Monica had decelerated to the odd forced and stiff call, endured more from force of habit than from any real desire to communicate. Apart from Danny, Kitty could not help but feel more and more isolated, and she had begun to wonder if, perhaps, it really was time to call it a day with that relationship too – but then she would catch the confused, haunted expression in his gaze as he looked at her – and all the old feelings would come rushing back so that she alternated in a flux of love and resentment, back and forth, day by day, night after night. It was a neverending oscillation, the pained effects of which were clearly etched on both their faces.

And when he left, three mornings ago, with his eyes studiously avoiding hers, she had wondered if anything, anything at all, could be worth this cold, empty toll it exacted. But gazing around the yellow walls of the flat, the all but dead plants and the coffee-stained sofa, she was pragmatic enough to know that there was nothing else. Nothing left of her old life. And at that moment, she experienced a longing so great for her own home, it left her standing by the living room window, motionless for hours, staring out at the bleak slate rooftops across the street and the blur of colours down below from the passing cars of strangers.

The same window, she now realized, had come to represent a contradiction, a four-paned paradox, permitting her, on the one hand, a glimpse of life outside and beyond their flat, while on the other hand, it compounded with its sterile unchanging view, her seclusion.

The music stopped. She lay still for a while and listened instead to the sound of an infrequent car swishing through the rainswept streets below. When the silence grew too intense, she got up and flipped the tape over.

There was little point now in trying to sleep – she knew that it would be a physical impossibility – so she went to the bathroom and splashed cold water on her face, enjoying the icy feel of it against her skin. She opened the mirrored door of the little cabinet above the sink and studied for the tenth time at least, the instructions on the box she had purchased earlier that day. She ripped the box open and began to lay everything out in preparation for the morning.

*   *   *

The following day was a Sunday. Kitty sat around waiting for Danny to call from a phonebox. She had been tempted to run out to get a newspaper and some milk but she was afraid that she would miss his call, so she sat by the phone, staring at the little glass phial with the blue-tipped stick within. Her first emotion was one of blind panic – for so many reasons, now was not the best of times to discover that she was pregnant. But as the day wore on she got quite used to the idea and even found herself giggling a couple of times at the thought of Danny's reaction. She imagined that he would be terrified at first, then like her, he would find the prospect more and more attractive. Perhaps the timing was really fortuitous in some respects in that it would force decisions which had been pushed into the background for the last few months.

She lifted the receiver to call her mother; she was desperate to tell someone, then decided against. Eleanor's predictably dry reaction was not what she needed while her own feelings were still so mixed up. Throughout the day she paced up and down the length of the living room, afraid to allow herself to grow too happy in case Danny's reaction was negative. If that was the case, she decided that she would not hesitate to abort. There was every possibility that he would return this time and tell her that Eamon had managed to get employment for him in Belfast – she had been deeply suspicious about this Easter trip from the outset.

The course of the day presented her with a series of mini quandaries – should she smoke or not – what about caffeine – why wasn't she feeling sick yet? It felt good to be concentrating on something other than Danny's absence. She began to feel quite hopeful and scrunched her cigarettes into the bin, retrieving a butt minutes later when the hopeful mood evaporated for another while, until her eyes began to rove around the flat, mentally redecorating. It would suffice for a while until they found a bigger place with a small room for a cot. The thought of a cot made her heart give a little flip again. She was passing the point of no return, she realized, once she began to rattle names off, trying them out for sound.

It was growing dark outside and still Danny had not called. She decided to call Monica, who could get a message to Danny to call Kitty urgently. He was probably in the bloody Snooker Hall. She imagined the wariness in his voice when he would call and then the stunned silence when she told him. For the first time in months, Kitty felt as if she had a sense of purpose again – something to aim toward. She quickly tapped out the digits, Monica's phone rang for what seemed hours before she answered.

'Monica – is that you?'

'Kitty . . . How're you doing girl?'

'Fine. Fine . . . listen can you . . .'

'. . . Hold on a second, Kitty,' Monica interrupted. There was so much background noise she was shouting into the receiver and Kitty had to hold her end away from her ear. Monica returned. 'Can you hear all the commotion going on behind me? I think I'm losing my head and so I am. Every toy in the house is out on the kitchen floor – I just this second tripped over your bloody Transformer – on the way to the phone. You should see the state of the place, bits of half melty Easter eggs all over the sofa . . .'

Kitty laughed politely. She had forgotten that it was Easter Sunday.

'I'll let you get on with it – Listen, if you could just do me a favour . . .'

But Monica was away from the phone again, laughing and bawling something to her boys. Kitty listened patiently.

'Paul! Kevin!' Monica was roaring. 'Get off your Uncle's back – NOW – d'you hear me. Eamon – that's my one good saucepan, in the name of God . . .' She addressed the receiver again. 'Sorry, Kitty. You just wouldn't believe the madness here today. As I'm talking to you, Eamon's playing the "shredder" or something with my good saucepan on his head, my lads are the turtles and our Dan . . . Jesus, you should see him.' She broke off into a wheezy laugh. 'The lads insisted that he be April O'Neill or some such a one. Anyways, they've done him up in my skirt and high heels and his face is covered in make-up. Actually, I have to say, it quite suits him . . . I'd be having my doubts about him if I were you and so I would Kitty . . .'

'Danny's there?'

'Oh aye. Sure they all came over at midday for the lunch. It's a shame you didn't come yourself this time – Dan says you're working too hard. You should learn to relax a bit more, Kitty. No job's worth spending the holidays working all alone . . . Kitty? Are you still there? Did you hear what I said?'

Kitty swallowed hard. It was inconceivable that Danny had been there, all afternoon, with access to a phone and he had not bothered to call her. Yet, she had to believe it. In her mind, she formed a clear picture of the scene in Monica's kitchen. She saw Danny pulling guilty faces at Monica as he waited for the phone; Ma O'Neill at the kitchen table, oblivious to the noise, calmly folding the Sunday newspaper into neat, concise quarters to read with her forefinger pinning back her glasses; and Eamon – playfully cuffing the boys, his ears burning as he listened to Monica's conversation, a smug little smile playing on his full salmon-pink lips.

'I'm here, Monica,' she managed to say finally.

'I thought we were cut off there for a sec . . . Listen, I'll get Dan for you now. Hold on . . .'

'No! Monica – I think I can smell something burning under the grill – I have to go. Just tell him to give me a ring later, alright . . . ?' She slammed the phone down just as she heard Danny's voice call her name, then she immediately lifted the receiver off the hook and as she stared at it and listened to the dial tone change to a long monotonous hum, she made her decision.

* * *

Danny called on Wednesday evening to confirm his return the following morning. The relief in his voice was palpable when she finally answered the phone. He had tried numerous times all through Monday and Tuesday evening but she let the phone ring on until the constant peals began to sound more and more desperate to her ears. He stopped trying around midnight, and then she was awakened from a few hours snatched sleep sometime just after dawn, by the insistent ringing again. She could not trust herself to speak to him for a few days. Every time she reached for the receiver, the thought of what she had done washed over her and a film of cold sweat broke out on her forehead. Then, as the phone persisted, she sat there, gazing at it through blank, unblinking eyes until it stopped and she could breathe again.

He was close to tears, she realized, as he called her name when she finally managed to pick up the phone. He said that he was going out of his mind with worry and where had she been? In a dull, flat voice she reassured him that she was alright. She would explain when she saw him.

They left it at that, and when she replaced the receiver, she sat very still for a while, gazing out the window with her hands on her lap. She tried to think of the best way to tell him, which words to use, a sentence that would help him comprehend – but there was no best way. How could she possibly explain an action to him that was incomprehensible now to herself? At the time, it was as if she were standing outside herself, a mere spectator, watching her own movements, listening to her own voice, but estranged in a way from her own actions. She could not now decide to what degree she was responsible when she made that call on Sunday night. Certainly, she had had the opportunity to stop herself in the time that elapsed, a considerable length of time, between directory enquiries and the actual dialling of the number. She could not now say that her actions had been entirely intuitive or instinctive; there had been time for speculation, time for deliberation, even for a cup of coffee and two cigarettes – but she would not admit that to Danny when she made her sordid little confession tomorrow morning. No, there was only one way to tell him and that was bluntly and without emotion. Apologies could wait until after she told him that she was pregnant.

In truth, when she had made the call, she had had no idea that just one hour later she would find herself being interrogated in her own living room. A hail of questions were directed at her by two men who looked almost comically clone-like, their eyes aglow with suspicion and hostility as one talked while the other sat back and studied her intently. They were as persistent in their questioning about Danny as they were about Eamon, and when they had questioned her motivation for calling them, she had searched her mind for something plausible or even just coherent to tell them but all she could manage was just another confused shrug. They had made their copious little notes about Eamon and the boy Liam Fogarty, and as they exchanged glances from time to time, she remembered Eamon's caution and her heart desiccated within her chest. Finally, after what seemed an age but was in reality less than an hour, they got up to leave, offering her tight smiles and reassurances that the matter would be investigated but naturally and, of course, understandably, she was to tell no one of this exchange. In particular, her boyfriend, which went without saying, but they were saying it anyway. She had closed the door behind them and staggered backwards into the living room with her hand to her mouth.

There were moments during the course of the next few days

when her mind went mercifully blank. It simply refused to think for hours on end, and she wondered if perhaps that was some sort of fail-safe mechanism it naturally possessed to prevent it from shutting down altogether. Her cognizance of her own naivety, above all, pulsed around the walls of the room like an unwelcome but persistent intruder, and the possible consequences of her actions, she could not even begin to imagine. The only thing she knew with any measure of certainty was that she would have to tell Danny. She owed him that much at least.

There was nothing she could do now but wait, as an unstoppable train of events gathered momentum around the unsuspecting O'Neill household.

*   *   *

By the time he blundered through the door on Thursday morning, first dropping his suitcase in the narrow hallway, her eyes were stinging from lack of sleep and she had little else in her head but the thought of confessing to him what she had done then slinking into the bedroom to fall into a deep dreamless slumber.

He slumped against the doorframe when he saw her sitting by the window. He appeared to hesitate for a moment before moving in her direction. She avoided his eyes.

'Dan.'

'Kitty – Kitty, for Christ's sake, what's going on? Why wouldn't you answer the bloody phone? Do you have any idea, I mean any idea what was going through my mind?'

'No. I'm sorry.'

'You're sorry?' He stopped to adjust his voice, a swallow to modulate his tone. He looked haggard. 'Listen – are you alright?'

'I'm fine. How was your trip?'

He stood in front of her. Gazing down with a slight shake of his head.

'Alright, I suppose. I mean as alright as it could be, what with your behaviour and what's happening with Eamon . . .'

She looked up.

'Eamon?'

He turned, passing his fingers through his hair.

'Yeah . . . He was picked up yesterday – for questioning. We don't know what to think, it was so sudden, so – out of the blue, you know? I would have stayed but I was worried about you . . .'

She tugged at his jeans then. He turned and looked at her. The blue gaze perplexed at first, distant and troubled, but as his eyes locked with hers she watched the cloudiness clear and his mouth opened soundlessly.

'Kitty. No.'

'I'm sorry.'

She put her hand to her mouth. He just stood there staring. She tried to utter the spiel she had practised for three days and nights now, but nothing but one solitary gagging sound could escape her compressed lips.

'I'm sorry,' she choked again.

'Jesus Holy Christ.' He grabbed at a chair and sank into it with his head in his hands. His eyes appeared strangely turquoise when he looked up. 'Why?'

She held onto the silence for a while. There really was no easy answer to that. No way to explain away her actions. She could say that she did it for them, for their future, for their unborn child; she could be more honest and tell him that her motives were instinctive, impulsive, perhaps vindictive; she could lie and say that she was struck by some more noble and humanitarian compulsion. But, holding his gaze, she realized that it did not really matter what reasons she gave, there was nothing she could say that would be comprehensible to him. She opened her mouth to say the practised line, the sentence that might bring them through this, but she felt too tired and too disgusted to prolong the charade. She sighed and shrugged. The lift of her shoulders seemed to incense him.

'Do you have the slightest idea what Eamon will do when he finds out?' he said coldly. She noticed that his voice had dropped to a whisper.

'And how will he find out, Dan?'

'When I go back of course . . .' He frowned in disbelief, 'Jesus – you didn't really think . . .'

'. . . What?'

'You didn't think –' He stopped and shook his head. 'Jesus,

191

maybe you did. Maybe you really are that blind – Kitty! Kitty –
Listen to me – you didn't think that I'd just go along with it, did
you? I mean, how naive can you be?' He stood up, kicked his
chair back and paced the room while she watched through
narrowed eyes. 'I mean – what were you thinking of? How
could you be so fucking stupid – so fucking naive? How could I
let this happen? I should have seen this a mile off. I should
have been prepared for this. Jesus!'

A strange feeling came over Kitty, similar to the night she had
made the phone call. It was as if she were a spectator. Divorced
in a way from his anger and from herself. She watched him in a
curious detached manner, knowing that she should be using the
words to excuse herself, to apologise, to mitigate – but the truth
was, she really did not feel sorry in the slightest. If anything, she
was glad that Eamon was being questioned. It was the only thing
that actually made sense in the past few months. But then he
voiced the harsh reality again:

'What about Liam Fogarty?'

'What about him?'

He cast her a contemptuous look.

'You know the danger you've put him in.'

'I wasn't thinking about him.'

'And what about me . . . ?' His voice had faded to a whisper
again.

She wanted to sleep. To close her eyes and ears and possibly
never wake up. She shifted on her chair and sent him a silent
pleading glance to make him stop, but his mouth was open again,
his feet were scuffing the carpet again, his shoulders were up so
high she could no longer see his neck.

'Kitty.'

'No. Please . . .'

'I have to go now. Listen – Listen to me – you'll have to get
these people to send you somewheres . . . Don't – don't talk –
there's no point now, just listen, for Christ's sake . . . All I ever
did was to deliver a few packages. That's all I did. So help me
God. I never asked any questions – nothing more than that – but
I can't stay now. You can see that much, can't you? I'm only
telling you this so you'll see how serious this is and see that you

have to make these people look out for you. Alright . . . ?'

'Danny . . .'

'Shut up a second – Kitty, look at me – I'm going now, alright? Watch me, I'm getting my bag and I'm going . . . Believe me when I tell you that Eamon, my brother Eamon, he won't forget . . . Most likely, nothing will happen to him with the help of God, it all depends on whatever the young lad says, but Kitty, Eamon watched his own Da die in his arms . . . Please . . . Just listen to me – His Da, Kitty. My Da. And it was because of someone like you. A tout. He won't ever forget, Kitty. Like you won't ever forget – wherever you are. So I'm telling you – now. I'm telling you the way it is . . .'

She followed him to the hall. He stood, shaking, by the door. She opened her mouth but still the words would not come.

'You know,' he was saying, 'the – the funniest thing is that I came here this morning to tell you that I was finished with all that. I told Eamon I'd had enough. I wasn't going to be a pigeon anymore. I don't know – maybe I was just being romantic or idealistic or something but I thought we might have a chance someplace else. Just you and me – together . . .'

'Wait, Danny – just wait a second . . .'

But he was opening the door. She leaped forward but he held it open, resisting her. She took a couple of steps backwards but extended her arms, feeling his body with her hands, moving her fingers up and down his chest and abdomen, and her heart twisted as she realized what she was doing – she was memorizing him. His final look was bleak and uncompromising but there was something in the velvety blue gaze that gave her a moment's consolation – he still loved her.

Whatever that was worth. She stepped back. Two words and she might have made him close the door again, but she could not say them. Not now. She said:

'I can't say goodbye – it sounds too ridiculous.'

He smiled. The slam of the door made her shudder. She listened to his footsteps down the stairs then ran to the window to look out. He was striding across the street. Someone bumped into him at the corner. He stopped and looked back towards the flat for an instant – then he was gone.

October

She walked along the street with her head down and her hands
buried deep within her pockets. At the junction with the traffic
lights she turned up right, careful not to look up in case she had
to return a greeting. It was cold. Her breath steamed out in front
of her. She opened and closed her mouth, forming imaginary
smoke rings. As she approached a large white clapboard house
she could hear the noise from within already. Her hands flexed
within the pockets, eager with anticipation, in a moment or so
they would hold him. The rest of her body tingled in a state of
expectancy too. It was always like that, as though there was a
gaping empty socket where a limb should be – a feeling of incom-
pleteness until he was attached again. Balloons with funny faces
waved in the air, tied by string to the front door knocker. She
climbed the wooden steps and looked inside the large picture
window. She gave the glass a little rap with her knuckles. A riot
of screams came tumbling out through the hallway toward her.
The door opened, a woman carrying a crying toddler shouted a
greeting and rolled her eyes at the little crowd formed behind
her. She looked half demented.

And there he was. A huge grin splitting his face. He ran at her
and she scooped him up, burying her face in the sandy curls, breathing in his sweet sugary scent. His fat little legs pedalled in midair,
he wanted to get down again. She released him but not before her
lips clung to his cheeks, making loud wet smacking sounds.

'Party bag,' he said and disappeared into the throng, returning
seconds later with his prize.

She could barely get through the niceties, the thanks and how
was its with the distracted woman, she was so anxious to be off
with him. Alone together with him skipping down the street in

front of her, looking back over his shoulder from time to time with a mad, wild look in his eyes. They had the rest of the day together. Before she could let him off she had to hold his hand for one small portion of the journey, just to get her feeling of completeness, then he could go. He skipped beside her, chatting, chatting, chatting. She wondered how it was that he did not seem to need to draw a breath. The soft pad of his hand within hers was like a covenant, a gift given in trust. She could feel each tiny bone flexing and retracting beneath the velvety surface. Sometimes when she yanked it harder than she meant to, at an intersection or turning suddenly in a store, she could feel the little wristbones pulse and elongate to accommodate her pull.

They were almost up at the intersection now. Kitty called to him and gestured with her head at the drugstore. He whirled around and came crashing back at her, head down, hands flying out behind him – a plane. She closed her eyes and thought of his teeth smashing against concrete if he fell headfirst, but she did not say anything; every day carried a thousand such potential disasters.

The face of the woman behind the drugstore counter would have appeared friendly enough except for the small purse of her mouth and the constant shift of her eyes. She possessed a proud, unmistakable perm. Tight curls that no wind could penetrate. Like many of the matrons around here, she appeared to be stuck in a Fifties' time warp; the only thing they eschewed was the winged glasses of that period, though Kitty had seen one or two of them about too. This one was impervious to the wiles of three-year-olds but for all that, Kevin did not desist from his efforts to charm. Blue eyes took her in, measured her, then drifted idly to the lollipops. He licked his lips. He would prevail on his mother in a minute, but Curls was worth a try. Her trenchant resistance to him offended his sensibilities.

Kitty picked a few items, Kevin was drifting along the candy counter, pressing his nose against the glass for all the world as though he spent his life in deprivation. He stopped by the red packages of M & M's, the stubby nose snuffling faster and louder. 'Don't you think you've had enough – you've just been to a party, for God's sake,' Kitty said, adding the red package to her purchases.

Outside, Kevin began to dance in anticipation. She pulled the bag apart. He stopped dancing.

'You can have a couple now,' she said, 'the rest when we get home okay?' She handed him a brown and a green.

'No – yellow and red,' he protested.

'They all taste the same inside, it's only colour.'

'Yellow and red,' he insisted.

She plucked out a yellow and red and gave them to him with a weary sigh. He beamed and she ruffled his hair.

'What do I get?' she asked.

'Later,' he shouted over his shoulder. He ran up the street in front of her as she reminded herself for the hundredth time to get the kiss before he got the sweets.

He was still quite short and plump, waddling ahead as fast as he could, which was not fast at all. She waited for him to stop and check on her with that excited light dancing in his eyes, and when he did she signalled him on with a nod of her head. She observed, not for the first time, how his left leg turned inwards slightly and made a mental note to bring it to the doctor's attention on her next visit.

He had been going to kindergarten for the last year. She was pleased with his progress. He knew the beginnings of words from the phonetic alphabet she had taught him herself, and he could count past twenty. So far, he did not show much of her, possessing neither her height nor leanness. His hair had a faint hint of Danny's rufescence but it was darker, though not as dark as her own. His skin still retained a shade of honey from the past summer but it was the eyes, huge and cobalt blue, fringed with ridiculously long lashes, that were most reminiscent of Danny. At times, when he gazed up at her and crinkled a smile with his eyes while keeping his thumb firmly in his mouth, she had to catch her breath and look away.

Even when they had told her about this place, and efficiently, with an almost frightening smoothness, oiled everything into sequence for her, she had still briefly entertained thoughts of ridding herself of excess baggage. Now, the very thought made her lie awake at nights with her heart palpitating, and she had to place her fingers to his mouth to check that he was breathing.

196

He refused to move into his own bed in the next room, and she did not try very hard to persuade him. Every morning brought with it a moment of intense, almost heady joy – it never abated – as she opened her eyes to two blue saucers directly above, his nose pressed against hers. Then she tickled him and he protested loudly but always came back for more. They dressed and ate breakfast together while she riffled through the newspaper, repeating over and over again through the toast clamped between her teeth – 'Don't you ever shut up – even for a minute?' And – 'Eat up, will you? We'll be late again. Just another bite, no, a big one, not that big, don't be such a smartypants . . . Yes yes, that will do. Told you you'd drop it. Oh for God's sake just eat up will you?'

There was an implicit agreement between them that he should attempt everything possible to slow her down and she should moan suitably in response while stealing little kisses from the back of his juicy neck which he brushed off with a look of disgust on his face.

They gave her a box number in London for mail which they would forward. She sent a couple of notes to Eleanor but there were no replies. She sent a photograph of Kevin a few days after his birth and that was returned, torn, without a note.

Ahead, Kevin had run into the waiting arms of a tall, broad man clad in a check shirt and jeans. It was Joe, a half-Indian married to Marge, a half-Innuit, here where everybody seemed to be half something or other. Marge looked after Kevin when he finished in kindergarten while Kitty worked in the nearby granary. The work was mind-numbingly boring. She did the wages and sent invoices ahead of the trainloads of grain shunting down the track. That was the purpose of the town, if town it might be called, a few wide wood-fronted streets. A pitstop on the highway, a trainstop with grain elevators all along the railway. The people were hard, laconic and naturally uninquisitive. She had wondered if it was the climate or the boredom that made them that way. But she was glad of it. Now that she had Kevin, she didn't need anyone else. She was not unaware that it had been that way with Danny too, but now it did not seem to matter how much love she poured into one person. Kevin was a bottomless vessel.

He was shrieking, hysterical with giggles as Joe tickled his soft fat belly, twisting him under one arm then the other as though he were no heavier than a bag of sugar. When he saw his mother laughing freely, Kevin spurred Joe into further activity with his eyes trained on her, but she had turned her face up to the sky.

'Aren't you cold?' she asked Joe. Already Kevin and herself were wrapped up in their winter coats.

'Not yet,' he said and sniffed the air. 'But winter's in.'

She caught his hastily lowered eyes. He had been glancing at her again with that faint hint of curiosity she had seen in Marge's eyes too. But they never asked a question. Neither did she ask any questions of them. She assumed they had their own history. They were the only people she knew with any degree of intimacy here, and she knew them hardly at all.

Kevin was tugging at Joe's ponytail and whining to get down. Joe released him and he began to drag his mother by the hand, anxious for the rest of his sweets. Kitty allowed herself to be dragged along. She called her goodbye over her shoulder.

'Catch you later, Cathleen,' Joe shouted, laughing.

When she did not turn up right toward their wooden apartment building, Kevin groaned. She caught his hand and hauled him toward the edge of town which was not far.

'Bo-oring,' he said.

'Just for a minute. Just a minute . . . please,' she said.

She gazed ahead. Kevin muttered under his breath and scuffed at lumps of black earth with his shoes. Flat, black, rectangular fields stretched into the distance. The horizon seemed very far away, a huge grey expanse of sky finally curved to meet it. A few straggling homesteads with red barns and pylons broke the linear lines of the landscape here and there, offering sparse circles of already denuded trees.

Everything had a very definite quality in this place. Cerulean skies of summer gave way quickly, with little preamble, to the harsh white glare of winter. Golden, undulating wheatfields to shorn black overnight, then endless white. The air was pungent with the rich sweet smell of the humus-filled earth. Angry coarse stubble extruded from the ground, a reminder of the pre-harvest yellow.

Her first summer here, Kitty had stood on this spot gazing out

198

on the wheatfields. When she narrowed her eyes, the rippling sheaves were like the sea. The slightest puff of wind carved hollows and conduits in the grasses. An unexpected rush of hot summer wind from the south suddenly swayed the gold toward her as if in one gigantic tidal wave. She had stepped back, terrified, and never tried turning wheat into ocean again.

Kevin was jiggling up and down.

'You've got a pee,' she said, 'you can do it here, just there – see?'

'I have not,' he said.

'You know you have.'

'Have not.'

'Fine then. Wet yourself. See if I care.'

He glowered at her, then raised his shoulders defensively and stuck his hands in his coat pockets, the blue eyes were sparkling with momentary resentment – every gesture so evocative of Danny she had to close her eyes for a second and turn her head away. When she looked at him again, he was smiling happily.

'I'm going,' he said casually.

'Are you now?'

'Yes.'

'Off you go then,' she teased.

He hesitated then waddled away still muttering to himself. She felt such a spasm of intense love, staring after his wounded, retreating figure with its dragging, forlorn footsteps, that she thought she would never again love him as much as at this moment; but then at every such moment, she felt that. He stopped and turned, still scowling with his mouth pursed up. Kitty raised her eyebrows then knelt with her arms wide to receive him. He ran to her.

'I can't go without you – you fool,' he said.

'Don't say fool, it's not nice,' she said happily.

As they walked back toward the edge of town, a sharp high wind, promising snow that night, cut into their faces. They held hands and Kevin skipped. And Kitty looked back over her shoulder for a final glimpse of the tossed black earth. Tomorrow and for the long months to come, it would be sheathed in white. But Kevin would not mind.

December

Eamon parked the car and pulled the removable stereo from its slot. It was not a concession he made lightly but there was no point in actively courting theft. He was fortunate in that apart from locking the car, a new Ford Escort, he had no other provisions to make toward security. Unlike every other car in this and surrounding streets which regularly suffered the loss of hubcaps, wheels, even seats, Eamon's alone nightly stood in pristine white splendour, untouched. All Eamon's cars were white. He had experienced a few discomfiting pangs when it was brand new, and sat by his bedroom window every night for hours, watching it across the street. But it withstood the vagaries of time and proclaimed testimony to his status. He was very pleased.

In the hall, voices and the scent of freshly baked bread drifted out to him from the kitchen. He peered at his reflection in the chipped hall mirror, humming lightly as he flattened back his wind-ruffled hair with the palms of his hands. He was pleased that evening too. And wondered when he might deliver his little slice of cherished information onto his mother's plate; before or after tea?

In the kitchen, Monica was holding a knitted sweater against her chest. Ma had knitted it for Christmas for one of her boys. It looked enormous. Ma stared at it with her head to the side thoughtfully.

'Too big d'you think?'

'A wee bit.' Monica pulled a face.

'Eamon, come here a minute – put that up against you there – maybe it would fit you,' Ma said.

Eamon obliged but shook his head when he looked down.

'No. Too small for me. Maybe Dan?'

'Oh aye,' his mother said, 'you're right. But he's seen me knitting it . . .'

'I saw you knitting it too,' Eamon said plaintively.

'What?' Ma was turning her head this way and that, envisaging the sweater on Danny.

'You've hurt Eamon's feelings, Ma,' Monica laughed.

'Oh get away with you.' Ma pulled the sweater from Eamon and bundled it up. 'Danny.' She decided with a nod of her head.

'Where is he?' Eamon asked.

'Where do you think?' Monica responded. She cast him a disgusted look and began to gather her things, ready to leave.

'Excuse me,' Eamon said, extending a finger to poke her in the chest. She would not meet his eyes. 'Excuse me a minute here – why am I getting the dirty look?'

Monica ignored him and zipped her shoulder bag.

'I've got to be going,' she said. 'The boys will be wanting their tea.'

'Hang on a minute,' Eamon insisted and blocked her path to the door. 'I tell you I'm sick to my stomach of your looks and the little mutterings under your breath like I was to blame or something. He's had plenty of time to get his act together . . . Isn't that right, Ma?'

'Aye,' Ma sighed over her shoulder. She was busy extracting food from the fridge.

'He's had plenty encouragement,' Eamon said.

'Maybe it's not the right sort of encouragement.' Monica studied the floor. Eamon poked her again in an effort to get her to raise her head. He clenched his jaw, he was white-faced.

'And who are you to say that, eh? Eh, Madam?'

Monica flushed deeply. She finally lifted her gaze.

'I do my best for our Dan,' she said quietly.

'That's enough the two of yous – I'm sick of listening to it. What's done is done. Dan will just have to get on with it. And he will in time with the help of God. Now Monica, if you're going – go – or if you're staying for your tea, set the table there for me, will you?' Ma said briskly.

But Eamon was not to be put off so quickly this time. He was weary with Monica's asides and the implication that it was all his fault that Danny had changed so completely.

'It's easy for you.' Eamon's face hovered inches from Monica's. 'You can breeze in and out of here as it pleases you – Me and Ma – we have to live with him. In and out of that Snooker Hall and the stink of stale beer off him every morning turning us off our breakfasts . . . Isn't that right Ma?'

Ma O'Neill was silent.

'He's only hanging on to that job of his because of me,' Eamon continued. Monica's head drooped. 'I tell you that young Fogarty lad is of more use to me than my own brother – a hell of a lot more use . . .'

Monica slowly lifted her head. She cast him a look of contempt. Eamon was still shaking with rage but suddenly his expression changed. He took a step backwards with a smug smile on his lips.

He raised his eyebrows and spread his hands wide.

'Well – are you stopping or going?' he asked quietly.

'Going,' Monica said. She looked at him and shook her head. She grabbed at her bag and left.

Ma O'Neill began to place mugs and plates on the table. She signalled to Eamon with her eyes toward the fridge.

'I forgot the cheese,' she said.

They sat. Ma gave thanks for what they were about to receive. Eamon watched her from under his lashes. He waited until she had split a scone and buttered both sides, scraping excess butter from her knife onto the side of her plate. She cut herself a wedge of cheese. Signalled again with her eyes toward the teapot. Eamon lifted it. He leant forward slightly, holding the teapot aloft. He did not pour immediately. Ma raised her eyes to check on his delay. She saw the expression on his face, then lowered her gaze again, waiting.

'Saskatchewan,' he said softly.

A slight raising of her eyebrows was all that showed that she had heard him. She placed the wedge of cheese on one side of the scone. The teapot was heavy. It trembled in his hand. She did not look up again. But nodded her head. Once. Eamon poured the tea.